Gray Wolf

J.W. Webb

Acknowledgement for:
Susannne Lakin for editing
Roger Garland, for the illustrations
Ravven, for cover design www.ravven.com
Debbi Stocco, for book design MyBookDesigner.com

ISBN 13: 978-0-9987736-4-3 (Paperback)
ISBN 13: 978-0-9987736-5-0 (Digital)

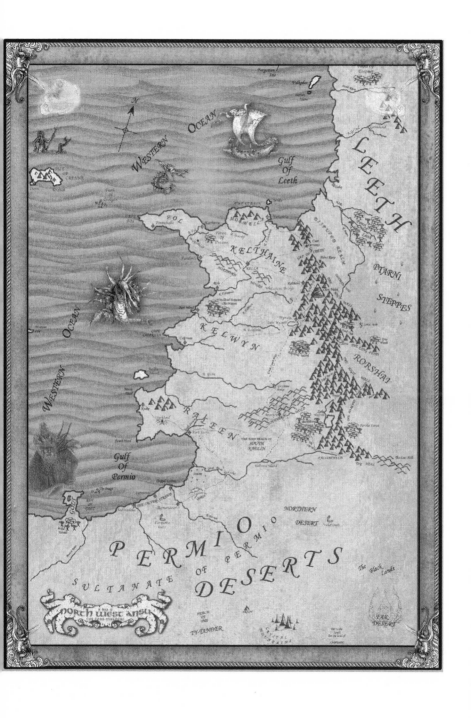

For Roger Garland, Tolkien Illustrator and Artist;
a man I'm privileged to know.

Table of Contents

Part One
Wolfling

Part Two
Wolf

Part One

Wolfling

Prologue

Raiders

They came at dawn, and it was Corin who saw them first. Three ships emerging as sleek gray shadows piercing the mist, their oars dipping and raising in measured silence. These were no fisher craft; their narrow hulls and brightly colored sails gave them away. Crenise Pirate ships. Corin had often heard his father speak of these vessels while trying to hide the loathing in his voice. He watched as excitement, anger, and fear fought to control him. Raiders had come!

Corin froze, his hands at his side, witnessing the three vessels beach the strand and shaggy figures wade ashore. He could hear their laughing and curses as they slung shields across their backs and made for the nearest houses of Finnehalle, his village. He'd been out early this morning before his kin were up. Corin usually slept as late as he could, but this morning he was restless, so he'd risen early to stroll the town and watch the sunrise from the harbor. Corin was a scarce hundred yards from his cottage when the ships emerged through the mist.

He stood, hovering and fretting until at last the fear won, and Corin sped up the hill to where the warning bell hung above the well, at the corner of the square. He tugged the rope, and the bell clanged and tolled until Corin's arms shook. The raiders were yelling now, rushing toward where he stood pulling on the bell cord.

There were perhaps twenty or thirty—it was hard to tell as the mist still clung to their ring-mail and furs. They carried shields across their backs, and in their hands were axes and curved swords.

Corin felt terror churning inside him. His stomach griped, but he was determined not to let his terror show. Out at sea the mist had cleared, and Corin could see other ships far across the water. He tugged the bell cord a final time and then turned for home.

Corin ran, picking up speed as the panic rose again in his belly. He heard shouts and the sound of breaking timber. Horrified, Corin turned and witnessed two bearded raiders crashing through the doors of his neighbor's house below. Shortly after, he heard screams from within. Shaking with rage, Corin turned away and sped up the hill. His long legs brought him level with his own front door, just as it burst open to reveal his father, Tollan, standing with bloodshot eyes and rusty blade in hands.

"Boy, get inside!" Tollan growled at his youngest son.

"I'll fight beside you, Father!" Corin felt angry and proud despite his fear. He wanted his father to know he was brave.

"Get in—idiot boy!" The burley fisherman yanked Corin by the hair and shoved him into the house. Corin's three brothers were in there, and his eldest sister, Ceilyn. His mother, Alize, stood by the hearth, her brown eyes wide with horror and her arms wrapped around the sobbing Daliene, Corin's little sister. Corin watched as his father strode out into the street and closed the door behind him. "Bar that door!" he told Corin, who complied swiftly, lifting the heavy metal rod and dropping it into place.

Inside the cottage, his brothers looked at Corin, their faces frozen in the misery of uncertainty and terror. They weren't like Corin. They were fisherfolk, as were their father and mother, and sisters too. Corin was different. A fire burned within him—always had. He couldn't stand here and let Father face them on his own. Corin stared at the door, the rage and terror conflicting inside him.

"Who are they, Corin?" Ceilyn's eyes were wide with terror as he turned and gazed at his sister.

"Crenise Pirates." Corin almost spat the words out as his hatred soared inside.

Noise and shouts filled the morning. The screaming was the worst. Corin heard babes crying, their yells silenced by steel. Dogs howled, snapped, and scampered, and a woman screamed somewhere close by.

Corin pushed past his horror-stricken brothers and stared out their only window, his kin too terrified to watch. Down there near the harbor, he could see the raiders had already put torch to the first two houses, and Corin could hear the screams of those trapped inside. Daliene cried out, and their mother held her tighter than before, her own tears mixing with her child's.

Corin gripped Ceilyn's hand in his own. "It will be alright," he told his favorite sister. They both knew his words were forlorn hopes, but Ceilyn nodded bravely and bit her lip until it bled. Corin could stand it no longer. Mind made up, he approached the door and lifted the heavy bar. "Stay here!" Corin yelled at his family. "I've got to help Father. Bolt the door behind me!"

"We're coming too!" Gordellen, his eldest brother, shook himself from his trance.

"No." Corin bid Gordellen to stay inside. "You three protect Mother and the girls!' Corin turned the latch, pushed the door wide open, and ventured out into the street. The raiders were closer now.

A shout turned his head. Three raiders were running toward where this father stood with the old sword gripped tight with sweaty hands. They slowed their advance when they saw his blade. The closet and biggest laughed.

"Looks like this one wants to fight." He grinned, and the two with him grinned back. Corin was dimly aware that his brothers had ignored his command and now joined him, while his mother and the two girls were fleeing up the hill toward the woods. Corin could see men already giving chase. He wanted to follow, but the raiders were circling his father now.

The three Crenise stood laughing at Corin's father. "Gut him, Brokka." The middle one revealed rotten teeth as he urged the biggest to attack Corin's father first.

"Be glad to." Brokka laughed and tossed his blade through the air, deftly catching it, his eyes never leaving Corin's father.

His father, hiding his fear well, swung hard, his sword slicing air as the raider, Brokka, jumped clear, laughing again. He was still laughing when he slid his curved blade between Corin's father's ribs. Corin watched in horror as his father dropped the sword, his big hands cupping the rent in his chest.

Corin screamed as a second blow severed his father's neck and his head rolled back into the empty house. Corin could hear his mother scream as she witnessed her husband's death from the edge of the village. He glanced up briefly, seeing her ragged face before she turned and fled out the gates. Corin turned as one dreaming. He looked up at the savage men now gazing upon him

Time froze. Corin's senses twitched as though he were primed by lightning, and a deep slow rage, like bubbling magna, filled his veins. He was dimly aware of his brothers' yells as they fled with the two other raiders hard on their tails. Corin focused on his father's killer, who stood with feet braced apart, his broad face clearly amused as he surveyed a skinny lad glaring up at him with hate-filled eyes.

"You're a fiery little shit." Brokka's eyes were bloodshot and his voice raspy, as though he smoked too much. Like his comrades, he wore chain mail and leather and stank of tobacco and stale sweat. A salt-and-pepper beard framed his heavy face, and he carried a round shield slung casually across his back. But in his right hand was the short sword that he'd used to kill Corin's father. Corin glared as Brokka pointed the seax at his chest and grinned. "Time to join your old man in Yffarn!"

Brokka swung hard at Corin's neck, but Corin was quicker. He dived low and rolled across to where his father's sword lay abandoned in the dusty grime.

Corin seized the hilt with both hands, then rolled again as Brokka hacked down hard upon him. Corin lashed out with a kick and—by sheer luck—caught Brokka between his legs. Brokka stumbled, allowing Corin the seconds he needed to find his feet and plunge his father's sword deep into Brokka's side.

"We gotta go!" one of the marauders said. Corin saw Brokka's companions looking out to sea. "Torval said to waste no time!"

"What about Brokka? We cannot leave him here."

Corin saw that the other raider had turned away and was running toward the gate.

"Yffarn take Brokka and that boy—it's the women we want. You coming?"

Corin was dimly aware of them leaving.

He watched Brokka twitch in agony beneath him. Corin savagely twisted the blade, and his father's murderer screamed. He pulled the rusty blade free with a savage tug of his palms, then he stabbed down again. And Again. And five more times, until a blow sent him reeling in the dirt, and Corin an Fol knew no more.

***

Corin woke to pain and silence and the distant sound of breakers combing the shore. He was alive, yet where was he? In a clean bed surrounded by windows filtering in sunlight and birds chirping outside. Corin saw a woman leaning over him. She was tall and willowy with long copper hair. She wore a smile like other women wear silk, and her eyes were calm. A thin green dress clung to her curvy body. She was beautiful and mysterious.

Corin tried to cry out, but the woman just smiled, and strangely his pain faded, as mist departs when kissed by morning sun.

She looked so beautiful and kind and wise, and Corin wanted to be with her. All this he discovered in the long warm seconds he gazed into her eyes, which were the most wonderful mix of green and gold.

"Who . . . are you?" Corin's voice squeaked, betraying his fourteen years. The woman's smile widened, and she placed a warm brown hand on his brow.

"You need to sleep." Her voice was summer breeze over heather, and her scent spoke of honey, roses, and wine. "Time to get your strength back. You were very brave yesterday, Corin an Fol."

"Who are you? And where is this place?" Corin glanced around but saw nothing familiar, and he'd been in most of the houses in Finnehalle during feasts and celebrations.

"It's a cottage close by the village—a place of peace and contemplation. I come here for both when the mood requires. As for who I am? That you'll learn in due course. For now you need rest!" She soothed his brow again, then reached back for something on a table close by.

She produced a goblet filled with steaming liquid; it smelled of mint and lavender. "Here's a brew that will ease your hurts, both inside and out. Drink deep and then sleep." She bade him to sit up and placed the chalice to his lips.

"But what about my family? They killed Father—"

"Drink first—you need strength."

Corin drank. The liquid tasted of honey and wine and earth and laughter. He had so many questions, but the woman's lovely face and her potent cup drove them far away, as sleep reached out and pulled him in.

When next he woke, the cool of evening filled the room. Corin's limbs ached but he felt stronger and swung his legs free of the bed. The room was empty, but he could hear someone singing outside. Corin noticed a robe lying on a chair close by. He wrapped it around his body, tied the cord, then Corin yanked the door back open and saw the woman hanging cloth on a line as bees buzzed all around her.

The mystery woman who had saved him. She glanced across and smiled, and Corin was filled with curiosity and wonder despite the worry in his heart.

"Do you feel stronger? Good. I'll make you something to eat."

"First tell me what happened to my family," Corin said as the autumn breeze sent goose bumps up his thighs. Corin noticed how she watched him intensely, and he blushed as only a teenage boy can. She seemed not to notice.

"They are dead—most of them," the strange woman told him, her huge eyes sad yet calm. "Though your sister still lives. I fear for her most. The others are free now—but Ceilyn—"

"Dead? Mother?" Corin stood shaking in denial. "I saw her running for the woods. How can she be dead? The others . . . I—"

"I'm sorry. Here, take this." She produced a blanket and bid

Corin to wrap it around his skinny frame. "Rest and grieve. Let the tears come; there's no shame in that. Meanwhile, I'll bring you another drink." The woman urged Corin to take a seat by the door. Close by, the hearty smell of roasted coney and potatoes reached his nostrils, but Corin wasn't hungry. He sat rocking and weeping and cursing the brutal men who had murdered his family.

Minutes later she returned with a hot bowl of soup. "They caught up with your brothers and killed them." The woman's face looked stern as she recounted the events of yesterday. "Your mother and young Daliene they carried to their ships, but they were spared the worst, Corin—trust me. I know! A freak wave drowned them as they left the shore. That reckless water took two of the raiders' ships too. Sensuata avenged you, Corin! The Sea God took their souls as slaves, even as He released your dear kin to rest in the Halls of the Maker. They are at peace now, Corin an Fol. Ceilyn was not so fortunate. They caught her last as she sought refuge in the woods. I fear their captain Torval has her now."

"Ceilyn? What will they do to her?" Corin tried to stand but the woman steadied his shoulders and urged him to sit back. "Who were they? Crenise?" Corin felt the anger return amid tears until her smile drove both away again. "Why did they come here? Finnehalle is so poor. Ceilyn . . ." Corin pictured his sister's pretty face and gulped back a sob. *What have they done with her?*

"Crenise pirates—yes. They have become bold of late, and many villages have suffered like Finnehalle. Corin, you need to sleep now. Drink up and rest. There will be time for questions later."

Corin clutched his soup bowl and numbly raised it to his lips. "I'm not hungry," he said, but he did as she bade him and scraped the bowl dry. After that he sank into an exhausted slumber, waking often to find her sitting over him.

***

A week later Corin felt stronger. He wanted answers now.

"Did they burn my village?" he asked the woman as they strolled outside the cottage, the bees buzzing all around and the bright spring sunshine casting motes beneath the trees.

"No, Finnehalle fared well—all in all. They were in and out quick, before the sea took some of them and swallowed them whole. Part of a large raiding force led by an infamous pirate chief named Torval. He operates out of Storn—it's on the far coast of Crenna. A rebel town at odds with the magistrate in Kranek Castle. Torval and his thugs are mostly rogues, brigands, and murderers. They range as far south as Permio and have a base there too. They were returning from raiding the Kelthaine coast. The three ships that beached here were strays from the main fleet. Their captains knew they wouldn't get much from poor fisherfolk, but doubtless slaves could be sold, south in Permio, or else in the nameless lands far across the sea. We will never know what their plans were."

"I hate Crenna!"

Corin had heard of the island but knew little about it, save that it lay somewhere west of Fol, his homeland—a stark spur of rock, cliffs, and heather lying just beyond the high king's domain. "I am going to learn to fight and kill as many as I can!" Corin stood, but the exertion made him giddy and he choked on his mead. "Then I'm going to find Ceilyn and save her from them."

"Perhaps . . . though I fear it's already too late for that poor girl. I am sorry, Corin—I truly am."

The woman stroked his hair, and Corin relaxed back into his chair, his eyes blinking back sleep. She was a sorceress whose words eased the worry worm inside him. Corin didn't question who she was or how she knew what she did. She was kind and mysterious and beautiful, and Corin had no one else now. He was an orphan and a stray.

Corin felt the tears dampen his cheeks again as the grief finally found him.

That night she told him stories, and after a hearty meal and more mead, Corin fell into a deep calm slumber, the strange woman's warm gaze on him until he faded into nothingness. The following morning she was gone.

Chapter 1

Finnehalle

Five Years Later

"And you haven't seen her since that night?" Holly traced a line down Corin's back until he rolled and grinned at her. They lay on the short grass, close by the cliff edge awarding sweeping views of village and ocean far below. He often came here, sometimes with Holly but mostly alone. This was Corin's favorite spot—a wild, windy clifftop a mile from town where he could watch the ocean and try to forget the loved ones he'd lost. It was early summer, and the smell of heather mixed with salty brine and the cry of gulls weaving above. Holly poked his ribs demanding an answer.

"What? Oh—her." Corin's grin faded. He liked Holly, but there were things he still preferred not to talk about—the golden-eyed woman being one. He regretted he'd mentioned her when first he'd lain with Holly in the heather high above the cliffs.

"You still love her?"

"I do not."

"I can see it in your eyes." Holly teased, until Corin, grumpy and fidgety, stood and strode across to the cliff's edge. He clenched his fists and let the fresh breeze whip his skin and salt his eyes.

"I don't really know if she existed at all," Corin said to the wind.

"Maybe she was a dream. Everything was so vague back then. I was just a boy having boyish dreams. Now I'm a man, Holly—almost twenty. But the memory still haunts me. And the guilt. They took my sister, and I let that happen. I can never forgive myself for that."

Holly, joining him, slipped a warm hand inside his and gazed up at him with sunny blue eyes. "What could you have done, and why didn't that wise lady help you, back then? She seemed to know everything." Holly sounded resentful. She was trying to help, but Corin had heard all this before. As he always did, Corin blanked out the memory of that dark time.

"Well, I love you, Corin an Fol, even if you still mooncalf after that dream woman. She's not coming back, but I am here."

Corin turned and smiled at Holly. "I love you too," he said. But the truth was, he was fond of Holly, but there was a raw restlessness that tore his insides and left scant room for love, save the fading memory of she who had saved him. And the hurt of how she had left him and simply disappeared. So cruel of her to do that. Since that morning almost five years ago, Corin had taken to brooding and steering away from most of the other villagers. He wasn't popular and didn't care.

At nineteen summers, Corin was so much stronger than he had been then. Stronger and angrier. The world was his enemy, his only comrades the sharp wind and stormy tides. Holly soothed him, but she could never understand the loss he felt. Her family had survived the raid, as had most, whereas Corin's kin had been obliterated—with the exception of poor Ceilyn, who doubtless suffered a worse fate—leaving him orphan and wastrel, with enough hate to fill this troubled corner of the world.

"We should get back." Holly tugged his shirtsleeve. "Father will be looking at opening The Ship. I'll be in trouble if I'm not there to help him."

"You go," he said. "I'll stay awhile and watch the ocean."

"And dream." Holly shook her head. "That's all you bloody well do these days." Holly's lips twisted, and she turned briskly. Without further word her strong tanned legs led her down the path back toward Finnehalle, their village far below.

Corin watched her leave. "I do love you!" he called after her, but the wind stole his voice. Besides, the lie was meant for his own ears. Corin hoped if he kept saying the words, they might prove true. So far that hadn't happened.

The years had passed slowly since that terrible time. Corin barely remembered how Holly's father had found him wandering witless through the streets of Finnehalle. The innkeep had been close to Corin's father and took in the lost boy as his own, much to the disapproval of his wife. That first year Corin did as little as he could, but soon after, Holly and Corin were given tasks in the village. She worked hard; Corin shunned his duties. And he didn't like his peers, those dour, tough fishers' sons. A curt word here, an insult there, and Corin took to fighting. It wasn't long before he got the reputation of a troublemaker—something he was now quite proud of.

He turned back to watch the ocean again, standing poised for more than an hour as wind whipped and seabirds whirled circles, mocking his silent vigil.

At last, done with his moping, Corin turned and ambled back into town just as evening quieted streets and smoke drifted up from cottage roofs, darkening sky and clogging his nostrils. He made for the harbor, as was his habit. Once there, Corin watched the boats bob and dance as their ropes and anchors kept them in place.

As dusk deepened, Corin returned to The Last Ship, his home these past two years—one of Finnehalle's three taverns, kept clean and smart by Burmon, Holly's father, the former friend of Tollan the Fisher, who had died in the raid, leaving Burmon no choice but to take in the only surviving member of that lost family. A decision that had had its consequences, as Corin had upset many of his customers with his sour expressions and snide remarks.

Corin seldom insulted anyone on purpose, but he masked his pain with an arrogant smile, and many thought him sly. Despite his protestations, they took him the wrong way and mostly steered clear, Burmon and Holly being the only exceptions. As time passed Corin grew more restless. He needed purpose, a world bigger than Finnehalle with its quaint charm, rain-washed lanes, old stone harbor, and narrow minds. He was wild and angry and ready for change.

Heavy with those thoughts, Corin opened the shabby door and entered his foster father's tavern. He noticed Burmon look up as Corin stepped inside.

***

Burmon rubbed sweat from his eyes as he watched the pale youth saunter into the taproom. "Supper's in the back." Burmon urged Corin to go eat before the food got cold. Close by, Holly was serving piping-hot fish and ale to three travelers seated near the roaring hearth. Outside the wind grew in strength, and a drumming on glass announced the rain's arrival.

Burmon spent a few minutes among his guests, checking that their comforts and needs were met and sharing natter and chuckle with some of the friendlier ones. Not the traveling trio—they were glum. Satisfied he'd done his duty, he ventured into the kitchen, where Corin slumped at his meal. Burmon sighed; he hadn't been looking forward to this.

"You need a shave."

"What?" Corin appeared lost in thought and hadn't noticed Burmon leaning over him. He grinned at Burmon and carried on with his stew. "This is good; Teri's best yet."

Teri was Burmon's red-faced short-tempered wife, who seldom surfaced from the kitchens except when Corin was about. Burmon knew Teri had scant time for Corin. She thought of him a wastrel—an opinion shared by many in Finnehalle.

Burmon sighed. He never found this easy. "So. The thing is"—Burmon wiped grease from his chin with a rag he kept for the purpose—"What are you going to do?"

"What do you mean what am I going to do?" Corin looked puzzled by the question. Burmon knew Corin had mistaken his meaning. His foster son would do what he always did—pester Holly, have a few ales, and then venture to bed.

"Find a quiet corner, I suppose," Corin mumbled when he realized Burmon expected an answer.

"You misunderstand me, laddie. I'm talking about your life." Burmon folded his arms and brought his brows together in a meaningful frown.

"Shit, but that's a bit heavy." Burmon watched Corin wipe stew from his mouth with the back of his hand and belch. "One day at a time, you always say. I'm just following your advice, Foster Father."

"That advice was not aimed at you but rather is a reflection on dealing with issues. I like to be pragmatic. But we need to talk, Corin." Burmon knew that if he left things as they were, Teri would find some way of getting rid of Corin. Burmon couldn't blame her, but, like his daughter, he believed this wild young man capable of more. And he owed Tollan's memory his best in helping Corin.

"Why?" Corin was avoiding Burmon's probing gaze. Corin always did this when he thought Teri had been complaining about him again. "Oh, alright—as you wish it," Corin said. "But can we do it around a beer? Truth is, I'm thirsty this evening."

"And short on coin too, I suspect."

"Funny you should say that. I was going to ask to tab it tonight. I'll work the nets in the morning and pay you back." Corin grinned, and Burmon gave in, as he always did.

***

Late that night Teri confronted Burmon in their bedroom.

"He cannot stay here indefinitely." Teri's pale eyes awarded no quarter. "You're too soft on that boy. Corin is indolent and wayward. That's bad enough, but he's also affecting Holly. She's gotten mighty lippy of late."

"She loves him—what can we do?" Burmon was worn out. It had been hectic in the taproom, and the hour was late. He just wanted to sleep but harbored little hope of that. Teri was not one for quitting.

"Throw the idle bugger out." Teri poked her husband in the ribs. "Let him earn his keep."

Burmon winced. "Corin helps out with slops and stuff. He does some work with the fishers too. Truth is, I've thought about this a lot, but with all that lad's been through, I haven't the heart to abandon him. He'll shape up in time—just needs some guidance."

"What about Polin the smith? He could knock some sense into that lad."

"Not sure Corin's ready for that." Burmon rolled over and showed Teri his back. "Now, Wife, I beg you—let me sleep!"

***

Later that week Corin dozed in a corner of the inn, close by the roaring fire that lulled his senses, as did the thick ale he'd drunk throughout that evening. To his right, a great hound lolled and drooled at his master's feet—a stranger Corin hadn't seen before. The traveler tucked into his evening meal with enthusiasm, ignoring both Corin and the dog.

Corin drained his tankard and yawned. He looked up, hearing voices, and recognized three young fishermen entering The Ship. The Toon brothers: Big Lorgi and his younger siblings, Dim Dooly and Gublet the Sly. Corin didn't much like the Toons. They were wet, grumpy, and thirsty for ale. They were also in a foul mood, as the day's catch had no doubt proved elusive.

The three dripped across to the barrels, where Holly poured them pints. Corin sniggered. He hadn't meant to; it just happened. The men stood leaning and dripping and looking so glum it caught Corin as a tad humorous. The youngest clocked his grin and nudged the biggest to his right. Lorgi was three years older than Corin and a bit broader. The other two were Corin's age, though hardened by long days at sea. None had much time for Corin an Fol. Lorgi in particular.

"What you grinning at?" Lorgi slung some ale down his throat and glared at Corin.

Corin, realizing his mistake, shrugged indifference. "Nothing —just thinking about life in general."

"You're a tosser." This from Gublet, the smallest of the three, who was known for a stirrer. "You wouldn't last a day on the sea, would he, Lorgi?"

"He wouldn't." Lorgi nodded sagely. Corin should have left it there, but the anger worm was stirring between his ears.

"You three are too stupid to do anything else." Corin shouldn't have said that, but truth willed out. And, besides, he'd drunk enough ale to no longer care what he said

Next moment, Lorgi was straddled over Corin, punching and kicking him, as Gublet and Dooly held Corin down.

Corin's head slammed against the slate flag as Lorgi's meaty fist bloodied his nose. Enraged, Corin jabbed his knee up fast and hard, catching Lorgi square in the groin. Lorgi rolled and whined, giving Corin the opportunity to wriggle free of the other two and find his feet.

Gublet dived in, but Corin used his knee again, bringing it up under Gublet's chin and sending him sprawling. Lorgi still nursed his groin, and Dooly kicked out at Corin's.

Corin's right calf trapped that kick, and in a nifty maneuver, Corin swept Dooly off his feet and booted him in the side of his head. Dooly's eyes glazed and he slumped. By now Holly and Teri were yelling, and Burmon and three customers were wading in. Within minutes fists were abundant, crockery was breaking, and, furious, Teri had near clubbed an innocent spectator witless with her stew pan.

But Lorgi had recovered. His next punch found Corin's jaw, knocking back into tables and chairs. There he sprawled akimbo, as the ale-fuddled hound slunk through the mess to lick and dribble slime across Corin's face.

Somehow Corin found his feet. The fight had spread outside now, and Corin noticed Burmon holding his nose as blood streamed down his face. Holly was kicking out at someone next to her father.

Lorgi launched another fist. Corin braced himself, then blinked as he saw a huge hand wrap itself around Lorgi's fist and, lightning fast, proceed to twist Lorgi's arm behind his back until he winced and yelped in pain. Gublet produced a knife and slashed at Corin's face. Corin jumped back, and the hound growled beside him.

All fighting and noise ceased when a heavy voice spoke. "I'd drop that can opener, laddie, else I shove it up your arse."

Corin had heard that gruff voice before. Polin the smith was in town again. Nice of him to drop by.

"Hello, Master Polin," Corin saw Teri grinning at the huge smith standing with mallet-sized fists on hips.

Polin still had a grip on Lorgi's arm. The big fisher was twisted forward, panting and sweating and begging to be released. Corin laughed seeing Gublet gulp when he saw the size of this newcomer. Things, it appeared, had gotten out of hand.

"Are you deaf as well as daft?" the heavy voice growled—a sound that put the hound to shame.

Corin watched Gublet shake his head and let the knife slip through his fingers to clatter onto the slate below. Polin nodded and then shook Lorgi free from his bear lock. "Good, now you three should bugger off, lest I change my mind and skewer you with this." He held up a broad seax, which, until now, had lain hidden beneath his woolen coat.

Teri was the only one smiling. "So nice of you to visit, Master Polin. I've a proposition for you."

Chapter 2

Polin

Polin's smithy was a cluster of buildings seven miles outside town, a hamlet enclosed by the same woods that could be seen from the cliffs above Finnehalle. Beyond it rose the moors, a bleak windy region that ranged for miles, finally folding into wooded valleys above the River Fol. Beyond that rose the dark hills of Kelthaine.

Corin had been to the smithy once during a brief visit with his father. Some business about a cart horse. It had been years ago, and he'd yawned through the encounter, hardly noticing the resin-soaked surroundings. The brick cottage, stone smithy with its crooked chimney, and cluttered compound with dry stonewalls enclosing it—all now very familiar as the smithy had become his new lodgings. Thanks to Teri and her bright ideas.

Corin wasn't happy with Teri. He'd seen how she fussed over big Polin and filled him with ale until the smith agreed to take in her "wastrel" and make a man out of him. "Teach him some skills, and that way he might be of use to somebody, though I can't really see it myself," Teri had said while Corin watched on in horror. Corin determined he'd get back at her one day.

He got to go home once a week. Aside from that, Corin was

up before dawn, scrubbing, cleaning, mucking out stalls until dusk brought release, when he eat stew, and—if he was lucky—drink some excellent ale. Polin brewed his own because he didn't like people and seldom ventured into the village taverns—which, in Corin's opinion, was not seldom enough.

Polin was an ox—broad of face, square of jaw, with heavy shoulders and massive hands. He spoke no words he deemed surplus and had a dim view of most things. The smith's wife, Inne, had died giving birth to their only child. That was twelve years past. Now Kyssa was a bright-eyed redheaded troublesome tangle of legs and giggles—most her attentions focused on the new hapless apprentice from the village.

For his part, Corin scarce noticed the girl. He scarce noticed anything. Polin had him running ragged, with never a chore done to the smith's satisfaction and always a new one to start right away. Nor was he forthcoming on praise.

"You're as skinny as a sun-dried bean."

"I've seen more strength in a sparrow."

"You're like a man made of tea leaves."

Those were but a few of his chosen phrases. Corin learned that complaining got him a swift slap across his head from that iron fist. Polin wasn't big on sympathy. The smith's customary frown was hidden behind thick black whiskers. He wore his beard square at the throat with his hair cut shoulder-length to match. He wasn't big on fashion either, though Corin wasn't about to tell him that. His teeth were good, though blackened by the tobacco he chewed. He had a wolf's head tattoo on his left bicep.

Corin had never imagined himself working like the others in the village. A dreamer, he'd always thought he'd find something different to do. Something important. It was a big world, and there were lots of ways to make a living—not that he'd any plan as such. Maybe travel and learn to fight with a sword. Find the pirate Torval if he still lived and then kill him. Find out what happened to his sister. A soldier's life would be honorable and something he could aspire to. Not for Corin an Fol the drudgery of fisherfolk and their daily chores.

He had explained this to Polin, who had laughed at him and handed him a bucket. "Go clean the stables," Polin had said, biting on his pipe.

After the first week, Corin had aches attached to his aches. When his weekly chores were done, he'd hobbled the seven miles into town and found Holly at work in the marketplace.

"Don't go in The Ship," she warned him. "Mother'll skin you alive."

"She got her bloody wish," Corin complained, feeling even more bitter about his banishment "And when do I get to see you, sweetling?" Corin put on his pouty, long-faced pained expression, much like a hound whose bone is confiscated without cause.

"We'll find time." She kissed him quickly, then turned back to her tasks. "I've much to do. Best you be about your day too." Corin watched as Holly handed out trays of piping-hot fish to hungry market-goers amid cheerful banter. He stood hovering, but she just ignored him, so Corin's face grew longer until he decided on a stroll through Finnehalle.

"Bugger it." Corin strolled along the quay and distanced himself from the market. He was determined to enjoy his first day off as best he could, and Polin needed him back before dusk. Maybe he should do a runner? But where to, and what was the point? Suffice it to say, Corin felt lost and disappointed with how things were turning out. After glum moments dwelling on his options, he decided The Last Ship was his only solace, as the other inns would have gotten word of the trouble the other night and he'd be banned. Burmon might be more sympathetic.

He was, to a point. "You can have one pint, and then you're out. If Terina catches you in here, she'll pull your ears off and then fill mine with shrieking." Corin nodded thanks, and Burmon joined him at table, taking a short break from his busy day. "So. How's the smithy?"

"Stinks." Corin stared morosely at his ale.

"They usually do."

"I hate it there. He works me ragged and never a 'Thank you, Corin, nice job, Corin,' or 'You're so good to have around, Corin.'

No, mostly he just calls me a tosser."

Burmon chuckled at Corin's expression. "Polin's a good man—hard, I'll grant you that. But then, he's got cause to be. Besides, you'll shape up in time and learn good skills. A smith is seldom out of work. You should be grateful he took you on."

"But that's just it—I don't do any smithing." Corin wiped froth from his mouth and worried that his ale was nearly gone. "All I do is run around fetching stuff, wiping horses' arses, and getting sworn at for the privilege. And I don't want to be a bloody smith. I hate the job."

"You hate work."

That was entirely of their conversation, as at that point Teri appeared and the men promptly fled the taproom.

***

Back at the smithy, Corin was glum. The rain kept coming down as he struggled to hold the horse's hoof in his hands as Polin swore at him while prizing the old shoe off.

"I've seen more strength in a bloody kipper! Hold her leg still."

"I'm trying!"

"Very." That did it. Later that evening Corin stormed into the cottage to vent his feelings. He would not put up with this nonsense one day longer.

"It's not working out." Corin loomed into Polin's smoke-filled sitting room. The smith looked up gruffly from his chair. He was half drunk and mellow but still managed a special scowl for his "useless" apprentice. Close by, the girl Kyssa grinned at Corin and hiccupped while twisting a ginger lock free from her hair. Kyssa didn't say much, but her saucy look made Corin wonder if she wasn't older than her twelve years. Future trouble, for sure.

"Eh?" Polin stared at Corin, who shuffled his feet and chewed his lip.

"This . . . contract between us. It's not working out."

"Contract?" Suddenly Polin burst into explosive laughter, squirting beer through his teeth until even the giggly Kyssa looked startled at her father's mirth and decided on wearing a more serious expression.

"Contract." Polin shook his head. "You're a caution, to be sure. This ain't no contract, boy. This is me keeping you out of shit. Now go back to bed and get some sleep. I need you up at first light to see to the beasts."

Corin left crestfallen and pouty as Polin's chuckles faded behind him as he shut the door. Time to change tack. But what to do? No point going back to Finnehalle without any chance of work. He couldn't stay in The Ship, and no one else would take him on. Kelthaine? Foreign country, but maybe his best bet. One thing for sure, Corin wasn't staying at Polin's smithy any longer than he had to.

***

But things took a fortunate turn. For some inexplicable reason, that following morning the smith had a change of heart. Polin found his unwilling apprentice mucking out the stables, spade and bucket in hands, accompanied by his habitual sour expression.

"I've been doing some thinking," Polin said.

Careful, Corin almost replied but managed to hold his tongue.

"What happened to your father's sword?" Polin ignored the look in Corin's eyes. That smirk fell away after that question, as suddenly Corin was interested.

"I don't know. I don't recall much after the raid." Corin pictured the woman's beautiful face again and fell silent. His face grew hot. Polin studied his charge with rare interest for a moment and then nodded.

"I'll enquire in town."

"What's this about?" Corin's mind always blanked over that fateful day, but the mention of his father's sword had him all ears. "It's just a sword. Maybe it's lost or else stolen?"

"You've got strength enough." Polin looked thoughtful, and Corin wondered what was on his mind. "Cocky enough, for certain. And quick—I'll give you that. You can move when you want, laddie—though most times you're a slug."

"Quick enough for what?" Corin placed the bucket on the straw, wiped his grubby hands, and wondered where this conversation was going.

"The Wolves." Polin awarded Corin a meaningful glance.

"Not heard any lately." Corin scratched his ear. "But I'm sure they're around. I've—"

"I don't mean those wolves. I'm talking about the Wolves in Kella City.'

"I don't know about any wolves in Kella City. What's so special about them?"

Polin rolled his eyes and mouthed a curse. "Spent your life asleep, boy? The Wolves are one of the three elite regiments guarding our high king. I should know—I was one once."

"You were a soldier?" Corin stared at Polin with a new respect.

"I was. And a good one, until I had a falling out with a man of rank. The choice was kill him and hang for it. Or else leave. I chose the latter."

"Well, what's this got to do with me?" Corin felt the edge of excitement as he already guessed the answer. "You think I should join these Wolves? Become a warrior?" Corin added after receiving no response from his charge-hand.

Polin brought his brows together and chewed his mustache. "Fancy an early ale?" Corin's eyes brightened, and he nodded emphatically. "Good, we'll take this afternoon off; I'll fare into Finny, and you can get ready,'

"Ready for what?" Corin couldn't believe his ears; he felt happier than he had in weeks.

"A trip east next month to the big city. Come, let's stop for a brew." Corin grinned and followed Polin inside his cottage, where the smith poured them both a tankard of ale.

"So, aren't you curious?" Polin asked him as Corin slurped, his mind racing between excitement and concern. Why was Polin doing this?

"But I've only just started working for you. Won't you miss the help?"

"Not really—your heart's not in it, and I don't think it ever will be. I did this for Tollan, boy. I liked your father; he was a good man. Honest and kind—both are rare virtues in this world. But you are different, Corin. You've a bad attitude, and I can't say I blame you for that after losing your kin and all. But you need to acquire some special skills if you want to avenge your kin. Torval's still out there killing and raping." Polin looked at Corin meaningfully. "Somebody needs to kill him."

"He took my sister." Corin's said. "I've never forgiven myself for not going after her."

"No, instead you caused trouble in town, and now no one is your friend. Except soppy wolf Burmon and that lass you're tupping."

"You know about Holly?" Corin was surprised. "So Teri told you?"

"Nope, the whole village knows that girl mopes after you. Poor lass, Holly won't tame that restlessness, though I daresay she'll try. You need to hone that temper, Corin an Fol. And because I liked your father and was once a wild lad myself, I'll teach you the basic moves. But first we need your father's sword."

"But why would these Wolves be interested in me?"

"Maybe they won't, but it's worth a visit, and I've not been to Kella City in years. We could do some sightseeing. What say you?"

Corin agreed that this was a good idea. Maybe he could get a look at these Wolves before making up his mind.

***

Unusually focused, Corin worked diligently that entire afternoon, achieving more than he had the week before. He was fired up with thoughts of Kella City, Wolf warriors, and swords. He had never felt so excited. He even found time to hug Kyssa and make her squeak. When Polin came back, the smith found Corin tidying the yard with a broom.

Polin raised a brow and then leaned to swing something heavy onto a bench next to the stables.

It was swaddled in wool and lashed together by old rope. It was obviously a sword. "Is that . . . ?" Corin stared at the bundle.

"It is." Polin started untying the cord, cursing, as it proved tough and unwieldy. "That old tosspot Burmon had it secreted in his attic. Said he was worried to let it near you, case you got wild one night and started swinging it about and hurt yourself. I told him we're off to the city next month, but first I'll teach you not to hurt yourself with this."

"What did Burmon say?" Corin felt his hands shake in anticipation. His father's sword—the weapon Corin had used to kill Brokka. He'd thought it lost, like so many things back then. Emotions flushed his face as Corin watched impatiently as Polin finally gave up and took a knife from his belt and sliced the rope in two.

"Sodding thing could have rusted away in that attic," Polin muttered. "He seemed worried," he added after a moment. "Thinks the world of you, boy. Gods alone know why." At last Polin peeled back the shroud of wool and cobweb revealing a solid-enough sword sheathed in faded leather with a steel cross-guard, leather hilt, and heavy iron pommel. Polin tossed the sword to Corin, who caught it deftly with both hands and slowly slid it from the sheath.

Corin winced when he saw the cloud of rust accompanying the steel as its length revealed itself. "We can sort that," Polin said. "Just needs my oil and your elbow grease. Not a bad blade, in all. I've seen better, but this will serve until you know sharp end from blunt."

"You mean to teach me?" Corin was excited now.

"Just the basics. You'll learn more on the job, so to speak. Don't worry—the Wolves take in every loser and dropout they can find, so they won't expect an expert swordsman. The Tigers and Bears are more fussy, but Halfdan likes his boys rough and ready." Corin had no idea who the Tigers and Bears were, but the name Halfdan had his ears lifting.

"The high king's brother . . . yes him!" Polin grunted affirmation at Corin's wide-jawed gape. "Halfdan commands the Wolves— has for decades. So you'll get to meet him if things go to plan. Mind your bloody manners when you do."

It was too much: Corin was a-goggle to get at the blade and swing it in the yard. "Can I try it out?"

"We'll clean it up first. Then sharpen it some. Then we'll sip some ale and plan our trip next month. How's that sound?"

"Good" was all Corin could manage.

***

Next morning, Corin worked hard at his chores and finished them early. Smiling, he approached Polin in the forge. "You done already?" The smith looked up from his anvil, the hammer gripped in his hand.

"All finished and ready for my first lesson," Corin replied.

"Alright, give me half an hour, and I'll join you outside the stables. And make sure Kyssa's safely out of the way." Corin nodded as Polin returned to his task.

Corin was swinging the blade as Polin loomed into the stable yard. "You swatting flies?" Polin said.

"Just getting my balance." He turned to grin at Polin and then cursed as the sword slipped through his hands and clattered onto the ground.

"Danger to yourself," Polin said, shaking his head. "Give me the sword before you cut your own head off."

Annoyed with himself, Corin reached down and retrieved the weapon, then passed it over to the smith. Polin gripped the blade two-handed and made three clean, precise slices through the air.

"Two hands. That way you can't cut the other one off. And keep moving your feet." Corin watched Polin demonstrate by pacing backward and forward, the sword moving all the while. "It ain't easy, but practice works wonders. Here—your turn." Polin passed the sword across to Corin, who seized the hilt and gripped it with both palms. He braced his feet and swung.

"Better," said Polin. "Practice that for an hour, and then we'll have supper."

Chapter 3

The City

A month later, Corin felt stronger and fitter and had a new pride that showed in his walk and the way he held his head. He'd learned some nifty moves with the sword and considered himself proficient. In addition, the general work around the stables and smithy had developed muscles where he hadn't expected them. "It's just the beginning," Polin told him that afternoon. "So don't get smug. You're a novice, but at least you've some strength in those arms and an idea how to stand. Now go visit that girl—we leave tomorrow at sunup."

Corin borrowed a pony and left right away. He found Holly scrubbing dishes in The Ship's kitchens. There was no sign of Teri—not that Corin was worried about that today.

Holly wasn't happy when Corin informed her he was leaving for Kelthaine and soldiery. "You might get killed or something bad." Holly's eyes were moist, and she bit her lip.

Corin put an arm around her waist and kissed an ear. She pulled away and looked cross. "It's not funny," Holly said, seeing his grin. "I don't want you hurt, Corin."

"I'll be just fine, sweetling. I'll earn good, honest money for a while, then retire early and come back and build us a house. You'll be proud of me—so you will. I'll return whenever I can, so don't go a-flirting with no fisher boys!" Corin tickled her thigh, and Holly managed a smile. Corin knew she wanted more from their relationship, but he wasn't ready for that yet.

A hectic grope and tumble followed in the stables behind the tavern. They hadn't done it there before, as its closeness to Terina's evil gaze had terrified them. Neither cared today as passion drove worry far and wide.

Later Corin held her close as the gulls cried outside, announcing the fishers were back from the sea. They took to strolling arm in arm, down to the water's edge, watching as the sun fell crimson into the watery horizon, the sounds of voices, birds, and waves mingling with the soft breathing of their closeness.

"I do love you, girl," Corin said, and this time he meant it. "Only the gods know the future. Wait for me—I'll be back soon as I'm trained. And if you like, maybe you can join me in foreign travels." Holly had nodded, implying she'd think about that, and Corin left her with a kiss. He returned to the smithy with mixed feelings and spent a sleepless night tossing and turning, wondering about the next day.

***

Morning came at last. Outside in the yard, Polin had a horse saddled for each of them, plus a pack mule to carry food enough for the four-day journey to Kella City. Dawn paled field and sky as the two rode out, making for the old road that ran east across the moors until it found the only ford that allowed crossing the River Fol. They made that by late afternoon, and once clear of that stream entered the dark, brooding hills of Kelthaine—a land Corin had heard much about but had never seen.

Those hills rose higher and higher, and the road weaved a thread through wood, vale, and moor. It was wild country. Polin kept eyes open for bear and boar, and maybe the odd lone rogue or villain. But they saw nothing, though Corin spied an eagle high above the trees. Kelthaine seemed a wild, empty place, and for a brief moment Corin thought of Holly and hoped he'd made the right choice. But his excitement won through. This was adventure!

They made good progress, reaching the walls and towers of Kella City just as the sun sank behind the western hills. The gates were shut, but Polin rode up and struck his stick against the hardened oak.

"Who's that?" a gruff grunt announced inside.

"I'm a smith from Fol with apprentice, seeking tavern and ale ere nightfall."

"Bugger off!" the voice yelled, and someone else added. "Come back tomorrow!"

"Let us in!" Polin awarded Corin a pained look. "I've done work for Lord Halfdan. Special order—he's expecting me."

"Why didn't you say so?" The first voice sounded peeved. "Norris, open the bloody gates—there's thirsty men outside!"

More grumbles followed, then minutes of silence. Corin and Polin exchanged glances. At last they heard grunts and grumbles and the heavy jangle and rattle of keys. It seemed quite a process, but Corin felt a wash of relief as the oak-and-iron doors parted to reveal a cloaked and helmeted guard beckoning them inside.

"I lost the bloody keys," Gap-toothed Norris grumbled to his accomplice as they forced the gates shut again and then locked them, soon returning to a dice game. "The Wolves' barracks are furthest from the palace," Norris's sidekick announced helpfully.

"I know the way," Polin growled and bid Corin to guide his horse into the city.

His first impression was the size. Tall buildings leaned toward one another, almost meeting and making tunnels of the lanes as they rode through. Corin had never imagined so many people living so close together. They passed tanneries, stables, taverns, and shops. All looked deserted, and Corin thought the city must be asleep. The streets were cluttered in places and strewn with all manner of filth. Corin screwed his nose at the stench rising from the cobblestones below. After a mile, the lanes widened and ran straight toward a squat squarish building with a golden roof. Corin noticed a weird spike of a tower piercing the dark sky above.

"The palace where Kelsalion III resides." Polin gestured at

the golden-roofed building with his hand. It seemed a bit gaudy. "Things are not as they were. The high king still mourns his lost queen though she perished years ago. He seldom ventures out these days and leaves most of his decisions to his councilor."

"What's that weird tower?" Corin pointed to the crooked spike dominating the skyline.

"The Astrologer's Roost; it's where the high king's councilor studies the stars."

"What's he do that for?"

"Buggered if I know. I'm a blacksmith, not a magician."

"I was only asking."

"Shut up and ride." They made the stone bulk of barracks some twenty minutes later. Corin was amazed how big Kella City was, but, then, he only had Finnehalle and a few other villages to compare with. But the city was empty and the taverns quiet. That seemed odd to Corin. He'd expected a lot of life in such a huge place.

"Alright." Polin reined in and slid from his horse's saddle. "That there's the barracks; there's a good inn close by where we can overnight."

Corin followed suit and slid from his horse. Together they guided the three beasts toward a shabby-looking inn awarding pale-yellow glow from within, indicating someone was at home.

Polin rapped on the door. It creaked ajar, and a woman glared at him. "It's after hours." She yanked the pipe from her mouth and spat on the floor. "What you looking at?" The woman saw Corin's pained expression.

"He's reporting in at first light." Polin nudged Corin toward the door. "Wolves are expecting him."

"What they going to do with him?" The woman looked Corin up and down and clearly wasn't impressed with what she saw.

Corin was about to complain, when Polin added, "The usual. Now, are you going to stable these horses and let us have some supper? We've come a tidy way, and I've a big thirst for ale."

"Me too," Corin added but was ignored.

"Squirrel!" The woman shrieked, and a skinny boy popped

his head out the door. "See to these horses, and be bloody quick about it!"

The boy named Squirrel leapt through the door and grabbed Corin's reins. "You can go in now, master," he said cheerfully enough. Within moments the lad had all three beasts in tow and was leading them off to the stable yard, which was hidden somewhere behind the tavern.

"Enter." The woman offered a grand sweep of her hands, and Corin decided this city was a peculiar place. "There's stew. It ain't good, but good enough for such as you pair. Ale's watery, as brewery prices are crippling us. It's hard to make a farthing these days."

Corin glanced at Polin, who shook his head and motioned for his charge to take a seat with him at a nearby table in the dingy room. Three lolling hounds, a struggling fire, trapped smoke, and four somber customers rested within. A fat man dozed in a distant corner. Polin informed Corin that the man was the proprietor of this fine establishment and the scowling woman currently pouring them ale his lovely wife.

The ale was superb and the stew very tasty. Corin remarked on this to Polin, who explained that Kells—his name for people from Kelthaine—had their own way of doing things.

"They don't seem overly cheerful," Corin acknowledged as he slurped his ale. He hadn't thought much about the next morning but decided he'd drink as much as he could, and that way he'd sleep well.

"They're all miserable," Polin whispered. "Famous for it. I prefer Kelthara; they know how to enjoy themselves in that city. But Master Caswallon clamps down on festivities in Kella. He holds the high king's purse, you see."

"Caswallon?"

"The high counselor—the real power in Kelthaine, as Kelsalion III is not as he once was."

"Is the high king unwell?" This was news to Corin. Polin didn't respond. He deemed he'd said more than enough on the subject. Instead, he grinned at Corin. "You ready for the morning?"

"Of course." But Corin was lying and drained his ale. "Can I have another one please?" He smiled sweetly at the woman still manning the pumps.

She grinned, a rare sight that revealed three missing teeth. "You'll feel like shit tomorrow," she said cheerfully as she replenished his mug. Polin said nothing, though a wry smile creased his lips. Corin consumed several pints of the heady brew before he decided on bed. Polin had retired already. It was Squirrel that guided Corin to his cot and shut the door with a cheery "See you at breakfast."

Corin closed his eyes and thought about the morning. He gazed at the worn drapes until heavy sleep wrapped its cozy arms around him.

He woke once, his head throbbing and mouth as dry as ants' nests. His face turned to where the window's drapes had parted just enough to show a pale moon silvering the floor. A woman watched him with arms folded.

She stood by the window, her long hair braided and her green-gold eyes smiling.

Corin felt a rush of emotion as he recognized the lady who had tended him after the raid on his village. She had returned at last.

"You must be brave tomorrow," the woman told him. "Your life is changing, Corin an Fol." Even as she spoke, the woman seemed to fade to smoke and moonlight, and Corin blinked as he tried to rise from the covers.

"Don't leave me!" He sat up in bed and wiped the sweat from his brow. But his words froze on his lips. The woman had gone.

Chapter 4

The Wolves

He woke to the clatter and bang of pots close by. Someone—the woman, Corin suspected—was yelling at someone else—probably Squirrel. Bright sunlight assaulted his head because some kind individual had pulled back the drapes, thus flooding the room with evil sunlight and filling his throbbing skull with dazzles and dots.

"Get up." Polin loomed over him, as fresh as a daisy, grinning at Corin, who blinked back sleep from his eyes. "If you want breakfast, you'd better get moving. Sun's up, promising a grand day to start your new career."

Corin didn't feel like starting anything at that moment. Still, he shook his aching, shivering hide free from the sheets and staggered half-starkers into the kitchen.

The woman was there and promptly shoved a bowl of gray porridgy stuff across the table in front of him. Corin glared at it with suspicious eyes.

"It don't bite," the woman said, then ruffled his hair in an odd show of affection that Corin found somewhat alarming. "Big day for you today." The woman winked at Polin, who nodded and turned to his gruel.

A half hour later Corin stood with wobbly legs, as Polin

pointed to a gap in the long, low wall ahead. The short, brisk walk
had returned them to the barracks Corin had seen last night. They
offered scant fascination for him this morning, as the reality of
what he was about to do made Corin's stomach twitch. He'd never
expected to feel nervous, but he did now and tried to suppress the
urge to turn and run. Was he really doing this? Why had he listened to Polin?

"See that crack in the wall?" Polin pointed and Corin nodded.
"That leads to the back door. Tradesmen's entrance. Once there,
knock loud, else no one will hear. And keep knocking. It might take
a while, but someone should show up and let you in." He passed
Corin the sword he'd brought along—his father's blade, all shiny
and sharp. "I almost forgot—you might need this."

Corin had a sinking feeling. "What about you?'

"I'm off to market; it's why I came here." Polin grinned at
Corin's horrified expression. "Did you expect me to hold your hand?"

"No . . . but . . ."

"You're on your own, lad. Now off you go and good luck!"
Polin rammed a huge palm into Corin's and shook it three times.
"Farewell, Corin an Fol. I wish you well!" Without further ado,
Polin turned and trudged back to the tavern, which was hidden
somewhere behind the maze of brick and stones that were Kella's
cheaper side of town.

Corin gulped and gripped his father's sword, unsure how to
proceed with it. He shoved the scabbard and blade through his
belt. A rush of emotions flooded his head: excitement, anticipation,
fear, and worry that he'd made a big mistake. Too late to go back
now, so he'd best focus on moving forward, one step at a time.

Somewhere close a dog barked, making Corin jump, and the
sounds of approaching wheels scraping on cobble reminded Corin
he was standing in the middle of a street. A cart clattered toward
him, and its rider, all cloak and tatters, swore and hurled something green at Corin. He ducked as a cabbage sailed past his head.
More carts appeared around a corner as Kella's citizens awoke to
their chores.

Corin hovered at the edge of the street. He stole a wan glance toward where the inn lay hidden, then sighed and turned to face the wall of the barracks looming out at him.

Bugger it.

Corin walked along the wall until he found the gap again. He squeezed through, marking how the tradesmen's entrance was more of a dog squat. He found the door—eventually. He stood for a moment, hesitating, then rapped three times on the timber with the pommel of his father's sword.

Nothing. He tried again and still no response. Corin started to think no one was inside, which, to his shame, left him partly relieved. *I'm not a quitter—I can do this.* Corin steeled his heart and knocked a third time, much louder. Still nothing.

Corin waited an hour, then began rapping on the door like a mad thing. He was angry now. Everyone was pissing in his pot, and he'd had enough. A pox on Polin, the tavern woman, and everyone else in Kelthaine.

"Who's there?"

Finally!

The voice was close, and Corin almost jumped in alarm.

"Corin an Fol."

"Never heard of him."

"I've come to enlist."

A creak and grunt had the door parting toward him. Hinges grated and groaned as the door shuddered open. A man stood there, short in build but stocky. His feet braced parallel and he wore a taciturn look on his square-set jaw. "You're out of luck," the soldier said. Corin knew him to be one, for he wore a short curved blade at his hip and a long, fat knife slung adjacent. His eyes were flat and blue. Whatever Corin was selling, this one didn't want to buy. "So go away."

"Lord Halfdan expects me." Corin stuck his chin out.

"I doubt that very much. The man crossed his tattooed arms and smiled at Corin. The sort of grin you might see on a thief who'd just emptied the contents of your purse into his. "The boss is in Port Wind supervising the construction of the new barracks. Wolves ain't welcome in Kella no more."

Before Corin could enquire further, the gate shut and foot-steps announced the soldier's departure from their vicinity. Corin slammed his fist into the gate in sudden temper. He kicked the timber and yelled "Tosser!" but to no avail.

Dismal and twice deserted, Corin took to sitting in the grass, sword in hand, until ants stung his backside. He stood and bemoaned his state of affairs. With no other plan, he returned to the tavern. The woman was napping, but her husband let him in.

"Got any coin?" The fat man demanded as Corin pulled up a chair.

"Nope."

"He was in here last night, came with the smith." Squirrel grinned his way, and Corin decided he was the only worthwhile fellow in this entire cursed city. He smiled back at Squirrel and then looked sad.

"The smith paid well." The innkeep had read his mind. "You hungry?" Corin nodded. The innkeep turned to the boy. "Wake Nora. Get her on that soup." Squirrel nodded, and then minutes later Corin winced when he heard Nora's curses.

"What do ya mean he's come back?" Nora appeared with red hands thrust on hips and wearing her greasy crinkled apron. "Were you rejected?" Nora cackled. "Rejected from the Wolves? Never heard of such a thing."

"The soldier said they've moved. To Port Wind—wherever that is."

"Oh, that's right." The fat innkeep looked alert and interested for the first time since Corin had encountered him. "Halfdan's boys have moved camp on account of Caswallon promoting Perani's Tigers as First Regiment over both Bears and Wolves. Belmarius's Bears swallowed it, but the high king's brother is too proud. Hence he's led his boys west."

"Where is Port Wind?" Corin thought that a relevant question. He wondered if he could get there somehow. He should at least try to, but lack of funds was no small issue here. Things had not gone as planned this morning, and Corin felt both irritated and confused.

"Miles away." Nora waved an arm. "You had best go back home with the smith. Catch him before he leaves the market. No point staying here."

"I thought Polin was returning here tonight." Corin's heart sank further as the option of returning to Finnehalle fled before his eyes.

"No, he settled up his account before you left—said he means to ride out after he's spent some time at market. Doubt he'll purchase much—seems the frugal kind, if you ask my opinion." Nora cast Corin a shrewd glance. "He came here for your sakes, boy. That much is obvious."

"Not to me," Corin grumbled. "And now it's too late, and it's a long walk back to Fol."

"Don't look so glum." The innkeep slapped his back. He seemed more jovial than his wife and poured Corin an ale to make him feel better. "You might as well stay here another night, get fed, then maybe get some work to pay for lodging and a nag to get you back home. Plenty of work in Kella."

"Plenty of work for them that knows what work is,' Nora couldn't seem to resist adding. Corin thanked them and decided on staying put—at least until morning. Things hadn't gone according to plan, but he was in a new place, and after two more ales and his head clearing nicely, Corin decided a sightseeing stroll was due.

"Well, have a care; you stick out like a swollen thumb. Here's some coppers incase you get in trouble, not much but it will pay for a pie or a pint, should you need one." Nora spilled several small coins into Corin's hands and ruffled his hair again, and Corin decided she wasn't too bad. "And you'd best leave that sword here. Lord Caswallon doesn't allow civilians to carry weapons on the streets. You'd get arrested—or worse."

Corin thanked her, and she stowed the sword in a cupboard. "I'll keep an eye on it," Nora promised him. Corin didn't want to leave it with her but saw no other option. He needed to think, and to do that coherently he needed exercise. So, with that in mind, Corin left the tavern, making for the palace that he remembered seeing in the distance last night.

Corin passed through the marketplace just in case Polin had loitered, but, as he suspected, the smith was long gone. Besides, the traders were done for the day and clearing up amid natters and complaints about the narrowness, short arms, and deep pockets of most of their customers.

Corin ambled through broad streets, his mind working better as he decided his next best move. Perhaps they'd give him work in the inn, or else know someone who could use his skills—though Corin wasn't sure what his skills were, he knew he must have some. Stick with that for a week or so, then he could either return home or else—and his heart told him he should do this—find this Port Wind place and try the Wolves again.

Corin felt more confident as his plan took shape in his head. Things would work out, he was now sure of it. Perhaps the gods were testing him? It was a sobering thought but one that deepened his resolve. Everything happens for a reason.

Corin glanced around as he walked on. Kella seemed a dour place—dogs lurked and skulked in corners, and children played games in the streets, their mothers yelling at them. But it was all rather subdued, in Corin's opinion.

He entered a wealthier sector. He knew this because the doors to the houses were painted, and they had gardens in which birds chirped and fountains tinkled. Trees shaded the streets, and wide pavements hinted a slower, safer area. Corin thought this the place to invest in property.

A sudden clatter of hooves and thud of boots turned his head. Then clarion blasts filled the afternoon, and a splendid sight unfolded before him. Corin hid in someone's garden as he watched the cavalcade go by. He counted twenty soldiers—hard-looking men mounted on big horses, their cloaks striped white over orange. They didn't look friendly.

A man rode behind, his face lost in thought. He was smallish in build, but Corin felt a strange sinister power radiating from the rider. He wore a white woolen cap with a purple feather askew. His cloak was white too, and his black boots were highly polished. The rider turned and looked at the spot where Corin was hiding, and

Corin shivered. It seemed those dark eyes saw him standing there. The rider turned his face away. It was a face Corin would remember—heavily lined, bearded, and hawk alert. The horseman rode on in thoughtful silence, a squad of infantry marching in file some ten feet behind him.

Corin blew air in sudden relief. Then came the trumpet players, a portly drummer, and a score or so of lethal-looking individuals with curved swords strapped to their belts. Corin assumed they were assigned to protect whoever was hidden in the gilded cart they surrounded, an intricate contraption pulled by two huge horses. He wondered if the high king himself sat within in that cart. That would make sense. Corin felt a flush of excitement as he witnessed the spectacle. He wished Holly were here to see this with him

He remained hidden until the troop had vanished around a corner. Then, deeming it time, he vaulted from the garden and made his way behind the cavalcade, taking care to keep out of eyesight. That took him to the palace. There were many folk there, some cheering—though even these fell silent when the white-cloaked noble glanced their way.

Corin walked closer and mingled with the crowd. He watched with anticipation as a frail figure clambered from the gilded wain and, with a guard supporting him, stumbled toward the palace gates, soon vanishing within. Corin felt saddened at the sight. If this was King Kelsalion, then he was not what Corin had expected. He had always believed the high king to be a powerful warrior type. But perhaps this was someone else. He'd ask Nora back at the inn. She seemed to know everything that went on in this city.

The fuss over, Corin trudged on, taking in the sights comprising palace walls and tree-filled grounds. The weird spike Polin had called the Astrologer's Roost cast a shadow on the street ahead. The tower was creepy and unnerving and seemed unnatural to Corin, stabbing up into the blue above like an accusing finger. He turned away. It was all a bit much, and Corin decided another ale was needed. Just one pint to quench his thirst, then he'd head back to Nora's tavern.

There were no inns near the palace, so Corin kept walking. At last, just as it was getting dark and he knew he should turn back, Corin saw the warm welcoming light of an inn. A smarter-looking establishment than the fat man's tavern.

I'll just have the one . . .

Corin strode to the door. A sign above read "The Pikeman's Rest." Corin thought that a good name for an inn and without further thought ambled in through the door. A rush of heat and noise greeted him, and he squinted as smoke stung his eyes. This tavern was full, but that wasn't the best news. Every man seated within was a soldier, and most were staring at where he stood lurking by the door.

"What is that?" This from a big nasty-looking type with an oversized customized tankard gripped between sturdy hands.

"Looks like it crawled out from the gutter." The big soldier's companion was weasel lean, half his face ruined by some hideous scar and his left eye milky white. A third man motioned to another to block the way out. Corin turned to see a tall smiling fellow with folded arms shutting the door behind him.

"You've got some nerve coming in here," the tall man said.

"I don't know where here is, really. I'm sort of lost." Corin knew he'd made a big mistake but was determined not to show it. Maybe he could impress this lot by not being scared? The odds of that appeared slim.

"You're sort of stupid," said the big soldier with the customized tankard. He stood, slurping and scowling at Corin as his friend with the mangled face grinned beside him.

"Skinny bugger," Scarface said. "I think I'll shove my hand up his arse and see if he squeaks." There were several chuckles, and Corin decided he really didn't like Kella City. His stomach twisted, and again he felt the urge to run. Instead, he bit his lip and stood his ground.

"First we should strip him." The tall man shoved Corin deeper into the room. "Get Grunt to poke his bare arsehole—make a change from the donkeys he's usually walloping."

They laughed, and Corin felt a mix of rage and horror. He didn't deserve this. "Fuck you!" Corin let the outrage inside him build, give him strength. They could beat him to death, but he would take a few with him—at least he would try.

"Spunky little bugger." The tall man slid a knife from his belt. Corin threw up an arm to defend himself, but the knife hilt clubbed the side of his face, and Corin lay sprawled on the floor. "Take him to the table, lads. Let's have some sport. What say you, Grunt?" Scarface grinned at his huge companion. Grunt nodded.

"Strip him down," Grunt said. Corin tried to stand, but the tall man's boot slammed into his back. Two others joined in, and they threw Corin across a table. The tall man approached, flicking the knife through his fingers. "You're in the Bear's Den, boy—that's forbidden to such as you. Now, we're just going to mess with you, and then we'll let you go. You see, you need a lesson." He leveled the knife while Grunt found his feet and walked over to grab Corin's collar.

"You're prettier than some whores I've tupped." Grunt grinned, then froze when a figure blocked his way.

"Let him be."

Corin could see the door just yards to his right and focused on making a mad dash for it. He would run and run until he was outside the gates of this foul city. He'd go hungry and be lost but didn't care a jot. *Just let me get out of here!*

"Taskala." Grunt almost spat the word, and the men surrounding Corin stepped back to allow the newcomer close. It was apparent they didn't much like this interloper, but they seemed to respect him. "I thought your lot had left town."

"Most have." The man called Taskala gazed down at Corin as though he were a slab of meat. "Not me."

"You Wolves are barred from this tavern." It was the first time the innkeep had showed his face. He was a toothless skinny individual with a drooping eyelid.

"I go where I choose," Taskala responded. "And do as I do." He stared down at Corin, who saw a hard face, flat gray eyes, a badly broken nose, and a thatch of close-cropped silver hair. So this was a Wolf standing over him; Corin felt a flush of relief. Someone was on his side after all.

"You had best go, Wolf." The tall man inched closer to where Taskala studied Corin. "You are not welcome here." He twirled his knife idly between his fingers again.

Taskala glanced at the tall warrior. He nodded and turned slowly, then snake-swift he reached forward and grabbed the tall man's wrist, twisting hard until the man dropped the blade. Taskala pulled him close and rammed an elbow up into the man's nose. It cracked like chicken bones, and the tall man's face exploded as he slumped to the floor.

Grunt leaped toward Taskala, but the other man was quicker; he blocked the big man's punch and clawed his fingers hard into Grunt's face. Then Scarface produced a knife and hurled it at Taskala. The Wolf soldier knocked that aside and seized a chair, bringing it down hard onto Scarface's head.

Corin blinked, shocked by the speed and savagery of what had just occurred. Very impressive. Corin smiled at Taskala, who glared back at him as though he were a fool.

"Get up!" Taskala growled at Corin, who needed no further prompting and quickly found his feet.

Taskala yanked Corin's arm and pitched him toward the door. The minute he turned his back, Scarface produced a second knife and leapt upon Taskala, the blade inching toward his throat.

Taskala twisted and rammed an elbow back into his assailant's groin. Scarface coughed, and Taskala threw him from his back. Scarface staggered to his knees, knife still in hand.

"Watch out!" Corin yelled. Taskala kicked Scarface hard in the groin, and he crumpled unconscious to the floor.

A scrape of steel. Taskala saw Grunt's sword whistle through the air. He ducked beneath the blade and, finding his hidden dagger, stabbed hard and quick, piercing Grunt's heart. The big man slumped, and Corin watched in horrified fascination as Grunt's blood pooled across the straw-strewn flagstones.

Silence followed. Taskala eyed those watching him. Clearly, they knew Taskala's reputation and they knew Grunt's. But Grunt was dead, and though angry, they weren't about to join him. So they backed off, and Taskala, eyes cat-sharp, departed The Pikeman's

Rest with Corin close beside him.

Outside in the street Corin stood shaking, his mind racing as it tried to absorb what had just happened. He looked at the hard-faced warrior, who was still watching the men inside, lest any change their mind.

"Thanks," Corin muttered, still stunned at the violence he'd just witnessed.

Taskala looked him over. "Shut up," he said and pushed Corin further out into the street.

"I was looking to join the Wolf regiment," Corin shouted as he was pitched into the muck.

"You just have," Taskala replied, and without a backward glance strode off down the street. Corin shook himself and stood. His knees were shaky after the trouble in the inn, but he was still angry, and despite being grateful to this Taskala character, he wanted answers from him.

"So what happens now?" Corin demanded while jogging, which allowed him to catch up with his new companion. "I mean, do I have papers to sign or something?" Corin felt numb with shock at this new development. He knew he should be pleased but was worried what those other men would do once they got over their shock. There's was obviously some kind of feud between the two regiments, and, unwittingly, Corin was now in the thick of it.

Taskala slowed his pace and awarded Corin a hostile glare. "You keep your mouth shut and ears open. That way you might survive the next few weeks. I'm not your friend—don't ever make that mistake. You think those fuckers in the Pike were bad news? You are in for a shock, boy. I'm Taskala Swordmaster—your new worst nightmare."

Taskala turned and resumed his step, walking briskly and with purpose.

Puffing, Corin ventured another tack. "The tavern around the corner. The woman Nora. I need to thank her; she was kind to me. And she has my sword in her safekeeping."

"You won't see her again," Taskala replied.

"She has my sword! I have to go get it. It was my father's

sword!" Corin yelled but Taskala ignored his protestations and led Corin along the wall until they reached the front gates, some two hundred yards past where the crack lay leading to the rear entrance. Taskala shouted, and someone responded immediately. The gates opened, and Taskala strode in with Corin close behind. A gaunt narrow-faced man with a mustache nodded at Taskala before appraising Corin with indifference.

"Recruit?" The gate man asked.

"Lucky to be alive." Taskala grunted. "Found him in the Pike surrounded by Bears. Grunt among them."

"What was he doing in there?"

"Fucked if I know; said he was lost. He isn't from around here." Taskala left the gate man gawping at Corin and walked into an adjacent building. Corin glanced at the gateman, who shrugged.

"Best follow him, Sunshine, and get kitted out," the gaunt man suggested.

Corin nodded, and, nerves tingling with excitement and anticipation, he entered into the barrack stores. Taskala stood in a hallway lined with cupboards along one wall. Most were empty with doors ajar, but after checking, Taskala grunted as he found what he sought: a leather coat, leather trousers, well-worn boots, and a belt with a brass buckle.

"These will serve," Taskala said and gestured for Corin to don the trousers and strap the belt around his waist. "You'll have to keep that shirt as we're short of stock here. Hungry?"

Corin nodded.

"The canteen's at the end of this building. Find Dillen the cook and say you've just enlisted. Eat and sleep; we ride at dawn."

"Sleep where?"

Taskala didn't answer; instead, he slammed a cupboard door and briskly departed the hall. Corin watched him, wondering what the man's problem was.

He shrugged and ventured through several doors until he found the canteen. Like everywhere else, it appeared empty, but then Corin noticed three men seated at a far table, one sporting a grubby apron. And judging by his red face, Corin deemed him the cook.

He approached the three apprehensively.

"I've just joined up," Corin said as they turned their heads his way.

"What did he say, Dillen?" The man who spoke was as lean as leather and his face weather-beaten and hard, a half-round scar circling his right eye. The third man was bigger, though also lean and appeared as tough as wire. Dillen studied Corin and laughed.

"I've seen more flesh on a sparrow. You hungry, boy?"

"Yes." Corin shuffled his feet, and the three exchanged glances. "Taskala rescued me from The Pikeman's Rest," Corin thought he'd better explain. "Didn't realize I wasn't supposed to be in there. Not from around here."

The lean man clutched his beard and laughed. His companion joined him, and even the cook looked amused.

"You were in the Bears' den? Was Grunt there?" Dillen asked before wandering off to a table that held trays of piping-hot stew.

"He was."

"You're lucky to be in one piece," the scarred one said. "I'm Scolates, and this is Delemar, but you can call us Scolly and Del. That there's Dillen, the cook, and he's a tosspot." Dillen grinned at the insult and slammed a plate of gray stew on the table.

"Where you from?" Scolly asked, seeming the chattiest and friendliest of the three.

"Fol." Corin tucked into the stew; he was hungry enough to ignore the bland meat and weak gravy with watery carrots alongside.

"Didn't think anyone lived there," Scolly said. "Wind and warlocks—that's all I know about Fol."

"Lots of wind." Corin nodded between munches. "Not aware of any warlocks."

"He means that tower at the western end." Delemar spoke for the first time, his voice deep and slow. "They say a wizard lived there once."

Corin shrugged. "First I've heard about it." He looked up and frowned upon seeing Taskala enter the canteen.

"Ho there, Swordmaster!" Scolly greeted Taskala. "Want some stew?"

"I'd rather eat rat shit." Taskala glared at Corin and pulled up a chair beside the others. "Tell you where I found him, did he?"

"He did." Scolly nodded. "Lucky you were there."

"Grunt's dead."

"Fuck." This from all three at the same time. "That's not good," added Scolly. "I mean, yes, it's excellent news, but it means we'll have all his mates after us now. Grunt was popular."

"That's why we're leaving town at first light," Taskala told them. "I was planning on staying another week to see if I could find some more recruits, but this arsewipe has buggered that up."

"Why don't you like me?" Corin wiped his mouth and stared at Taskala, whose lips twitched, hinting violence.

"Wisen him up, Scolly, before he hurts himself." Taskala stood wiping sweat from his face with a sleeve. "I'm turning in. We ride at dawn, understood?"

"Understood," the others said, and Corin nodded.

He waited until Taskala had gone and then turned to Scolly. "I left my father's sword in the inn across the street. I need to get it back."

"We'll get for you, lad—don't fret." Scolly glanced at Del, who shook his head.

"Lost his sword already?"

"He wouldn't let me fetch it." Corin hinted at the door Taskala had just vacated. "He doesn't like me, does he?"

"That there is Swordmaster Taskala," Scolly replied. "He's a bastard, and he hates everyone. But he's the best friend you can have when the Permians are trying to slit your throat. "Just don't back-chat him, lad. Do as he says, and you'll get through. You're in for some sunny days, Folly Boy!"

"Aye." Dillen nodded, smiling. "Welcome to the Wolves, Folly!"

***

Several miles outside the city, Polin urged his horse toward a small hamlet that spilled welcoming light from the deep forest surrounding it. Time to rest up and reflect on his busy day. Once inside, the smith paid a tavern girl good silver and had the inn's snug all to himself. Not for him the noise and banter of the common room next door.

Polin lit his pipe, sucked in smoke, and thought about the lad Corin an Fol. The next months would be hard on the boy. But Polin knew Corin had the backbone and the tenacity to endure, as long as he kept that temper under control. And his mouth shut too.

Polin eased back in his chair. He'd done what he'd had to. Polin liked Corin despite behaving gruffly toward him. But needs must—the lad had required honing as much as his father's sword. Corin would be alright; Polin felt certain of it. With a rare reflective smile, the smith raised his heavy tankard and toasted his former apprentice.

"To you, wild laddie. Stay strong and keep your chin up. And steer well clear of that bastard Taskala!"

Polin took a long, slow gulp and sighed as the heat of fire, food in his belly, and mix of strong ale eased his weary bones. He'd purchased some hides and a couple of wood axes—nothing much. But he had enjoyed the trip. The following morning Polin was away ere daybreak, the miles crunching beneath his horse's hoofs. Yes, he thought, that had proved a worthwhile visit to Kella City, but it was good to be homeland bound again.

Polin stowed his pipe in his saddlebag and whistled the horse to kick up dust. If he was lucky he'd reach Fol by nightfall.

Chapter 5

Port Wind

Driving rain did nothing to raise his spirits as Corin guided his horse behind his new companions, Scolly and Del. The two older men appeared to have a soft spot for Corin and had taken him under their wing. Corin suspected this might have been because they knew what he had coming. Certainly they'd been dropping hints, which were seldom encouraging. The word *training* had an unsavory sound to it. But at least Taskala Swordmaster was happy to ignore him—something that suited Corin very well.

They were three days into their journey, and it had rained solid for two of them. Corin was soaked through—his cloak and leather beneath it were drenched, his horse and saddle dripping, and his nose full of snot. Summer in Kelthaine! He hoped he'd never visit during winter. Corin tried to focus on the positive, but warm, dry images of Holly naked in Burmon's hay shed did little to help.

They had left Kella City without incident, and long before the sun gilded the roof of the high king's palace. For his part, Corin was glad to leave. He hadn't overly enjoyed his abrupt stay in Kella and was happy for new horizons. He hoped he would eventually see them through the rain clouds.

Their road had run straight and clean for several miles until they entered the Northern Wolds, an area of low wooded hills that ranged across central Kelthaine. These they threaded, crossing woods and streams for many miles, while wolf and boar watched their passage from the safety of the trees. As he rode, Corin had time to reflect on his new career. He had mixed feelings but was determined to pass every test that came his way. These people were tough and enduring, and he would soon be the same.

A few months fighting would give him an edge. Then Corin could seek out news of Ceilyn and the bastard that had taken her. Corin was convinced she was long dead, but at least he could avenge her, find this Torval—if he still lived—and then cut out his heart. It was a thought that helped focus his mind as the dismal rain soaked and chilled his body beneath the heavy cloak.

The rain stopped when they reached the coast at a town called Reln. Corin had never heard of it, but, then, he'd never been overly curious about distant places. He regretted that now. Reln was a muddle of thatch and timbers perched on a windy cliff overlooking the marching flanks of gray breakers rolling in from the western ocean. To its south, the River Kelvannis looped neatly around wooded hills until greeting the sea in a sludge of green.

"Kelwyn." Scolly pointed to the far bank where trees shaded the river's southern side. Beyond these rose more round hills in what looked to be a pleasant country. "That's our new home." Scolly grinned at him conspiratorially.

Corin hadn't realized Port Wind was in Kelwyn but decided not to expand on the matter. He didn't know much about Kelwyn either, save that it was ruled by a different king, though that ruler paid homage to the high king in Kella.

"Lovely," Corin managed after a moment's wan reflection, grateful that the afternoon sun had helped dry him out. "How do we get there?"

"By ferry." Close by, Delemar looked at Corin as though he'd just said something beyond stupid. "It departs at first light, so we'll rest up in Reln this eve."

"Ale and lasses." Scolly winked at Corin, who grinned back,

until he saw Taskala guiding his steed to join them.

"Not for him." Taskala gestured at where Corin sat his horse. "He's in training." Taskala awarded Corin a half smirk and urged his beast forward.

"Bastard," Corin muttered beneath his breath. But he kept his cool. Corin knew he could learn much from Taskala. The man was a killer with lightning-fast reactions, and Corin, while disliking him, admired those skills.

Learn what you can, and then go it alone . . . The plan was forming in his head.

When they reached the desired tavern and stabled their horses, Corin was left to seek out his own supper in the inn and was then told to depart while the older men imbibed.

Happy to be alone, Corin walked for a time. The town was quiet now; evening had seen traders and dockers leave their stations to sup. The streets were mostly empty save for the odd skulking hound. Reln's apparent lack of attractive girls gave Corin some solace as he strode along the docks and quayside. After such busy weeks, he'd finally found time to reflect on his recent actions.

Revenge. One word, but it was enough and gave him purpose. Corin had loved Ceilyn back then, and the anger of her abduction had never left him. That, and the futility of his never knowing her fate though always believing the worst. Corin hated Crenna, though he still knew little concerning that remote island. He vowed to one day seek it out and thrust holes in a few of its occupants with his father's sword. First he'd benefit from the skills the Wolves would teach him. Learn fast and live hard. The tougher, the better; Corin was ready for this challenge. Besides, what else had he to do? That said, he was daunted by what lay ahead, and part of him wished he'd never left Finnehalle.

I have to stay strong . . .

He reached a jetty where fishing boats bobbed and strained against ropes. The tide was coming in fast. Corin walked to the end of the wooden dock, its planks creaking and groaning beneath his feet. From there he gazed out across the ocean as a wash of loneliness flooded through him.

Corin missed Finnehalle, and he missed Holly—more than he'd expected to. He was ready for this new life but hoped it wouldn't be forever and that one day soon he could at least return—if only for a brief while—and hold her in his arms again. It wasn't much to ask. Corin believed he was doing the right thing, but watching the calm lap of dark water tugged at his heartstrings. But what choices had he had? Polin had abandoned him in Kella, no doubt believing he'd done the right thing. A hard lesson for his ex-apprentice to learn.

Corin was surrounded by far tougher individuals than those he'd grown up with. He would have to work hard to prove himself and earn their respect, but he'd get there. Scant time for moping— look ahead and seize the adventure. Corin stood to gain much as long as he held positive.

Footsteps announced someone approached. Corin pulled a face, not being in the mood for snide comments from his new companions, or worse—insults from Swordmaster Taskala. But instead, a young man about his own age stood grinning at him.

"I'm Darrel," the youth said. "And you're Corin an Fol. We're to be mates."

"What?" Corin glared at Darrel, seeing a freckle-faced, red-dish-haired lad, small in build and looking younger than his own twenty years but cheery in demeanor and missing two front teeth.

"I joined up this evening." Darrel looked pleased with himself. "I was in the tavern with my uncle; we'd been fishing and had a rare thirst. I saw the Wolf brooches on their cloaks hanging on pegs by the door and went across and said hello. They laughed at me a bit, but after I spun them a line, they agreed I could enlist. Seemed like a good crew. They called me a ginger tosser and sent me out to join you. They said you'd be down by the water."

"You . . . enlisted?" Corin's frown deepened. Darrel didn't look strong enough to lift a sword, let alone mean enough to kill someone with it. "Why?"

"It's either that or starve as a fisherman. Or else perish of boredom. Nothing ever happens in Reln."

"That I do believe." Corin gazed at his new acquaintance for a few moments and then thrust out his hand. "Good to meet you, Darrel. I think we're in for some shit weeks."

"Has to get worse before it gets better." Darrel gripped Corin's hand, and his grin broadened. "Well met!"

***

Morning found them crossing the River Kelvannis in a barge constructed of logs lashed together with ropes and guided by an old gaffer with a wide-brimmed hat and shabby cloak, his scrawny hands tugging at the rope that linked north bank to south. Corin caught the old man's eye and determined him an unsavory fellow. The men stood beside their horses and waited as the barge edged onto mud and roots and they were able to disembark.

Taskala passed coin to the ferryman, who nodded and set about readying his craft for the return trip. Once ashore, they mounted: twelve men, including four new recruits, three fresh from Reln, and one late arrival from Kella City. Corin stared at the latest enlisters found in a tavern last night. They were a sorry-looking lot, with the exception of Darrel, who seemed to resonate cheerfulness despite dreading what was coming.

The three newcomers from Reln were thin and wiry: freckle-faced Jorl; skinny Clorte, who had a very crooked nose, badly broken in a fishing accident; and Sleagon, who spoke seldom and when he did, it was usually negative, like "this will probably kill us" or "they'll send us to Permio, and we'll all die down there." Corin steered clear of Sleagon most the time.

Then there was Tomarric from somewhere north of Kella City, whom Scolly and Del had already nicknamed as Tomato, much to the other recruits' amusement. Tomarric didn't seem to mind; he was cheerful, though not as idiotically optimistic as young Darrel.

They fared south through wood and copse, often fording streams and guiding their mounts through steep bird-noisy woods. It was pleasant country, and they were blessed by a warm summer sun. The countryside surrounding him was more pleasing to the eye than Kelthaine had been, its woods and folds populated by the odd hamlet and village that Corin spied now and then. They stayed clear of those; Taskala wanted to reach Port Wind by nightfall.

The woods began to weave tighter, but to their right Corin often glimpsed the blue glint of ocean, and during those moments the loneliness found him again. He kept his thoughts to himself and instead consulted with chatty Darrel about this region of Kelwyn.

"Why does everything begin with a K?" Darrel had told him that the river they had crossed had been the Kelvannis and that they were making for where the Kelphalos met the sea after mixing its clear waters with the mighty River Kelthara.

"Named after Old King Kell, as are most places I know. Didn't they teach you that in your school?" Corin knew Darrel couldn't fathom him out. To the younger recruit Corin must have seemed moody, distant, and grim. But then, Darrel knew nothing of Corin's past, and Corin wasn't planning on telling his new friend about that anytime soon. Corin liked Darrel, but some things he'd always keep to himself. The other recruits hardly spoke to Corin. Sleagon warned that people from Fol were untrustworthy. Corin had let that go for the time being.

"I never went to school; don't even know what one is." Corin glared at Darrel, who shrugged and cheerfully explained that this region was known as the Woods between the Waters, and it was one of King Nogel's—Kelwyn's ruler—favored hunting forests. "Nogel is a warrior king," Darrel told Corin. "Not like the high king. And Nogel doesn't much like Caswallon. There's been tensions between this land and Kelthaine of late."

Darrel appeared to be a trove of information, but Corin's curiosity had ebbed as his new friend seemed to fill every second with chattering. At last sensing Corin's disinterest, Darrel urged his beast ahead to where Scolly and Del were hinting to some of the others at what delights awaited them in Port Wind.

Taskala got his wish, and they reached Port Wind ere dusk darkened its streets. Bigger than Reln and south-facing, the town looked out across the wide blue waters of the Western Ocean. Corin could see three ships moored at the northern banks of the River Kelphalos where it greeted the sea.

They guided their mounts through windy streets, reaching

cliffs at the far side and a wide track that led up a steep incline into gorse-yellow hills. "The barracks are five miles from the town," Darrel had already told Corin, and it was evident the smallest recruit saw it as his new duty to gather information. A half hour later they crested the hills, and Taskala allowed a brief pause to settle mounts and share a flask of water. Corin gazed back down at Port Wind, seeing the ships he'd spied earlier, which were now distant blobs of movement.

Taskala clicked his tongue and bid his mount to approach the knot of ragged recruits who were all gazing back at Port Wind. "Yes, take a long, hard look, my lovelies. Port Wind is out of bounds to you six, so forget any thoughts of ale and lasses. We start your training tomorrow." He ended with a harsh bark of a laugh and urged his horse into a trot.

The wind picked up as they rode west toward a bleak promontory. Here, dark square buildings could be seen and a wide stockade ringed by a wooden wall. Corin stifled a curse; the barracks didn't look overly enticing. Slate-dressed walls and roofs glistened stark beneath leaden skies, and the wind whistled and whined like a kettle reaching a boil.

A man watched their approach from above the single iron gate. Tall, stern, and hard of face, he ordered two soldiers to open the gates and allow the new arrivals in. Taskala waved at the tall man, who nodded briefly and then turned away to continue his perusal elsewhere.

"That's Lord Halfdan," Darrel hissed in Corin's ear; the little fellow sounded overly excited. "I didn't know he was here. He's the high king's brother, Corin."

"So I've heard." Corin was unimpressed. He hated the thought of being hemmed up in this bleak place, knowing there was a town so close by. Maybe he'd slip out one night if chance allowed. That thought brought the ghost of a smile to his face—the first he'd managed that day.

Once inside the compound Corin looked about. It wasn't reassuring. Stables, armory, rain-washed fields muddied by boots and marching, and squat barracks, all of a similar size. He saw one tavern but realized that was for the veterans and not for such as he. There was also a bigger building to the left that afforded wide views over the ocean. Close to that, a long whitewashed hut with a badly rendered chimney proved to be the canteen.

After seeing to their horses, the new arrivals were shown their barracks at the northern end of the stockade. A single window allowed just enough light for unimpaired movement. There was no fireplace, and Corin counted nine blankets on the floor. Two were occupied, the nearest showing a mop of black shaggy hair.

"Brought you some friends." Scolly grinned down at the sleepers, then turned toward Corin, Darrel, and the others. "I'll show you the canteen, lads. Once you've filled your bellies, return here and get some kip. You'll need to be sharp in the morning." He flashed Corin a grin and then departed for the veterans' tavern, where Del and the others were no doubt already quaffing ale.

The cook shoved a gray slab of meat on Corin's plate and filled his pewter mug, care of Scolly, with some lukewarm water. The cook's name was Rodi, Corin learned. He was fiery and appeared in a foul mood. Just another fellow to steer clear from in this horrible place.

Corin hardly slept that night, and when Taskala crashed into the room before dawn, Corin alone was ready.

Chapter 6

A Sorry Bunch

"They appear a sorry lot," the commander said as rain beaded his window.

Lord Halfdan was seated at his desk, watching the parade of skinny arms and legs shamble into loose order. The high king's brother was in his middle forties, a serious man with a lean face dominated by heavy brow and blade-lean nose, with keen blue-gray eyes that hinted cunning and tenacity. Taskala respected this man above any other.

"Pickings are lean, my lord. Belmarius and Perani got the cream of the crop up in Kella—Caswallon saw to that. These lads are mostly strays from Reln and Port Wind. One or two might shape up in time. We'll do what we can in the coming weeks."

"I do not doubt it, Swordmaster." Halfdan shook his head, seeing one of the young men trip and tumble into the mud, then stumble back onto his feet, only to trip again. Taskala had ordered them to run for more than an hour. He'd added that if they stopped, he'd ban them from eating that night. To a man, they looked exhausted. "I am lucky to have you."

"Is Rana in camp?" Taskala noted the sour expression on Corin an Fol's face as he reached down and lifted the sprawling

Darrel to his feet. He would have to watch that one, Taskala decided. Halfdan had also noticed Corin, and he studied the youth
with interest.

"She arrives tomorrow; she sent word via pigeon two days
past."

"Good." Taskala flashed his rare grin. "She has her work cut
out with this lot. How fare things in Point Keep?"

"As well as can be expected." Halfdan's eyes still studied the
latest batch of staggering recruits. Two more had fallen, and they
all looked beyond miserable. Hard to imagine any of these holding up against a Permian war band. "The Keep's been deserted for
years," Halfdan added. "But the boys have settled in nicely and will
make things comfy before the rest of us arrive. But why are you
here, Taskala? I thought the plan was to remain in Kella City, glean
what news you could, and maybe find some more lads."

Taskala curled his upper lip. "There was a bit of trouble," he
allowed.

"Trouble?" Halfdan turned in his leather chair and awarded
Taskala a bleak look. "What kind of trouble?"

"That kind of trouble." Taskala pointed to the field outside,
where fresh rain was assaulting the red-faced recruits as they completed their one-hundred-and-fifty-second circuit of the drill yard.
Halfdan's shrewd gaze followed Taskala's hand until it rested on
Corin an Fol, now bringing up the rear, a murderous expression
on his face.

"Enlighten me."

"Found him in The Pikeman's Rest surrounded by randy
Bears," Taskala said. "Taken upon himself to wander inside demanding ale. Didn't get the reception he'd expected, so I hauled
him out before they buggered him senseless."

Lord Halfdan's frown deepened. "And why were you there,
Swordmaster? You know the fragility of the situation in that city."

"I do, my lord," Taskala replied awkwardly. "I'd heard rumors about Belmarius's lads stirring up trouble with Caswallon.
I wanted to discover all I could before leaving Kella. So I slipped
inside their inn, found a dark corner, and kept myself well hidden

with hood and cloak. Until that miserable creature out there ruined my disguise.

"I killed Grunt," Taskala added after a moment's silence.

"Well, that's not overly helpful," snapped Halfdan. "Belmarius was fond of that troll—the gods alone know why. I shall write him soon with our sincere apologies. Say it was a personality clash. You have been somewhat overzealous, Taskala. Your orders were to watch and monitor. Assess and not provoke. Caswallon will seize on this as an excuse to dismantle our regiment. Gods know he's wanted that for years."

"I'm sorry, my lord." Taskala's face was red with fury. He didn't like being reprimanded and determined that another reason to blame Corin an Fol. "That boy's trouble," he added vindictively. "You remember Big Polin from far-off Fol?"

"A good soldier, but not that flexible—what of him?"

"Short Tom the sentry said he saw Polin in Kella with yon lad." Taskala noted that three of the recruits had stopped running and were crouched on their knees coughing up blood. He smiled—no supper for those three tonight. The rest kept moving, though barely. "He said the boy had approached the gates the night before I found him, asking to join, on Polin's recommendation."

"I would fain talk with said youth." Halfdan's keen gaze studied the yard outside, while across from his desk, Taskala was puzzled by his commander's sudden interest. "Of course, I want to address them all," Halfdan added smoothly after catching Taskala's quizzical expression. "I think maybe you should let them rest for a time, then get them cleaned up. I'll see them this afternoon."

Taskala felt uneasy. There was something odd about his commander's sudden interest in the recruits. Most often he would scarce even notice them until Taskala and his second, Rana, had made some useful shape of them. That said, he nodded and kept his lips closed.

"That will be all, Swordmaster." Halfdan unfolded a parchment on his desk and studied it in detail. Taskala took the hint, saluted stiffly, then briskly departed from his commander's office. Outside, he was greeted by rain and gales and eight mournful faces.

"Stop!" Taskala boomed. They skidded to a halt, Corin crashing into Darrel's back and someone else bumping him from behind. "You three." Taskala pointed at Jorl, Sleagon, and the Kelthaine lad called Greggan, who had arrived in camp four days past. "No supper tonight. When I say run, that's what I mean. Now, off to barracks and get cleaned up. There's a hose outside; you may use it. Our commander wishes to address you this very afternoon—the gods alone know why."

***

Corin scrubbed dirt from his boots as he listened to Greggan complaining about missing supper. He'd met Greggan that morning along with Marric. Both came from some village in eastern Kelthaine. Greggan was likable enough, but Marric—the biggest of the recruits—had an arrogance that set Corin's teeth on edge.

"I only stopped because I had a cramp," Greggan complained. "That Taskala's a bastard."

"He is that," Corin added, noting how Marric was staring at him. "What's with you, big lad?" Corin continued brushing his boots while keeping a wary eye on Marric.

"Nobody wants to know what you think, Folly." Marric leaned forward and ruffled Corin's hair. "At least he doesn't have donkey ears." Marric grinned at Greggan and the others. "I'd heard they are all descended from asses in Fol. Or is it sheep?" He pushed Corin again, harder this time.

Corin refused to be goaded, and, annoyed, Marric soon tired of his game. Corin watched the big lad settle on his blanket and smirk at the ceiling. Corin smiled; he'd bide his time, but smirking Marric would pay for his comments in due course.

***

Darrel came out beaming from ear to ear. "He said I'd make sergeant in five years," Darrel whispered in Corin's ear as he practically jumped down the corridor leading from the commander's mess rooms to the yards outside. Corin wondered if Darrel was unhinged. Certainly he was blighted by an overdose of optimism.

Corin took a more philosophical approach. Taskala hated him, Rodi the cook disliked him, and Marric took every opportunity to mock him. And rumor was they would have a new instructor arriving in the morning who would most likely hate him too. So why would the Lord Commander prove different? At least Corin was getting a break from running in the rain. It mattered not what they thought about him. This was a temporary situation—or at least he believed it to be.

The others emerged one by one after their interviews with Lord Halfdan. Some wore smiles, a few looked perplexed, and Tomato and Jorl looked terrified. Corin's turn came at last. He grunted as Taskala yelled in his ear and ushered him inside the spacious office where Lord Halfdan was seated neatly at his desk. After a moment, Taskala closed the door and left them alone. Corin stood rock still for more than a minute before his commander deigned to glance upon him.

"Sit." Lord Halfdan gestured for Corin to pull up a chair and face him across the table. Corin obliged with a startled expression. He hadn't expected courtesy. Corin sat and fidgeted for several moments as Halfdan's gaze swept over him. "And how shall I serve you, Corin an Fol?"

"Excuse me?" Corin was puzzled by the question. He'd thought he was supposed to be the one doing the serving.

"Excuse me, *my lord*." Halfdan's eyes bored into Corin's and made him feel decidedly uncomfortable. Seeing Corin's constipated expression, he snorted. "Relax, boy." Halfdan almost smiled. "You appear as one in pain."

"I'm not understanding your meaning, my lord. I'm just a recruit but willing to try hard."

"We don't 'try' in the Wolves, Corin an Fol. We 'do.' Those who try often fail, and he who fails will probably die. Remember that snippet. So? How fared Master Polin when last you saw him?" Halfdan changed tack as Corin still fidgeted, pinned by his commander's steely gaze.

"Well enough, I suppose." Corin was still angry with Polin and didn't really want to talk about him.

"And you're from quaint Finnehalle on the north coast of Fol?"

Corin nodded. "You know of it, my lord?"

"I do," Lord Halfdan replied. Corin was impressed. But Halfdan's gaze hardened, and he dropped his voice to a whisper. "Swordmaster Taskala holds a dim view of you, boy. I'd tread carefully in the weeks ahead, were I you. Lest you make an enemy."

"Well, I didn't think I'd make any friends here," Corin responded, then wished he hadn't spoken. Quicker than he'd believed possible, Lord Halfdan's hand shot across the table and seized Corin's leather tunic, pulling him close.

"You are going to impress him, Corin an Fol. You are going to excel at every task he gives you. You won't complain, and you certainly won't cause trouble with that big fellow Marric. Learn humility. Self-discipline. Keep your mouth shut and ears open. That way you might just keep your head on your shoulders. Dismissed."

Lord Halfdan thrust Corin back in his chair and scowled at him. Corin glanced askance at the commander for a moment and then found his feet, and without further delay he departed from the man's office, passing Taskala in the corridor.

Corin had been right in his assessment—the Wolves' commander hated him too. There was a pattern forming here. But he was determined to take note of Halfdan's words. Corin would keep his head—though he might knock a few others about.

***

Taskala strode into the office and closed the door behind him. "That's them all, my lord. As you said this morning—they are a sorry bunch."

Lord Halfdan nodded. "Do what you can. Get them up to speed with the rest. I need them all ready for the autumn campaign in Permio."

Taskala smiled upon hearing that. "So it's on? We're going back there? I'm surprised, after the last debacle." The Wolves and Bears had joined in an attack to oust the rebel warlord Imbala. It hadn't gone well. Imbala was fox-cunning, and having gotten word of their combined attack turned the surprise against them by falling upon the northerners at the Craggy Passes west of Cappel Cormac.

The Wolves had taken the brunt of the attack, losing more than two hundred men, the Bears having fled the ambush. It was still a sore point between the regiments, especially as Councilor Caswallon had announced the Wolf regiment as hapless and un-dependable—a prod meant for Lord Halfdan, though he dared not accuse the high king's brother directly.

"Imbala's been busy." Halfdan gazed out his window as rain beaded the glass. The recruits were out there running again, he not-ed without much interest. "The wily old fox fell upon Agmandeur and slew the sultan's garrison there. That city has always proved troublesome, and now Imbala is using it as a base to raid from. They say he has over forty thousand tribesmen at his heel. Clearly an exaggeration, but the sultan is worried and has once again called on the Four Kingdoms for assistance. Belmarius is sending a unit down there in a few weeks. The Raleenians will help, Lord Starkhold has promised Caswallon."

Taskala grunted. Permio had been a thorn in their side for countless years. The vast desert country was in a state of con-stant war, usually with its own people when warlords like Imbala showed up. But now and then with the Four Kingdoms also. The First Permian War had ended a hundred years previously. A brittle peace had followed. The Permian Sultanate had relinquished its age-old claim on Raleen. For his part, Caswallon, the high king's voice in the south, had promised the sultan aid in fighting the ban-dits. Suffice it to say, there was little love lost between any parties involved.

"Our force is somewhat depleted," Taskala complained. "The Tigers should go. They haven't served down there for years."

"Nor are they likely to, with Perani as commander. I swear that man's in Caswallon's camp." The high counselor in Kella had become powerful of late, gathering allies from courtiers, politicians, and soldiers—General Perani a key member of the latter group.

"Someone should do something about Caswallon before it's too late," Taskala said in a growl. He hated the high counselor, whom he blamed for losing many companions in the desert. "It's already too late." Halfdan abandoned his perusal of the training yard. The rain was heavier now, and dark clouds hastened overhead. "Storm's coming," Halfdan added, though it was hard to know whether he meant the weather or the current situation. "My brother is a lost soul. I mourn for the man he once was."

"And we have no heir to the throne," Taskala added poignantly. Halfdan glanced at him sharply as if struck by his words.

"I meant no offense, my lord." Taskala knew, as did everyone else, that Halfdan's son had been the true heir to Kelsalion III, for in Kelthaine, nephew followed uncle in succession. But both Halfdan's son and his beloved wife, Celeze, together with Kelsalion's queen, Anyetta, and her eldest boy child had all drowned in the disaster off Fol more than twenty years ago. It was something the commander never spoke about, and Taskala cursed his lack of discretion. If Halfdan noted Taskala's discomfort, he showed no sign, being lost in thought. The swordmaster deemed that a good moment to take his leave and, after mumbling a few words, briskly vacated the building.

He found the recruits soaked and caked in mud. Scolly had taken a turn with them, showing them wrestling tricks and bidding them take on one another. Darrel being the smallest had not fared well, but despite a torn ear and blackened eye, he still managed a smile.

Taskala observed the sorry sight for a few minutes before heading to the tavern for an early ale. The news of their scheduled return to Permio had given him quite a thirst. Delemar joined him there and Rodi too, both wanting to hear the news he'd acquired.

***

A wave of weariness washed through Halfdan's veins. He gripped the table and willed it away. Truth was, he'd never recovered from that disaster all those years ago. But unlike his brother, the high king, Lord Halfdan had stayed strong for the Four Kingdoms that he loved and his valiant boys in the Wolves.

Was it possible? Halfdan thought about the young man called

Corin an Fol. Certainly he had the look. And there was no fear in the boy but rather a wildness that bespoke arrogance and anger. Finnehalle? Halfdan had gone there after hearing of the shipwreck nearby, where his beloved wife had perished together with their only son. Or had he? Did he dare hope?

Halfdan closed his eyes and shut out that dangerous thought. But it was too much of a coincidence, and the boy had his look.

Halfdan staggered to his feet and opened a drawer in his cabinet. He found the brandy and poured the bottle's golden contents into a large oval glass. He moved across to the window and sipped slowly, watching the rain and allowing the tears to salt his cheeks again as memory of that terrible day twenty-one long years ago came rushing back.

Chapter 7

Vendetta

Clearly she wasn't beautiful, but there was something oddly attractive about Yazrana. The woman had a feral, fierce-eyed look, enhanced by the bent nose and jagged scar cutting through her left eyebrow. She wasn't tall but rather stocky and well balanced, her sleek black hair tied back in an ordered ponytail and those huge almond eyes eagle sharp. Scolates smiled; It was good to have Yazrana back.

The lads called her Rana, lest she be confused with the swordmaster, though such a notion was completely ridiculous. A couple of the senior Wolves dared call her Yaz, her preferred nickname, Scolly and Del among them. The new recruits soon learned to call her "Boss Lady," and for good reason too.

Scolly laughed as he watched her throw the wild-eyed Corin an Fol on the mud as though he were a sack of potatoes. Yazrana was the strongest girl he'd ever known. She was also the toughest and a match for any man in camp, with the exception of Swordmaster Taskala and perhaps Lord Halfdan, the latter renowned as a formidable master of the feared Longsword.

She'd arrived late last night and had woken the recruits before dawn. Scolly grinned, having been witness to that occurrence.

Poor little buggers hadn't known what hit them.

"Get back on your feet," Rana yelled in Corin's ear as he staggered to his feet, blushing and cursing as Marric and a few others watched and laughed.

"Beaten by a woman, Folly!" Marric couldn't resist yelling. That was a mistake. Rana turned her back on Corin and awarded the biggest recruit a withering stare.

"And who might you be?" Rana stalked over to where the big freckle-faced youth stood with a greasy smirk smearing his lips. Rana stopped inches from him. "Are you the toughest here?"

She smiled up at Marric, her dark eyes filled with humor. She was a foot shorter than Marric, but the big youth shuffled awkwardly, pinned by that gaze. "Tough enough to floor me?" Rana purred. "Go on. Strike me! It's the only chance you'll get."

Marric looked pained. "I'll not hit a woman," he muttered. Rana's grin widened upon hearing that. "I mean, it's not the done thing." The other recruits were laughing at Marric, whose red face had turned almost purple in the rain.

Rana snapped her knee up hard and fast, crunching into Marric's groin, at the same instant her left hand shot out and gripped his right ear, yanking the big lad's head down low, just so she could knee him again but this time in the face.

Marric fell in the mud and lay there sprawled, groaning. "It doesn't matter how big you are!" Rana stood over Marric and yelled at the spectators, who stood grinning like loons, except Corin, who seemed fascinated by Rana. She caught his eye, and her own gaze narrowed.

Marric sobbed as Rana kicked him in the ribs, almost as an afterthought. "You lot are off to Permio soon as I can knock some shape into you. The women there aren't gentle like me. They'll slice your guts open and tie them around your neck, and then smile while the vultures feed."

Rana glanced down at Marric. "Hear that, fat boy?" Marric nodded. "Good, now get back on your feet!" Marric, sobbing, staggered to his knees, and then somehow found his feet. He stood there shaking with eyes focused intently on the ground.

***

That evening Taskala burst in on them as Rana sat drinking with Scolly and Del, the three of them discussing Halfdan's news about Permio. "His lordship requests your attendance," Taskala told Rana, who nodded and leapt to her feet.

"I was wondering when he would see me." Rana grinned at her drinking mates and left the tavern as evening claimed the windy hills. She found Halfdan at his desk reading parchments, much as she'd expected.

"Cold for the time of year." Lord Halfdan smiled slightly seeing Yazrana standing before him. She grinned back despite marking how weary he looked. She hadn't known the commander long, but theirs was a good friendship, and very occasionally something more. They'd met during a skirmish near Cappel Cormac late last year. Yazrana knew Halfdan saw her as a wild card who didn't fit in with the Raleenian Lancers with whom she'd trained. She'd upset a few prominent officers down there, so had been delighted when Lord Halfdan offered her a commission in his regiment despite evident consternation from people like Taskala. Yazrana knew she'd proved a comfort to him ever since. Especially as she sometimes warmed his lonely nights.

"You look older, my lord. Your hair shows more gray."

Halfdan smiled upon hearing that. He motioned Rana to sit, and she joined him at the table, where he poured them both a large brandy.

"I've missed you, Yazrana," Lord Halfdan said. He raised his glass and she followed suit; they clinked and sipped and smiled before sitting for a time and discussing the situation in Permio.

"It's about to flare up again." Rana had been in Cappel Cormac the week before, doing some reconnaissance work for the Wolves. She blended in down there and could travel freely without being challenged as a northerner. "Imbala's planning something big, and the sultan wants to stop the warlord before it's too late."

"What do you propose we do?" Lord Halfdan always listened to Yazrana's council, as he did the swordmaster's. She knew the commander considered them both shrewd tacticians.

"Scout the hills south of Cappel, as close to Agmandeur as we dare. I think Imbala's overconfident; the sultan's secure in his cities and along the coast. But the warlord holds the desert. That's how he sees it."

"Supplies?"

"The chink in his armor. Imbala has to rely on constant raiding to keep his tribesmen content. You know how quarrelsome that lot are."

Halfdan nodded. "So we lay low, get our bearings, and then start breaking up his supply caravans. Why hasn't the sultan tried that?"

Rana scoffed. "That lazy slug won't venture into the interior, and his 'special forces,' the Crimson Elite, are a bunch of tossers in nice red cloaks. Overrated. The Crimson are terrified of the desert—have been for years—hence Imbala's success uniting the tribes. The sultan might have relinquished the claim to South Kaelin, but the nomadic tribesmen never expected that. And now Imbala has promised that land to his followers, who see those fertile valleys as their divine right."

Halfdan sighed. "There'll never be peace down there. It's been on-and-off war for a thousand years—ever since your patron Kael of long-lost Gol founded Raleen as a province, and then later took the borderlands from the Permians and called that country South Kaelin. Kael's actions have proved costly over the years."

"Kael was securing our southern borders." Rana was quick to defend her ancestor. "Your high kings have never held sway down there. Raleen has always had to look to itself."

Halfdan let that go. Like all Raleenians, Yazrana was proud of her heritage. Her people were known for their stoic stamina and quick skill with the knife. A Raleenian could be your best friend in the morning and bitterest foe by nightfall. They were a proud but easily offended bunch. Added to that, they were fickle and almost as deadly as the Permians, whom they hated with a passion few northerners could understand. Hence, Rana knew she was proving an invaluable asset to Halfdan in the south.

"So we have ninety-six recruits divided into twelve troops of eight?"

Halfdan nodded. "That last batch arrived just yesterday. I know it's a big ask, Yazrana."

"Six weeks." Rana sipped her brandy and smiled. "Achievable. This is good stuff, by the way."

"From Calprissa."

"I thought so. I love that city. All that white marble, and those fountains . . . agh . . ." She placed her glass on the table and sighed. "Would that I had been born a fine lady." Rana chuckled; it had always been a joke between them. "Taskala's his usual charming self, I see. He told me to be hard on those boys out there. Your latest batch. Harder than usual. Did that come from you, my lord?"

"Aye, it did. I want them to stay alive, Rana. The others are weeks ahead in training. These new lads have a lot of catching up to do. With the swordmaster drilling them, and you showing them which end of a sword to hold, they might just survive down there. You know how I hate sending such striplings to war."

"Needs must—though I think the Wolves are doing more than their share. Have they fallen out of favor with the high king?"

"His counselor—which amounts to the same thing." Halfdan's tone was bitter. "Caswallon wants to disband us. He doesn't like me and will do anything to undermine my influence on my brother. Kelsalion III is not the man he was."

"Depressing." Rana sipped her brandy. "Tell me, Commander. Who is the tall youth with the wild eyes and dark shaggy hair? The one they call Folly?"

"A stray Taskala picked up in Kella." Halfdan's eyes were hooded, and Rana knew when to stop prying. There was something happening here. "Why do you ask?" Halfdan's cool gaze rested on his favorite confidante.

"He has potential; he's quick, got attitude, and I think would make a reasonable longswordsman if he could stomach the discipline needed to learn such a weapon."

"He already has a weapon."

"His father's broadsword. Scolly salvaged it from a tavern

near the barracks in Kella. The boy had left it there."

Halfdan frowned. "That was careless of him."

"Not his fault. Taskala refused to let him leave the barracks, then the next day they were away. But you know Scolates has that soft touch."

Halfdan grunted. "Keep an eye on that boy, Rana. I'd be grateful for that. We need to nourish talent," he added smoothly.

"I will," she promised. "Would you like me to drop by tonight?" Rana added in a quieter voice.

"I think not." Halfdan looked tired and drawn. "I need to think, Rana. I've much on my mind. Go now, assist the swordmaster, and I'll hear an update from you in the morning."

Rana nodded and rose to her feet. Without a glance, she slipped from his office and sprinted out into the rain, where Taskala had his most recent recruits doing press-ups in the mud. She glanced their way and frowned. Six weeks would pass all too quickly.

***

Corin scraped the whetstone along his father's sword as he watched the rain bead the barracks window. Rain and wind, and wind and rain. The weather was worse here than it had been in Fol, which was well known for its storms and frequent deluges. But this plateau of rock near Port Wind seemed to suck in foul weather from every direction.

Corin suspected Taskala had chosen the place out of spite. Scolly had told them it had been the swordmaster's decision to use this camp. There had been others available, and Lord Halfdan had been away in the east.

Corin had come to hate Taskala. He owed him his life, and that knowledge made him loathe the swordmaster all the more. Taskala knew it and went out of his way to goad Corin. He didn't do that with the others, Corin noted. He was harsh and crude. He bullied and cajoled. But it was mostly words. With Corin an Fol he took it further. But it was the day Taskala broke his nose when Corin decided payback was due.

Marric's fault. The big freckled oaf had caused the fight in the barrack room that night. Corin had been honing his sword by the window. It helped him relax and had become something of an evening ritual after the three weeks' intense training they'd been put through.

Marric had complained about the sound just out of spite, as the rest of the recruits were already fast asleep. Corin had ignored him, so Marric had taken it further.

"You're a whoreson, Folly. I heard how they tupped your mother, those rude raiders from Crenna. Taskala told us all about it."

That did it. Corin flung his father's sword across the floor and sprang to his feet.

Marric's right jab missed Corin's jaw by an inch, as Corin ducked beneath the blow before launching his palm up under Marric's chin, knocking him off his feet.

Marric crashed onto his back. He tried to roll, but Corin kicked him hard in the ribs. He kicked again. And again, until the others were awakened by the racket and yelled at him to stop. Marric's face was bleeding badly, and he'd spewed a tooth on the floor. That was when Taskala had arrived.

The swordmaster must have heard the rumpus when he left the tavern. He'd come crashing into the barrack room, and when he saw the state Marric was in, Taskala had yanked Corin away from the boy and shoved him on the floor.

Corin had rolled to his knees, his eyes blazing, then Taskala's boot had impacted his face, breaking his nose and snapping his jaw back. Corin had lost consciousness at that point.

Darrel, running to report, had found Rana in the mess room and explained what had just occurred. Rana had been furious and spent most of that night seeing to both Corin and Marric, though the latter had recovered somewhat. That had been two weeks past. Marric had avoided Corin, and he'd done the same with Taskala. But Corin was burning inside, and he was determined to address the swordmaster again before the training was over.

At least he was left alone in the evenings now. Corin spent

hours sharpening and cleaning his father's sword long after the other recruits had fallen asleep. This night was no exception. He was bone weary; his nose hurt, and his jaw still clicked behind his right ear. That said, Corin felt fitter than he'd ever been. He could run for hours without tiring, and he knew the basic skills of military horsemanship, sword craft, spear defense and attack combinations, and how to shoot a bow with some accuracy while mounted on a horse. Better still, he'd also had learned to wrestle using lethal moves taught by Rana, whom Corin had come to admire not just as an instructor but as a woman too.

She wasn't beautiful, certainly not pretty. But Rana had something about her, and Corin was fascinated by this dark-eyed, deeply tanned woman who could trounce everyone in the garrison, save perhaps the swordmaster. She had a sense of humor too. Corin had witnessed it on a couple of occasions when this or that lad messed up and ended up sprawled facedown in the shit. Rana was merciless, but she wasn't brutal. That was Taskala's domain.

***

It was just before midnight when Yazrana entered the barrack room and found Corin an Fol still working on his sword. "You should be sleeping, Corin." She alone addressed him by his name, and that was another reason he liked her.

"Plenty of time to sleep when I'm dead," Corin responded, noting how she studied his face in detail.

"You look thin and gaunt, like someone burning from within." Rana took seat on the floor and smiled at Corin. "How old are you now?"

"Almost twenty-one, far as I can tell. Don't expect I'll live to be twenty-five."

"Tush! I'll not tolerate self-pity in this camp." Rana rested a hand on Corin's thigh, and he almost jumped with surprise. "I've ten years on you, and I wouldn't go back a day. I hated being young. Felt so vulnerable. At nineteen my parents had just sold me in the Permian markets, and I was almost bought but managed to escape on the night before the slave auction."

"Permio." Corin was very aware of her fingers caressing his leg. "You're Raleenian."

"Adopted. Not even the commander knows. Were he to find out I was born in Syrannos, he'd be beside himself. Probably throw me out the regiment. Permians are hated up here."

"I'm sure he'd get over it." Corin knew the rumors about Lord Halfdan and Yazrana. "Why not tell him and be out with it?"

"You are naïve." Rana's hand left his thigh, and she rose to her feet. Corin watched her as a flood of confused disappointment surged through his veins.

"And you are beautiful," he said. Rana laughed at that, but Corin's face was serious. "I mean it," he told her.

"Let me look at that sword." She held out a callused hand, and Corin passed her the broadsword hilt first. Rana studied it for a moment and then screwed up her nose. "It's a reasonable blade, and I'm impressed with how dedicated you are to keeping it in fine fettle. That said, it's too short for your gangly arms."

"It's my father's sword." Corin face flashed anger. "I avenged his killer with it."

"So I've heard, way up there in windy Fol—wherever that is." Yazrana passed the sword back to Corin, and he grabbed it fiercely. "I've a gift for you, but you'll have turn earn it." Rana saw the excitement flush through Corin's cheeks and chuckled. "Not that type of gift, Corin an Fol. But a worthy prize nonetheless."

"What must I do to earn it?" Once again Corin failed to hide his disappointment. Rana rubbed her palms together and gave him a tight smile. "A longsword. You must learn how to wield it. Then, if you are good enough, it will be yours to keep."

"I already have a sword." Corin felt suddenly annoyed. "And why are you helping me? What's so special about me?"

"Suffice to say, Taskala cannot stand you, Corin an Fol. I merely seek to address the balance. So, each night after dark come to my cabin—behind the commander's—and I'll teach you how to fight better than anyone else in this camp. You're a stray, Corin. I am too—so I've soft spot for you. And don't be upsetting Taskala again. He will kill first and worry about the consequences later."

"Not if I kill him first," Corin couldn't help adding as he thrust out his chin.

"You are not in his league, boy. Stay alive. Learn and practice, and keep that temper under wraps else it prove to be your downfall. Good night." Rana leaned forward and placed a fleeting kiss on his cheek, leaving Corin flustered.

***

Yazrana hardly spoke to him the following day, as she and the swordmaster had the recruits battling one another bloody with hard wooden drill swords. But that night, while his companions snored through their exhaustion, Corin an Fol commenced his extra training with the former Permian assassin known only as Yazrana.

Chapter 8

Yazrana

"I can hardly lift this bloody thing!" Corin swung wide, and Rana stepped aside and tapped the back of his head with her rapier.

"Too slow," she told him as Corin puffed and wheezed, the sweat running down his face. "Get your breath back and we'll start again."

Corin eased the blade's tip into the dirt and rested his greasy palms on the crosspiece. He'd never seen a six-foot-long sword before, and now he was trying to master its use. To make things worse, Rana was armed only with a skinny rapier. But she was running him ragged, swatting him on arse and legs, and sometimes his head too, with the flat of her blade.

"It's too bloody heavy," Corin complained.

"Then grow stronger," Rana replied, as she had a hundred times before. Two weeks had passed since his secret training began, and still Corin couldn't master the huge, unwieldy longsword he had nicknamed Clouter. "It's just a matter of balance. Keep it swinging back and forth, and don't overreach. And remember: stance is everything—you have to move your bloody feet." To prove her point, she kicked Corin hard in the shin.

Corin groaned. "I'll give it another try."

They stood in the spare stable yard, a single lantern spilling just enough light and shooting weird shadows as the night winds rattled shutters and doors. Again it was late, and for the fifteenth consecutive night Corin regretted agreeing to this extra training. He was as skinny as a half-starved rat now and always hungry. His body ached with bruise piled on bruise, and though Rana had straightened out his broken nose with her strong fingers, it still hurt.

But Corin was too tired to fret about Taskala, and the sword-master seemed content to leave him be. The latest recruits were shaping up fast. Just as well, for the time approached when they'd be sent south with the rest of the regiment posted here—a garrison comprising three hundred strong, a number that included the ninety-six recruits. Most of Halfdan's Wolves were up in Point Keep, keeping an eye on the eastern frontier, where the barbarians of Leeth were always threatening war.

Not surprisingly, Corin lagged behind during most runs and exercises. Darrel remarked on this, and Corin replied that he was storing up stamina. He dared not reveal how shattered he was and just how many nights he'd battled to get through Rana's guard. Long gone was any thought of a tussle with her. Corin viewed her as his personal torturer now.

He braced his legs, tensed his arms, and slipped both hands around the leather-wrapped hilt. Eyes intend on Rana, Corin allowed the blade to rise, then started swinging slowly as she watched him, her rapier thrust in dirt. Corin stepped deftly sideways and swung hard and fast, for once catching Rana off guard. The swing went wide, but Corin's shoulder crashed into his instructor's back and sent her sprawling. Corin grinned. Unconventional or not, that was the first time he'd landed a blow on Rana, and it felt so good.

She rolled to her feet and flashed him a grin. "Better," Rana said. Then she kicked him hard in the right shin, and Corin swore in protestation.

"What was that for?" He hopped, and then thrusting Clouter point first in the mud lifted his leg and rubbed the bruise.

"You stopped." Rana's dark eyes shone in the lamplight. "The one time you have me at an advantage, instead of pressing it, you quit and congratulate yourself. Do that in Permio and you'll be shorter by a head."

And so it went night after night, and at last Corin was making progress. His balance improved as he became accustomed to the longsword's length, and his thighs and arms became as hard as corded wire. Corin was still using his father's sword during the day. But when he fought in the melees, in one-to-ones and in mock battles with the other recruits, that shorter blade seemed clumsy and limited.

***

A day came when Taskala announced their training was complete. They were needed in the south, and they would ride on the morrow. The camp was abuzz with excitement and chatter. Everyone had an opinion on how things would go. Darrel kept Corin informed with most of that. Not that Corin listened. Let them chatter; he doubted anyone knew what to expect. Hardship? Thirst? Battles and pain. And agony and death for some. It didn't matter; Corin was ready for Permio; this was destiny. Past time to hone his new skills and then find the killer of his sister.

That afternoon Lord Halfdan addressed them while Taskala, Rana, Scolly, and Delemar watched on and added the odd comment when asked by their commander.

"You lads have done well," Halfdan told the ninety-six recruits. "In just a few weeks you've shaped up nicely into soldiers. Look at wee Darrel there—even he has muscles now." Darrel beamed like a lighthouse after hearing his name.

"But I'll not lie to you boys. The next months will be dangerous and hard, and you'll need to support one another and watch each other's backs. Permio is a den of serpents. Once there, don't mix with the natives. Trust no one, especially the women." Rana grinned upon hearing that. "Treachery and villainy, murder and deceit—those are the currencies of Permio. You have been warned."

Afterward, recruits Greggan, Jorl, and Tomato stood discussing their future as Corin watched on. Darrel and the others, including the increasingly surly Marric, had departed for the tavern. They were allowed two beers each for completing their training, and once they were done, Corin and the others would follow in shifts. Corin couldn't wait.

***

After bolting his second ale and cursing Taskala, who had been responsible for capping their limit, Corin sought Yazrana and found her grooming the horses with Scolly and Del. Corin noted how Scolly looked annoyed.

"I've got something for you, Corin an Fol," Rana announced as he loomed in the stable yard. Del's eyebrows rose hearing that, but Scolly scowled. He seemed lost in thought.

"How was your ale?" Del asked Corin, as Rana beckoned him to follow her to the spare stables, the first time he'd been inside during daylight hours.

Del and Scolly let them be, and Rana closed the stable door behind her. "Your friends are all fired up," she said. "The commander's right about Permio, though not necessarily about the Permian people. There are good and bad folk in every land."

Corin didn't respond but instead watched as Rana strode across to where Clouter leaned against a straw bale. "This is yours now—you've earned it and might just be able to use it without harming yourself."

She pressed the longsword's hilt into his palms. Their fingers touched slightly, and for the first time in weeks, Corin felt a tingle down below. "Meet me after supper," Rana said. "For your final lesson."

"I thought I'd get tonight off." Corin pouted; he didn't feel like training tonight—not with good ale in his belly.

"Well, you were wrong. I'll expect you here after sundown. And do try to sober up."

"I'm not drunk; I only had a couple," Corin complained, but Rana smiled her secretive smile and turned away.

"Go get something to eat. I will see you later."

The recruits were gathered in the canteen when Corin appeared. Taskala was with them but for once said nothing when Corin joined them at table. "Remember what Lord Halfdan told you," Taskala said in a growl. "If you want to keep your heads, then keep your eyes peeled. I don't hold out much hope for you tossers, but some of you might survive. We leave at dawn, so turn in early." Taskala rose to his feet, shooting Corin a flinty stare, then strode briskly from the canteen.

Corin watched him depart and visualized a dagger protruding from his back.

"There's seconds for them what wants them." Rodi the cook was affable tonight. "I'd not have you lads hungry on your first march south." They ate well that evening and took to their beds early, though only Darrel and Greggan slept the night through.

Corin waited until there was no movement in the barrack room. Satisfied, he slid Clouter out from under his blanket, as it was still a secret only he and Yazrana shared. He'd tell the others in the morning, as a six-foot-long sword was not easy to hide. Corin wasn't looking forward to that, expecting some snarky comment from Taskala, and maybe Marric too; the big lad still harbored a grudge. Doubtless most of Corin's fellow recruits would resent the attention he'd been getting, but Corin couldn't care less about that. He'd put the hours in while they were sleeping. Hopefully those long sweaty nights learning the longsword would stand him in good stead in the desert.

Corin eased the door to and wandered out into the night. For once it was calm, and no wind or rain pummeled his face. He strode out under a satin-black sky, the horned moon and three stars glancing down on him from above. Close by, the distant roar of breakers reached Corin as he trudged across to the stables. He really wasn't in the mood.

Yazrana smiled as he entered. She was seated on a straw bale, and there was something different about her tonight. Then Corin noticed how her long black hair lay loose and tossed wild around her face. Her almond eyes flashed in the lamplight, and suddenly Corin thought her the most beautiful woman he'd ever encountered.

"I'm kinda tired," Corin muttered as he slid Clouter free of its heavy scabbard.

"That's a shame." Rana's upper lip curled slightly, and Corin wondered what she was up to. "I was hoping you had a reserve tank stored in there. Oh, and put that bloody weapon down, long-swordsman. We'll play a different game tonight."

Before Corin could grasp her meaning, Rana had slid free of the bale and now approached him, as lithe and graceful as a stalking cat. "I don't understand . . ."

Corin froze as Rana's warm hand fumbled with his draw-string, and she worked her nimble fingers until she found what she sought. Corin groaned, and Rana smiled as she knelt before him. "You should have heeded the commander's warning about Permian women. Too late now . . ."

***

He'd slept for a brief time, Rana's naked body on top of his own. They'd made urgent love three times, and Corin was spent and happier than he'd been in months. He hadn't even thought about the morning—plenty of time to worry about that. It was almost dawn when Yazrana rolled free of his embrace and slipped back into her garments. Corin gazed up at her, fascinated and wishing they had time for another go, though he lacked the energy and really needed more sleep.

"We'll ride out in an hour. I suggest you get ready." Rana placed a wet kiss on his forehead and turned to leave.

"Just answer one question before you go, will you?" Corin shivered. It was cold now that she'd left him lying starkers on the straw bed they'd made. Rana turned and gazed across at him.

"Go on."

"Lord Halfdan—are the rumors true? I mean, they say you are his lover. I—" Corin felt awkward, but she smiled away his worry that he'd overstepped the mark.

"You are not the only orphan in this world, Corin an Fol. I get lonely sometimes too. The commander and I are good friends. Sometimes that leads to other things; sometimes not."

"But . . . why me, and why now of all times?"

"Why not? I'm Permian, after all. We are capricious folk. And no man rules my heart, Corin. But I like Lord Halfdan; he's a good man and a lonely one too. We ease each other's pain. And as for you, boy . . ." Rana dusted off her tunic and smiled again, though this time there was sorrow in her eyes. "You remind of him, though I cannot think why."

She turned to leave but stopped at the doorway. "Look after Clouter, Corin. It was the commander's sword when he was a younger man. For some reason he suggested I give it to you. Life is strange, is it not? Good night!"

"Good night," Corin replied, though dawn was almost breaking. He watched as Rana faded into the gloom outside. Strange indeed. Corin was baffled by why the commander had given him Clouter. Maybe Halfdan had seen promise in him after all? Corin sat for a time shivering and then rolled to his feet, found his clothes and boots, and staggered wearily into them. Gods, he was exhausted, but he was also in love and therefore capable of anything.

Corin's mind was racing as he made for the stable door, and his focus was distorted now Yazrana had slept with him. Complications—he didn't need them. But she was so wonderful, and anyway, she would be there too, and they could share some time together. That thought was comfort enough for now.

Outside, the moon had fled behind racing clouds, and a pale glimmer of gray heralded a cold, bright morning. Corin was ready to leave this camp, if only to find summer again.

As he strode back toward the barracks, Clouter slung across his shoulders, Corin felt a tingle along his spine.

I am not alone . . .

Corin slowed his pace, half expecting Taskala, or else maybe Marric, to confront him in the half-light. He turned, wary and slow. Nothing. Then a sudden gust whipped straw in his face, and Corin blinked and choked. Looking up again, he saw her sitting on the stockade wall, her long copper hair lifting in the wind, and her green-gold gaze locked on his own.

"Be careful, Corin an Fol," the woman told him as Corin stood rigid and sweating, his cold lips welded together. "Yours is a dangerous road. I will see you in time."

Another violent gust of wind made Corin shade his eyes from dust and muck. When he looked up again, the woman was gone. Confused, and also a little scared, Corin returned to the barracks just as his comrades were stirring.

"You look like you've seen a ghost; are you worried about Permio?" Darrel almost jumped on Corin outside the privy.

"What? No, just got things on my mind. Now leave me be—will you?" Darrel obliged and Corin shut the privy door and closed his eyes. What was happening here? There were two women in his life. Three, if he included Holly—though he hadn't thought about her in a while. Yazrana—his training—the new life had almost erased Holly from his memory, something he felt ashamed about. And the copper-haired lady still watched over him. Why? Who was she, and would he ever know?

Corin sighed and rubbed his tired eyes. Outside he heard shouts and the sound of horses' harnesses jingling. Time to move and put these thoughts away. Corin was a warrior now—a Wolf. A man of strength and purpose. Holding that thought, Corin gritted his teeth and smiled as he left the privy behind and went out to face the morning.

He saddled his horse and joined the others outside the stable yard, where Taskala and Scolly were yelling and cursing as the recruits shuffled into order and readied their steeds. The buildings emptied as the garrison staff joined the others, and when everyone was assembled, Lord Halfdan guided his horse across to meet them. Scolly and a dozen others were to stay behind while the rest of the camp journeyed south. They rode out within the hour.

Chapter 9

Permio

Corin smiled as the hot sun melted the tar on the stays. Beneath his feet, the ship pitched and rolled over deep-blue waters, while high above gulls weaved and mewed through clear, bright skies. This was the life! One week out from Port Wind Camp, and at last they'd reclaimed summer.

There was little to tell of their journey thus far. They'd ridden out that chilly midsummer morning as dawn paled the sky and dew dampened grass. Three hundred horsemen—the ninety-six recruits, including Corin, among them. His troop of eight had ridden up front behind the veterans led by Taskala and Delemar. Scolly had been tasked with maintenance duties back in Port Wind and was missing out on this latest foray south. It explained his miserable face the week before.

A few days later they'd arrived in Calprissa, a city like nothing Corin had seen—set high on a cliff with white walls glistening like polished marble in the sunshine. Far below lay the harbor, their destination, hidden from the ocean by a tight twisting channel that guarded it from surprise attack. The road wound beneath those lofty walls, and Corin had gazed up, seeing soldiers looking down at them, the sun glinting off their armor and spear tips.

Once they reached the harborside, Corin had wanted to climb the steep path back up to the city to explore, but Taskala had ordered his new Wolflings—as he now called them—to stay in the harbor, though he did let them visit the quayside taverns in a rare show of kindness. After that brief recreation, they'd restocked with food, seen to the horses, and then started the tricky business of guiding horse onto vessel.

The Wolves had commandeered three large ships courtesy of King Nogel in Wynais, Halfdan having arranged that weeks before. Once the horses were corralled and settled, the men took to loading goods and water barrels—and the odd cask of brandy for the veterans.

The ships had sailed out the following morning, their white sails gleaming, and the water as smooth as glass as they glided through. Once clear of the narrow channels masking the harbor's entrance, the Kelwynian crew stowed oars and reefed the sails trapping the blow.

That was three days past. Now Corin's eyes were fixed on sandy bluffs flanking their east—the coast of Raleen, some ten miles inshore. He hadn't seen much of Yazrana since the night before they'd left. She was on the second ship, and Corin could see that and the third one sailing a mile or so behind them. Taskala and Del were on Corin's ship, but the swordmaster seemed content to let his Wolflings relax and enjoy the voyage. Their world would change soon enough, and Corin was certain some would die in the weeks ahead.

Lord Halfdan had accompanied his Wolves to Calprissa, but once there had bade them good luck and farewell. He'd then ridden east alone to meet with King Nogel in Wynais, his capital—also known as the Silver City—close by the mountains in the east of that realm. Corin had wondered what the commander would be discussing with Kelwyn's ruler. Doubtless politics and things that didn't concern Corin. Still, he was curious.

Most of the lads spent day on day playing dice, quarreling, and teasing one another, and a crafty few cheating. Corin was crap at dice; he lacked the patience. He avoided most games and instead preferred to watch the view from the bowsprit, as waves danced and dolphins pursued them in sheer joy.

The day came when they changed course and steered due east. The cliffs had fallen away. Instead, a wide, flat horizon eventually raised yellow beaches and the odd swaying palm tree, and later, a city comprising ruddy stone, with sandy walls crowned by a bartizan with square crenellations and a high round keep.

"Port Sarfe," cheerful Darrel told Corin in a rare break from his dice game. Darrel was both clever and quick, and he'd won several games and had a nice jingle of coins in his pouch "And this is the Gulf of Permio. We'll cast anchor in Sarfe and then ride south to the borderlands."

"Why not sail?" Corin glanced down at his friend, who grinned back as if his question had been stupid.

"We dare not enter Permian waters. They've slave galleys with ballistas and trebuchets on board itching for a fight. And there's vessels from the strange lands beyond Golt—none of them friendly. These trade with the Permian Sultanate, exchanging precious gems for slaves and such. And then there's the pirates. Crenise freebooters aren't outlawed in Permio like they are in the Four Kingdoms. They free-range down here."

Corin frowned upon hearing that. He fingered Clouter's hilt, which was now strapped to his back with a harness Delemar had showed him how to assemble. Perhaps he'd get a chance to use the longsword on some Crenise cutthroat before this year was out. That would feel good. He wondered if Torval the raider was still at large in the south. Corin held no grudge against Permio, but his hatred of Crenna was as passionate as ever.

They murdered my kin. Corin pictured Ceilyn's terrified face the last time he'd seen her, and again he heard the screams of his mother as Brokka butchered his father. Brokka, whom Corin had slain. But the raider's leader was still out there, or so Corin believed. "I'm coming for you, Torval," Corin muttered under his breath. "If you're out there I will find you."

"You say something?" If Darrel had noticed Corin's grim expression, he didn't let on.

"Nope. Just thinking."

"Well, there's plenty to think about. We'll be in Permio in a day or two." Darrel grinned up at him, still oblivious to the change in his friend's expression. Darrel was far too cheerful, in Corin's opinion, and he wondered how the youngster always seemed to know so much. But Darrel was a big talker and not afraid to question the veterans on board, even if that got him a cuff on the ear.

"I can't wait," Corin muttered after a moment and then returned his attention to the seabirds and dolphins and the constant creaking of timber strake and hemp stay. Darrel took the hint and returned to his dicing.

***

They reached Port Sarfe just as dusk darkened its grubby streets. Corin got a good look at the city while they were approaching. His first impression was that of a sprawling untidy mass of sandy stone dwellings; a wide, square harbor cluttered with all manner of craft; and at the southern end, a large sluggish river mingled its brown muddy waters with the with the clear blue brine of the Gulf of Permio.

Further south, smooth white beaches faded into haze. Beyond these lay the Liaho Delta, a maze of swamp and treacherous waterways, domain of waterfowl, frog, and snake—or so Corin had been told. To Corin it felt as if he'd entered a new world entirely. A place of sun and warmth. And a place of adventure. He decided he liked Raleen from that moment hence.

As they entered the harbor, Corin saw people everywhere: traders, hawkers, and the odd warrior striding arrogantly among them. There were sailors joking with their comrades, with their captains close by, dealing business with hard faces. He watched a troop of city guard file into one of the seedy-looking taverns and minutes later heard shouts, then witnessed some unfortunate sod thrown out into the street and clubbed senseless.

Most of all Corin noticed the girls. There were quite a few, strolling about on the quay, some selling perfumes and spices, others offering more intimate ware. They all looked beautiful, and

Corin recalled how often he'd heard men speak about the famed Raleenian women. Dark of eye and skin, quick with smile—though quicker still with tongue and dagger.

Fascinated, he stood poised as the sailors heaved to and Halfdan's borrowed ships cast anchor and awaited skiffs to collect them from the shore. Getting the horses on those small craft took some time and considerable effort. Eventually all reached the quay without mishap. Then the goods were off-loaded, and finally the men were allowed to venture into town.

Taskala paid and thanked the three skippers from Calprissa, and these started readying their vessels for the return voyage in the morning.

"You've got an hour," Taskala growled at his Wolflings huddled together on the quay. "No fucking about. Anyone drunk or caught with a wench will have me to answer to."

Corin made the most of his hour. He found the grubbiest-looking tavern at the southern end of the harbor. He downed five ales and a scat of rum and decided Port Sarfe was a city of quality.

Yazrana found him ordering his sixth ale. She frowned at what she saw, and her almond eyes showed no mercy. "Leave that, stupid! You've had your quota." She grabbed Corin's hand and dragged him from the taproom into the dusky street outside.

"Hello, sweetheart!" Corin leaned forward, attempting to kiss Rana on the lips, but she gracefully stepped back and smacked the side of his face with her iron-hard palm. "Ouch. What's was that for?"

"Taskala's on the prowl." Rana slapped his ear this time, then stamped angrily on his foot. "If he sees you in this state, you'll be on latrine duty for the next six months. What's the matter with you, Corin? Have you lost your wits? This is no game."

"I thought you and I . . ." Corin felt shocked and a little wobbly on his feet. The ale had been strong, and the rum perhaps not the best idea.

"That was just a moment's light relief after some intense and hardworking weeks. We had fun, and we might again sometime if you survive the desert. And If I'm horny, I'll seek you out, unless of course I find someone better." Rana slapped his ear again, this time playfully. She grinned at his wan expression. "Ugh, you're a sorry sight, Corin an Fol. Don't worry; I still like you. Now stop looking so glum and shape up. Your friends are gathering at the quay, ready for the ride south. If you're not there soon, the sword-master will be made aware."

"I thought we were staying here."

"In Port Sarfe?" Rana rolled her huge dark eyes and snorted. "Taskala isn't stupid. Setting you lot loose tonight would draw in every cutthroat, cutpurse, and whore from every gutter. This is a dangerous city. A bad place when you get to know it. A worse one when you don't. No, we are to camp three miles beyond the walls so we can get an early start in the morning. Now get a bloody grip and go join the others!"

***

Corin obliged without comment, though his face was longer than his sword. Yazrana left him and patrolled the quayside taverns, eventually finding three more strays. One still had his wits about him and got off light. The other two were not so fortunate. These would face Taskala's wrath in the morning. Rana almost pitied them. Almost.

***

Corin saw nothing of her for several days. The Wolves were on the move again. That first day they'd ridden hard, passing through the disputed region known as South Kaelin and arriving at the bridge that spanned the wide River Liaho. Corin had been stunned by the sight. A huge steel structure arcing up in a single curve with no evidence of strut or support.

"The Golden Folk built it in millennia past." As usual Darrel had the details. As the smaller Wolfling rode alongside Corin, he'd chattered ceaselessly about the ancients and their wars. It was all a bit beyond Corin, who had never paid much heed to history.

"So who were they?" He tried to show an interest.

"The Golden Folk?" Darrel shrugged. "Magicians and warlocks mostly. Clever bunch but not very nice. They waged war with their evil cousins who lived beneath the mountains. The Dog People. But of course you've heard of them?"

"I haven't."

"Really?" Darrel looked shocked. "Shapeshifting necromancers—very unpleasant," he explained, summoning patience. "Mother used to tell me about them when I was tiny. Nasty lot, the Dog People. But they were all destroyed, thank goodness. The Golden Folk had flying machines, you know."

"I didn't."

"Anyway, the war dragged on until most of that lot perished too, and then our ancestor, Kell the Conqueror—"

"Your ancestor," Corin corrected. "I'm from Fol. It's a free state and not part of your Four Kingdoms."

"—arrived and everything changed. That's all I know." Darrel went on for several minutes until Corin's mind began to wander.

"The bridge is impressive," Corin said as they approached the narrow arch of steel and dismounted. The horses were nervous, so to avoid disaster they'd had to lead them over the bridge. A process that took some time, and Corin cursed the ancients for not making the bloody thing wider.

He'd stopped at the bridge's apex and gazed down and across to where the sluggish Liaho wound west like a lazy, fat snake bound for the Gulf of Permio. Corin couldn't see the ocean though it wasn't far. Instead, the river faded into green haze of mangrove, treacherous channels, and swamp. Word was the Liaho Delta was best avoided.

Beyond the bridge's southern end loomed a brown arid region comprising shrubby hills, with the thin gray ribbon of their road winding through. Beyond those hills, the vast Permio Desert stretched for mile upon mile. An empty, desolate region, save for the odd treacherous tribesman and nomad. Their journey was almost over.

Three days later, the Wolf army reached the outskirts of another city. Even Corin had heard of Cappel Cormac. As vicious a den of iniquity as could be found anywhere on this earth, or so he'd heard. They steered clear of the city, instead turning south along another road that flanked the fast-flowing River Narion, eventually leading down to Agmandeur on the edge of the High Dunes, a huge desolate region rumored impassable.

Agmandeur was in enemy hands now. Held by one Imbala, the warlord they were tasked to tame—or at least to shake up—and deter his attentions from the sultan's cities, which he was currently raiding from time to time. Sounded simple enough, but few among the veterans had any idea how difficult their task might prove.

Chapter 10

First Blood

An arrow thudded into the dirt inches from Corin's head. He ducked instinctively, and a second shaft pierced his horse's saddle. At least he'd had the sense to pull his beast low and use its body as a shield. To his left and right, Corin's companions were lined up awaiting the inevitable charge. He could just make out the screaming savages hopping and jumping in the heat-hazy distance.

More arrows zinged and whined. Corin lay on his stomach, covered his ears, and kept as low as he could. Three hot, fly-buzzy, sun dazzling, sand scorching hours they'd waited in ambush only to have the tribesmen surprise them and turn their day upside down. Corin was thirsty and his head felt hollow; his mouth was dust dry, but he dared not drink much more, lest he run out of water like some of the other lads had. Corin didn't hold out much hope for them. Water was life down here; you had to savor every drop and ration your thirst. If he was lucky, this would be a long day. And if not? An arrow struck the saddlebag of his horse, and Corin jumped.

"Attack, you bastards—come on, let's get this over!" The suspense was eating Corin inside. That, and the fear churning his belly as the shafts kept coming.

His teeth rattled, and his guts were tied in knots as the fear rose up threatening to loose his bowels a third time that morning. Corin stayed put; he wouldn't let the monster unman him. Focus the fear; feel the hate. Feed that hate, and it would reward him with strength.

Beside Corin, Greggan was retching in the dirt. "You alright, mate?" Corin grinned at Greggan, who glared back at him as though he'd lost his mind. "We'll get through this," Corin told him. "Hold to courage!" Greggan just nodded and then threw up again. He wasn't the only one; every recruit was beyond terrified, Corin included. And for good reason—they were surrounded by screaming murderous tribesmen; their first encounter with the Permians was looking like it might be their last.

Corin heard a scream close by. Turning, he saw a recruit he didn't know clutching at an arrow protruding from his gut. The boy kept screaming and screaming until Taskala found him and slid a knife across his throat to end his misery.

At last the arrow assault ceased. Corin rolled to his knees and witnessed the next onslaught. This time the tribesmen came yelling and whooping toward the defile where he and his comrades waited, most frozen beyond terror with greasy, sweaty hands clutched around their weapons. Some of the Permians rode horses, and a few were hunched on camels—bizarre-looking beasts that Corin had never encountered before. But most were on foot, yelling and spitting, with scimitars and heavier tulwars cutting circles in the air.

Corin rose to his feet despite someone yelling at him to stay down. "Fuck that," Corin muttered as his teeth rattled. Let them come! "I'm ready for you." Corin yelled, stabbing Clouter's point into the sand and summoning the rage boiling within him. He pictured Brokka's ugly face, and that helped push the fear back inside his belly.

I will survive this day . . .

They were closer now, just yards away. He could see their dark hate-filled eyes as they whooped and yelled insults with words he couldn't understand.

Corin counted to ten and slowed his breath as Rana had taught him. He had no idea where she was, though Taskala seemed to be everywhere at once. Corin glanced right and saw the swordmaster kicking Clorte to his feet. "Plenty of time to shit yourself later, lad!" Taskala roared and went on to kick another terrified Wolfling. "Get ready—they're coming!"

And so they were. More than a hundred strong. They wore shaggy robes and baggy striped trousers, and most had colored scarves shrouding their faces and protecting them from the fierce sun.

Corin tightened his helmet strap and ran slippery fingers down Clouter's hilt, as he willed back the urge to flee.

I must . . . stay . . . calm. Fear is the enemy within. I shall master my fear.

Corin bit his lower lip until blood filled his mouth. He gripped Clouter's hilt and leveled the weapon at those rushing toward him. *Feed the hate; conquer the fear. . .*

And then the tribesmen were on them. Scimitars scythed through hot desert air, slicing muscle and cracking bone. Men screamed. The few veterans present took the fight to the nomad, allowing the Wolflings scarce seconds before they received the full brunt of the Permian attack.

A man raced toward the place where Corin stood with Darrel and Greggan. His friend's eyes were huge with terror. They remained put, but Corin leapt forward and, bracing his legs, swung out hard and fast with Clouter.

The Permian ducked low and launched his lean body like a missile into Corin's chest, knocking him backward. *Stance . . . remember your stance . . .*

Bracing his legs, Corin regained his balance and brought Clouter's pommel down hard on the tribesman's head, crunching his skull open and sending him sprawling. Corin yelled, "Bastard!" and felt a mixture of horror and triumph as he witnessed the Permian's seeping skull. Corin's nostrils were filled with the stink of death, and he watched with morbid fascination as fat black flies settled and crawled across the dead man's ruined face. A cramp tore inside him; he buckled forward and spewed, stopping only when a rough hand shook his shoulder.

"Well done," gasped a stunned Greggan as Corin still gaped at the twitching enemy, whose blood and brains were oozing into the sandy dirt. Corin straightened and gulped the last drop from his water gourd. Get a grip! No time to think about what he'd just done, as a dozen more Permians were racing at them.

Corin willed his legs to move; they felt as heavy as blocks of wood. He jumped back as the next assailant swung his scimitar at Corin's throat. Corin countered hard and fast with Clouter, knocking his enemy's smaller sword aside and then smashing pommel and cross-guard into his face. "That's for Ceilyn!" Corin roared at the tribesman and swung again.

The Permian was knocked backward by that blow. He recovered, and though his vision seemed blurred by blood, the Permian attacked again, his scimitar slicing at Corin with alarming speed.

Again Corin jumped back, but this time he swung Clouter two-handed in a wide arc, slicing the Permian's neck and head free of his shoulders. Corin was dimly aware of the man's scarfed head rolling past his feet and settling on a tussock. A surreal sight under that desert sun. Then the next man was on him.

Greggan and Darrel had each killed a man, though Greggan had received a nasty slice along his arm and Darrel a blow to his head that had sent him sprawling. Corin was unscathed, and his wild, ragged temper had served its purpose banishing the earlier terror and allowing him to kill and kill, until six enemies lay sprawled bloody at his feet.

Again Corin saw the pirate cut down his father on that beautiful morning. As the rage consumed him, he heard no sound and saw nothing that transpired around him. At last the enemy stopped coming, and someone yelled in Corin's ear.

"They've gone! You can stop now, Corin an Fol!"

Corin's eyes were filled with tears, but he could just make out Marric's big frame standing beside him. "We saw them off, Corin," Marric yelled. "You did well," he added, his freckled and blood-splattered face showing new respect for his former rival.

Corin allowed Clouter's point to settle into sand as he leaned hard on the cross-piece. Exhausted, Corin gazed about at the carnage. Everywhere, corpses lay sprawled, tribesmen in brightly colored garb oozing lifeblood alongside his Wolfling companions and the odd seasoned warrior. So this was war? Part of Corin was horrified by what he saw. But a small triumphant part of him reveled in the death surrounding him.

I am a warrior now. This is where I belong . . .

It had felt so good to fight after those long hours waiting, but as the rage slowly subsided inside him, Corin glanced at the corpses sprawled everywhere and questioned his actions. Those men lying there were not his enemies; they hadn't murdered his kin. They were just warriors like he was now. Brave men, with wives and children who would be weeping their loss by nightfall. It made little sense. Corin shook his head; he was bone weary and his emotions were shattered.

But he had survived, and that was all that mattered.

***

"They fled when the Bears arrived and took their flank." Darrel wiped fresh blood from his head with a wet cloth. He was smiling in disbelief, and Corin noticed he'd lost two front teeth.

"Are you alright, Darrel?"

"Happy to be alive, Corin. That was touch and go. My head hurts though, and I feel a bit queasy." After saying those last words, Darrel leaned forward and spewed violently onto the dirt. Nearby, Greggan's arm was being tended to by Delemar.

"You lads did good," Del was saying. "Bloody good, and now you've survived First Blood. It's always the worst, is that. Soon you'll be vets like the rest of us." Del ventured to where Corin stood still shaking with anger, his bloodied hands resting on Clouter's cross-piece.

"You fought well, Folly. I shall tell Taskala." Del rested a hand on Corin's shoulder, but Corin pulled away.

"Fuck Taskala." Corin spat bloody phlegm and felt his rage muster again. "He murdered that recruit as though he were a goat at market. He's a cold, evil bastard."

"That he is." Del nodded. "But Taskala also knows the right thing to do. That poor lad had a skewered gut. It would have taken him hours, maybe days, to die. It was a mercy killing, Corin." Delemar shook his head at Corin's wild expression and ventured off along the defile, congratulating all those he encountered. Corin watched him go, Delemar might be right about the swordmaster's actions but Corin had seen Taskala's eyes. The man was a psychopath who enjoyed killing. A brutal wicked bastard.

Corin saw the swordmaster away off to his right. For a moment Taskala caught Corin's hostile expression. He smiled slightly and then turned away.

Corin was suddenly gripped by a wild rush of weariness, and he almost collapsed as it flooded through his veins. He clung on the cross-guard until the moment passed. An odd sound turned his head. Corin looked up and saw a large raven had settled on a small rise. It faced him and cawed three times.

"Go away." Corin flicked sand at the bird, and it hopped backward but remained close. "I said, fuck off!" Corin reached down and picked up a stone, then sent it flying. This time the raven took flight, its mocking croak fading with it up into the merciless blue.

Corin heard rough laughter behind him. He turned and saw an old man standing there, his features shadowed by a wide-brimmed hat. His long bony fingers clung to the ashen shaft of a long spear. "You are mine, boy. I shall come for you in time."

"Who the . . . ?" Corin blinked and coughed in dust. "What did you say?" Corin choked out the words, but the old man vanished in the shimmer of heat as Corin's exhaustion finally claimed him and he fell face-first into the sand and lost all consciousness.

***

When he came to, Corin realized he was in camp. "What happened?" Corin asked Greggan, who was seated on a cart close by with his arm bandaged; the shaggy-haired recruit looked to be in reasonable shape.

"You were gone, Corin." Greggan rubbed the bandage masking his arm. "Del tossed your long shanks onto a cart, and you rode with me and Darrel, whose head still ain't right—though I daresay he'll mend."

"I saw . . . shit . . ." Corin remembered the old man and the raven. Had he imagined them?

"Dehydration." Greggan waved his good arm. "It will fuck you right up. You need to keep drinking down here." He reached back awkwardly behind him and grabbed a flask from the cart. He tossed it at Corin, who uncorked it and swallowed the lukewarm contents with sudden giddy thirst.

"Thanks." Corin tossed the flask back after taking a few long swigs. "I thought I was losing my marbles back there."

"A good few lads have." Greggan looked reflective. "Some fled too, though Taskala caught up with them and hung the poor sods this morning."

"He did *what*?"

"Discipline, Corin. It's the only way we'll survive." Greggan's expression lacked conviction. "Lord Halfdan would have done the same."

Corin didn't believe that, but he let the matter rest. He was still exhausted and needed to get his strength back. Instead, he questioned Greggan about the attack, his memory having faded from the last few days.

"We were onto them," Greggan explained. "But the sly bastards got wind and sent for help from Agmandeur, including those sodding archers who caused most of our problems. We lost sixty men, Corin. Most of them Wolflings, though a few vets too. Would have been worse if the Bears hadn't arrived. Now Taskala owes Belmarius's boys, and he ain't happy about it."

"I didn't know the Bears were here." Corin rubbed his tired eyes. He didn't much care for the Bears he'd met thus far, but was grateful for their timely intervention on the road south of Agmandeur.

"They're on their way to Syrannos, where they have a cushy little number. Guarding that fine city from would-be raiders. Most likely they'll be loafing about in taverns and not stuck on filthy desert duty like us lowly Wolves. Still, I'm glad they dropped by."

"That's big of you, Greggan." Corin looked up, recognizing the swordmaster's growl.

Taskala had loomed into view; his short-cropped silver hair was shiny with sweat and his hard face already heavily tanned. He turned to survey Corin with icy gray eyes. "And how fare you, Folly?"

"I'm alive," Corin replied.

"I'm alive, *Swordmaster.*" Taskala approached with scolding eyes, until he stood scarce six inches from where Corin perched on the cart. "Am I going to have trouble with you, Folly?" Corin didn't respond, and Taskala tired of his goading and continued on his way.

"You did well there." Delemar said. "He wants you to snap back at him. That way he's got you. Don't take the bait."

"I will kill him one day," Corin hissed under his breath.

"What say you?" Del loomed close. "Have a care, Corin an Fol! You showed some promise today; it would be a shame to lose potential talent in the regiment."

Corin let that go; he was too tired to argue.

They'd set up camp the previous day some twenty-five miles north of the rebel city Agmandeur. Taskala had found a good site set upon a low ridge hidden from scouts by shrub and thorn and affording good views of the road for more than a mile each way. A stream struggled some hundred yards below their camp, so there was water for horses and men. It would serve well enough for the time being.

But Taskala's plan was to keep his Wolves moving. They'd been caught out by Imbala's attack that morning, so he was determined that wouldn't happen again. That evening they dared a small fire, and those who had healing skills helped the wounded get some comfort and eventually find sleep.

Beside him Greggan, Jorl, and Darrel snored, but Corin found sleep evading him. A worm of loathing rose like bile inside his belly. Again he pictured Taskala rounding on that youth and slicing his throat as if he were meat at market. It might have been the right thing to do, but it was the callous way the swordmaster had done it that rankled Corin so.

He rolled and fidgeted until deciding it was no good and got to his feet to relieve himself in the shrubs. Having dealt with that, Corin turned to find Swordmaster Taskala standing behind him.

"What's your problem, Folly?" Taskala's sinewy arms were folded. He was dressed in shirt and trousers, a single dagger at his belt.

"Just answering nature's call," Corin responded. He was aware of Clouter close by, leaning up against a rock.

Taskala smiled as though guessing Corin's thoughts. "Think you a match for me, Folly?" Corin fiddled with his drawstrings and made to push by, but Taskala shoved him back hard into the scrub. "Lost your tongue, or are you too shit scared to speak?"

"I'm not scared of you." Corin snarled at Taskala and made to pass him again.

Taskala blocked his way a second time. "Well, you should be. This will help act as a reminder!" Quicker than Corin could blink, Taskala had grabbed his dagger and leapt at him, steel in hand. Corin jumped back, but this was no tribesman attacking him. He was quick, but Taskala was quicker.

Corin saw a flash of blade, then cried out in agony as the dagger's point cut open his face, slicing a curved line just above his right eye and up through his brow to his hairline. Corin fell back, gripping his face as the red pain seared through him. He couldn't see anything and swung his arms about in panic.

Corin smelled the swordmaster's hot breath, and his rasping voice growled in Corin's ear. "I'll teach you to lip back to me, you lanky shite. I've a good mind to slice off your balls."

"He still needs those," a sultry voice whispered. Taskala whirled around and saw the dark shape of Rana standing a few feet behind him.

"This doesn't concern you, Yaz. I'm teaching the shiteling a lesson. Best you go back to bed, girl." Taskala showed her his back.

"Don't turn your back on me, Swordmaster," Yazrana hissed. She slipped a dagger into her own hand. Snake fast, Taskala spun on his toes, his dagger lunging hard and fast to where Rana had stood. But she was behind him now, and her own blade rested on the nape of his neck.

"Do it," Taskala grunted. "Go on—protect your plaything. I know you've had his cock up your arse, Rana. You like 'em young, don't you? And old too, if we include Lord Halfdan. So go on—stab me, slut! Then flee with your lover and hide until they find you and peel the skin off your hides."

***

Rana refused to be drawn in. Taskala broke people this way. She knew he was confident she wouldn't stab him. So instead she pricked his neck with the dagger and hissed in his ear.

"I'll not sink to your level and gut you here, Taskala. But touch this boy again, and I will kill you, swordmaster or not. Now go—before I change my mind." Rana launched her foot between the back of Taskala's legs, catching his balls and sending him sprawling.

He uttered no sound, but straightened, gave Rana and Corin an Fol a withering stare, then strode off into the night. Rana watched him leave, then satisfied he wasn't coming back anytime soon knelt beside Corin and cradled his bloody face. She tore a strip off her shirt and wiped it as best she could.

"You are lucky he missed your eye." Rana cleaned the oozing blood from Corin's face and dabbed at the tears of fury descending his cheeks. "You made an enemy today, Corin. Not only for yourself but for me too. I don't plan on leaving the regiment anytime soon, so methinks it best we both keep a healthy distance from that bastard."

"I'm going to kill him," Corin sobbed as she tried to staunch the blood that seeped from his wound.

"It's just a slice and will leave a nice scar—so what? We've all endured worse."

"Fuck the scar, Yazrana. I don't give a shit about that. I'm going to kill Taskala for what he called you. I'll face him alone one day and cut the smile from his lips." Corin stood and angrily wiped fresh tears from his face.

"I do not need you to defend my honor, Corin an Fol." Rana studied his face and frowned. "Wait there. I'll be back with needle and thread."

***

Corin willed the rage inside him to still as he waited for her to return. He was shaking with anger and wished he could face Taskala there and then. Moments later Yazrana emerged from the darkness with supplies in hand. "This will hurt," Rana told him.

It did. But Corin made no sound until she had knotted the last stitch and kissed him softly on the cheek. "As I said, you're lucky you've still got that eye. Now get some sleep while you still can." Rana turned away but stopped when Corin called her back.

"I didn't mean to insult you, Yaz. I know you're a match for that bastard or any man here. I'm sorry. I meant no offense."

Rana smiled then. Not her fierce smirk but rather as a lover smiles. Corin noted how it made her look younger. "Thank you, Corin an Fol. It's good to know you're there for me. We'll both need to watch our backs in the coming weeks. Best we sleep together from now on—unless you have a problem with that."

"No problem at all." Corin felt a surge in his groin, but she laughed at his expression and bade him return to his blanket.

"Not tonight, my young darling—you need to rest and time to let that face heal. I'll catch up with you in due course. Good night!" Rana left him then, and feeling happier than before, Corin staggered off to his blanket. He rolled inside, and this time sleep pounced on him and stole him away.

***

Yazrana stalked warily through camp for several minutes until she spied the swordmaster's shadow resting against a rock.

A time will come, Taskala, when I will cut out your heart for what you said to me today. But I can wait, and I'll not throw away a good career for one such as you.

Rana watched from her hide for several more minutes, then slipped back to where Corin an Fol lay snoring with the others.

She studied his sleeping face kissed by firelight's flicker. Truth was, his words had touched her deeply. Yazrana had never let a man close enough to love her, though many had claimed to do so. But Corin was different, and when she stared into his ravaged face, Yazrana was hit with the terrifying truth.

She was in love with this gloomy northern boy, and that would most likely prove their ruin.

End of Part One

Part Two

Wolf

Chapter 11

Cappel Cormac

Six months later Corin was seated in a seedy coffeehouse in the poorest quarter of Cappel Cormac, his bloodshot eyes studying the letter that he'd received this morning from Yazrana; she'd been gone two weeks now, and she had some big news.

Torval was here.

Corin read and reread the parchment. It was written in code—something he'd learned to decipher over the last months while they were stationed as a "watch and wait" crew here in Cappel Cormac. Corin had endured seven more clashes with Imbala's rebels until about two months ago, when things had quieted down. Word was the situation was changing.

Halfdan visited once, and when he left he took Taskala with him. The swordmaster had returned a month later and announced that most of the regiment would return north to Point Keep due to some recent trouble with Leeth. He'd asked for a hundred volunteers to stay in Permio and keep an eye out. Yazrana and Corin had been first to apply.

After the main force had departed, the rearguard broke up and filtered into Cappel Cormac, their task to keep eyes and ears open until Taskala returned. For Corin this was a change for the better. No more desert ambushes, and though Cappel was as grubby and murderous city as could be imagined, it was better by far than being camped out there.

Yazrana had left without explanation after they had quarreled one night, Corin having no notion of the cause. This letter was the first he'd heard from her since then. When he read the contents, Corin could hardly believe it. Code deciphered, the words read as follows:

Corin dearest.

I regret our last conversation, but enough said. Big news. After you told me about the raider Torval who took your sister, I did some private work, asking the right people and learning about Crennise activities here in the south. They have a new ruler on that island, a man called Rael—a cunning killer who's brought that unruly lot into line, mostly by murdering all his rivals. Torval, being on Rael's hit list, got wind and fled south. He's here, Corin— in Cappel Cormac. Torval has three ships just outside the city hidden in a smugglers' cove his cutthroats have used for years. Wait for me to return before you take action. I will be back this evening. This will take some planning. Do not do anything stupid!

I love you, and I'm sorry we fell out.

Yaz

Corin leaned back and wiped sweat from his face. *So bloody hot in here.* A girl approached and blinked at him; she was almost pretty, but her eyes were flat and her dark cheeks hollowed by years of drudgery. "Fill your flask?" The girl gestured at his coffee.

Corin shook his head. "I need something stronger," he told her. "I've just had some big news, Sulisa." Sulisa nodded and came back with a flask of brandy and a shabby tumbler. "Thanks," Corin said and pored himself a large one.

An hour later Delemar joined him and three others that were

part of the "watch and wait crew" stationed in hovels and squats surrounding this coffeehouse—their favored meeting place. His three companions sought some female attention in the rooms above, but Delemar chose to sit with his friend. He looked excited, though Corin hardly noticed.

Corin and Yazrana had been lucky enough to get a room upstairs, adjacent to the whores, mainly because of Yazrana's Permian background and her knowing Sulisa. It was noisy at times but worked, particularly as Rana had made some show of winking and flirting with customers below. Something Corin hadn't approved of. "Helps us blend in," she'd told him when first they'd moved in.

"Imbala's dead," Delemar said as he took a seat next to Corin and helped himself to some brandy. "That's good; you're starting early today." Corin shrugged; he was still thinking about the letter from Yazrana and had hardly listened to Delimar's words. "Didn't you hear me? The bastard's dead." Delemar stared at Corin and then shook his head. "This changes everything, Corin. Killed by the sultan after they ambushed his camp outside Sedinadola. Slipped the net, but they caught up with the wily fox and flayed his skinny hide. Belmarius was involved, so they tell me."

"No doubt he took the credit."

"He did, but the sultan took it back from him. Poor Belmarius has been left out in the cold—serves the tosser right. One thing though—one of Imbala's sons escaped."

"So . . . ?" Corin tried showing some interest as his mind struggled with his own news.

"Baranaki—a right clever little fucker whose fled deep into the desert and will be plotting revenge. More dangerous than his father, they say. They might have chopped the head of the beast, but the legs will still come after them."

"Well, I suppose that's a good thing," Corin said without much interest. "I mean, Imbala dead—not his son on the loose. Del, excuse me—I've heard from Yaz. I'm poor company at the moment; I cannot think straight and need time alone."

Del laughed. "That's what love will do to you. Glad you two are talking again." He glanced up at the ceiling, wincing as the grubby lantern swung to and fro, casting shadows, and the floorboards creaked and groaned in time with the shouts and moans accompanying them. "I don't know where those fuckers get their energy from," Del complained. "We've been up since four this morning watching the docks. I'm off for a kip, Corin an Fol."

Corin watched Delemar vanish behind the door leading to the rooms upstairs. The news of Imbala's fall would affect them all, but he hadn't time to digest that now. He couldn't think straight, and the brandy hadn't helped. So Corin decided on a walk down to the quayside to get his thoughts together.

Torval here. After all these years it seemed the time for Corin's vengeance had arrived. Corin strapped Clouter to his back and strode outside, where the fierce stab of afternoon sun almost blinded him.

Mind fueled by emotions, Corin walked briskly down to the harbor. There he watched the fishing vessels and slave ships bobbing in the breeze. All was quiet in the heat of the afternoon. He stayed until dusk watching from the old tower at the western-side roof the quay. It was usually deserted, as the city watch spent most the day sleeping, and Corin had come here often over the last two weeks just to kill some time.

He watched the sun spill crimson on distant water as it slid from view. Time he started back; he wanted to scrub his body and clean up for Yazrana's return.

Deep in thought, Corin wandered back through the crooked lanes of the city, Clouter strapped jaunty across his shoulders and all around the evening sounds of a deep and dirty city. The air hung heavy—the usual mugginess clung to his nostrils, as did the stench of night soil and stale smoke from cooking fires. But there was something else. An edginess, a feeling of disquiet. Corin felt invisible wires of tension stiffen his back. Something wasn't right here.

Corin should have read the signs: the small hairs lifting on the back of his neck, a sudden chill running down his spine, and the creepy sensation that he was being followed. You had to keep your guard up in this life. When Corin stepped into the side alley, he realized his mistake at once.

There were four of them, their dark crimson cloaks marking them as the sultan's elite. One fellow carried a short stabbing spear, while the two creeping up behind him held their scimitars low. But worse by far was the grinning leader with the yellow sash across his tunic and loaded crossbow fixed on Corin's chest.

Corin slowed his pace, eyeing the crossbowman warily, and allowed his arms drop by his sides. He could hear the other two closing on him from behind. No room to swing Clouter here, even without that crossbow aiming at his heart.

Corin felt as tense as cord; the Crimson Guard were feared in Cappel Cormac. The sultan's soldiers had a reputation for brutality and ruthlessness. Corin hadn't come across them before, and his mind raced for a way out of this situation.

He slowed his walk and then stopped ten paces in front of the leader, who signaled to his men who were following to wait. Just behind him, the spearman leaned on his spear shaft and smiled unpleasantly. Corin ignored that fellow and instead focused on the leader with the crossbow.

"I thought we were friends," Corin said, grinning and holding his hands wide in parley. "Comrades against the desert scum."

"You're the scum." The leader wasn't smiling. "Your vile kind has been infesting our cities for far too long. Northerners don't belong in Permio. Never have."

Corin could tell they were bored and just looking for something to liven up an evening's duty. He dropped an arm, allowing the small dagger to slide into his palm.

"Except when we are winning your wars for you." Corin's smile fled his face as a chill entered the alley. He felt the rage burning inside. His long-awaited revenge was close, and he'd not have that stolen from him by arrogant fools in dark-red cloaks. Sod their reputation. Corin didn't have time for this.

"Haven't you heard there's a new warlord on the loose? Imbala's son slipped your net while you were sleeping." Corin watched the leader's fingers on his crossbow; this would be touch and go. "They say he's going to feed your Crimson arses to crocks in the Narion, then nail your heads to spikes all along its banks."

Corin watched as the leader's face twitched and his finger inched toward the trigger. But the Crimson Guard were overconfident.

Corin's knife tore into the crossbowman's throat just as he loosed the shaft. Corin hurled himself against the wall as the bolt skidded past his left ear and stuck in a post. The leader might well have been dead, but the other three were on him now.

The spearman yelled as he hurled his weapon. Corin knocked it aside with his forearm and whirled to face the two attacking him from behind.

It was close-quarter work in that alley, and their scimitars were too long to be effective. In their rage to get at him, the pair ill timed their attack, and their weapons clanged off each other. Corin shoulder-charged the nearest, knocking him off his feet, while the other one took a firmer grip on his scimitar and lunged hard for Corin's chest.

Corin dived over the fallen man and forward-rolled, launching both feet up and knocking his assailant's sword aside. Then the spearman was on him from behind. He'd reclaimed his weapon and was stabbing down at Corin, who kept rolling this way and that as he dodged the thrusts; the spear tip sparked and scraped as it dug deep into the cracks betwixt the cobbles.

Corin smiled up at him, and the startled spearman stopped for the briefest instant. Corin used that moment to grab the man beneath him by the cloak and heave him up just as the spearman lunged down hard and gasped, witnessing his spear goring open his comrade's chest.

Corin rolled free of the corpse and kicked up, tangling the spearman's legs and tripping him. As the spearman tumbled, Corin grappled with him and pushed him hard back against the wall. He relaxed the grip when cold steel pricked his back.

"And now you die!" the second swordsman said as he readied his scimitar for the killing lunge. Corin closed his eyes, cursing the capricious gods who had stolen everything from him again.

Just make it quick . . .

***

Corin heard a grunt of pain followed by the sound of some-thing heavy settling on the street. He opened his eyes, then blinked. The spearman slid down the wall, his guts torn open by Yazrana's blade. The second swordsman lay across his companion, both now spilling lifeblood on the cobblestones. Yazrana stood glaring at him, her hair wild and eyes murderous. She wore black leather trousers and a linen shirt and held the bloody rapier in her hands.

"Well, I'll be buggered." Corin grinned in disbelief. "I thought I was a dead man." He almost sobbed the words in relief. "Gods—but I've missed you, lass."

"You very nearly were buggered." Rana wiped her knives clean on the dead spearman and then punched Corin hard in the belly. "Why am I always getting you out of the shit, Corin an Fol?"

"I had them on the run," Corin said as relief flooded through him. "They just didn't know it yet. Anyhow, glad you happened along. Where have you been? It must be three weeks since last we shared an ale. Torval—tell me everything."

"Almost a month." Rana stowed her knives and flashed Corin a wicked grin. "I'm amazed you're still alive, quite frankly. What with your bad habits and me not around to nursemaid you. As for Torval, I've already thought of a plan. We'll need Del and the others."

As they walked, Rana told Corin that she'd been working alongside another woman—a native of Yamondo and a feared as-sassin called Zukei. "A real professional; I learned a lot form her," Rana said. "She's been contracted by some foreign king who had a vessel raided by pirates. She suspected they were Crenise raiders and caught up with them—killing the lot. She doesn't mess around. I asked, but it wasn't your Torval. However, Zukei said she knew of his whereabouts and pointed me in the right direction"

"Is she helping us?"

"No, she had to return south to her country—Zukei moves around a lot. I shall miss her." Yazrana's lips hinted a secretive smile, but Corin didn't notice; he was just happy to be alive and back with his lover with everything patched up.

"Things have been pretty dull since you left. Tonight was the first bit of action I've had in a while."

"And very nearly the last." Rana threw her dark arms around Corin and kissed him long and hard. "I've missed you too, although, you're the stupidest ass I've ever encountered. What have you done to piss off the Crimson Guard? And why are they here? They're usually stationed at Sedinadola or close by along the Silver Strand."

"I don't know," Corin replied and then kissed her back. He slid a hand up her trousers and tugged at her drawstrings until he'd loosened them enough to reach inside.

"We can't do it here," Rana breathed as he worked his fingers deftly between her legs. "It's too . . . dangerous," she sighed as he probed deeper.

"Just don't scream." Corin kissed her ear and slid his spare hand under her tunic, at last cupping a breast.

"You're not that good." Rana chuckled as she pulled and tripped him and he crashed on top of her. Corin took her hard and fast scarce inches from where the Crimson Guard lay motionless, their lifeblood still seeping into the gaps between the cobbles. Neither lover paid heed to them as they laughed and tumbled in the filth and clutter. It was good to be back together again.

Chapter 12

Dawn Raiders

Corin raised the spyglass to his head and grunted as the pink predawn light allowed just enough vision for him to see the three men seated on the rear of the nearest ship. They were playing dice, obviously at ease as morning light spilled into the deep cove where their ships lay hidden. Ten miles east of the city, this forgotten cove had been used by smugglers, pirates and slavers for hundreds of years. The odd merchant ship too—when they were in trouble.

Yazrana had informed Corin that her contact had scouted the cove's occupants while reporting back to her foreign king. This Zukei woman had left the Crenise be, as she'd had urgent business elsewhere, so Yazrana told him.

Corin studied the other vessels bobbing gently in the breeze. Nothing stirred down there. Just another peaceful morning on the edge of nowhere. Corin grinned; they were about to change that. Rana nudged his arm. "The third ship—the one with the blue-and-white striped sail—that's Torval's vessel."

Corin was still amazed by how happy his fellow Wolves had been to help him seek out the leader of the men who had murdered his kin. It wasn't their concern, but they'd been happy to oblige— not just Delemar but his three companions too. Men Corin hardly knew, as they'd been veterans in Permio for years now.

"You're a Wolf, Corin," Del had told him. "We are brothers—your enemy is our foe too."

As for Yazrana? Corin couldn't fathom her: sometimes she was so passionate and other times distant and cold. Yaz had her past as did he, and Corin assumed she was helping him because she loved him. Though there were times when he wondered about that too.

"How many?" Corin passed the glass to Delemar, who grunted thanks and pressed it to his eye.

"Zukei told me Torval had over a hundred men, but most were away raiding with his other ships. This three are undergoing repairs; they got caught in a storm off Golt. Torval stayed behind along with two dozen men. That's what she told me."

"Two dozen?" Del said. "There are only six of us, Rana. Granted, we are Wolves, but fuck—those are not good odds."

"We have surprise and Corin's destiny—we will succeed, Delemar. Hold to cheer."

"I always do." Del looked anything but cheerful. "You three ready?" Delemar's companions, whom Corin now knew as Rigan, Thruster, and Shagger—these last two named for their legendary prowess between the sheets—were cheerful big lads, all around thirty, with scars and dents to match. Corin smiled up at them, again grateful for their aid.

"We're ready if you are," Rigan said.

"Good," replied Yazrana. "Let's do this thing. Corin, pass me that bow."

***

Torval the Strong, recently of Crenna but now on the run, sat in his carved rocking chair on board *The Red Kraken*—his pride and joy and the only thing he'd ever loved. Torval had worked hard as a young man back in Kranek Harbor. He'd completed every task his masters had given him, eventually earning enough money to go it alone, doing what Crenise did best—pirating and plundering.

He'd built the *Kraken* himself with some help from his brothers—all dead now. But Torval was a survivor. That's why he'd taken the hint when the old regime came crashing down, allowing the "Dark Prince" Rael Hakkenon to seize control in Kranek Castle. An old thorn in the former ruler's side, Rael was said to have been tortured under that fortress. It would explain his treatment of prisoners after the coup. Rael had ordered them forced into wicker cages, and these were then set alight, filling the harbor and beyond with crackle and screams.

Cartez had witnessed that but never spoke of it. Torval's first mate had been tardy in leaving the island; he had a good woman there. Rael's cruelty had seen to her death in the chaos, so Cartez had fled and joined his former captain way down in Permio. Cartez didn't say much these days, but this morning he was up before dawn with his captain. They had much to discuss while the others slept soundly in bunks under the canopy at the stern of the ship.

"I don't like this place." Cartez gazed at the dark cliffs surrounding them. "I feel trapped here. We should move on, Captain. Take to the open sea and join the others. Roll the carpenter says the ships are in good enough shape after his work."

Torval gazed at his mate, noticing the shadows behind Cartez's eyes and the wild unkempt state of his beard. Cartez was a mess. Torval, at nearly sixty, still had pride in his bearing. He was six feet seven and as broad as an ox. Master of sword and ax, he'd never lost a fight and never spared a foe. He considered himself a bold leader of men, cruel as he'd had to be but no worse than many.

"We stay here." Torval stroked his pointed beard and sipped the warm ale in his cup. "At least for a few more days. The others should be back by then. I'll not risk three ships alone in these waters. The Dark Prince has paid good gold to the sultan, allowing him free range in the south. That evil bastard will make sure we'll be hunted down and butchered—whether by his raiders or the Permian galleys. Either way, we're dead men if we stick around."

"Which is exactly the point I'm making." Cartez glared at the cliffs again. Torval knew something was bugging his mate this morning. Cartez appeared edgy, and his bloodshot eyes flitted between his captain and the shore. Already the pink light of dawn was banishing shadows into corners of the cove.

"Relax." Torval lit his pipe and leaned back in his chair. "When they're back, we'll have nine ships. Even Rael Hakkenon's boys won't threaten us, knowing they'd lose a good few men, and maybe a ship or two. They know Rael would have their heads on spikes once they returned to Kranek. He's not the forgiving type. That man's twisted, Cartez."

"We are all twisted," Cartez responded. "It's the life we lead."

"What choice did we have? Starve on the streets, join the harborside gangs, or struggle for copper coin under the docker's lash. I've had a good life, pirating and murdering. I ain't got no regrets."

"Well, I suppose that's a good thing, considering what's about to happen." The voice was a woman's, husky and velvet.

Both men looked up in shock. She stood beside the mast, scarce ten feet away. Her feet were braced, and she clutched a slim rapier in her left hand. She was dark, not tall, and rather stocky in build, but appeared comely in her tight black boots, leather trousers, and loose-fitting shirt. Her hair was glossy black and tied behind her neck in a long pigtail.

"And who the fuck are you?" Cartez said. It was the last time he spoke because a second later the woman's hidden dagger tore out his throat.

***

It had actually been ridiculously easy. Corin had watched as Yazrana's arrows skewered the three guards before they'd known what hit them. After that, the six Wolves had waded through the cool water and clambered up the side of the nearest vessel. No one on board, so they moved on to the next. Here they found a pirate snoring alongside a saw, a chopping ax, and some random tools, marking him as ship's carpenter.

The carpenter's eyes had opened just in time to see Delemar's dagger plunging into his heart. Then they'd left the second ship and crawled along the rope ladder that the Crenise had tied between that vessel and the third one. The last ship's blue-and-white striped sail fluttered briefly as the dawn breeze drifted in from the ocean. Corin saw a strange golden dragon creature painted in the middle of the sail.

Ready?" he asked Yazrana, who stood beside him with hands on hips.

Of course." She smiled. "I was born for this sort of work.

Corin watched Rana carefully slide her rapier into its scabbard and take to the rope ladder, deftly pulling herself across. Corin followed with Clouter swinging from his back and dragging him down, making his passage across tricky. But he made it without mishap, and Del and the others followed close behind.

Grizzly knife work followed as Del and Rigan quickly found the sleeping pirates in their blankets under the canopy and swiftly commenced slicing throats. One or two woke and struggled to their feet, but Corin swatted them back down with Clouter. After ten minutes, twenty-six corpses oozed gore on decks and strakes.

***

Corin and Yazrana had crept along the rail to the stern, where they'd found Torval and his mate. Rana whispered in Corin's ear that she recognized Torval from Zukie's description. A huge bear of a man with gray forked beard, his thick arms snaked with tattoos and scars, and his face heavy set and ruddy.

"Stay back; I'll handle this," Yazrana told Corin.

"No way; this is my affair." Corin took a step forward, but Rana grabbed his arm.

"Let me get them talking first, then you can take over," Yazrana said.

Corin looked at her for a moment and then nodded. He slipped out of sight as the woman approached the two pirates.

The mate challenged Rana, and Corin saw her silence him with a flick of her right wrist, the hidden knife piercing his throat. Torval just looked at her. For moments woman and pirate chief glared at each other while Corin watched. The silence broke when the others arrived, fresh from their butchery.

"So you're Torval the murderer?" Corin approached the pirate chief and stared down at him. "You don't look much to me."

"Torval the Bold." Rana nodded with a wry curve of her lips.

Corin leaned forward and spat in Torval's face. The giant didn't blink. Instead, his slate-gray eyes were filled with contempt.

"Assassins in the night. Worst kind of scum. The Dark Prince sent you, did he? Or was it that fat slug—the sultan in Sedinadola? I hear they're best of friends these days."

"Neither one," Rana said.

Corin loomed by her side, his face flushed with emotion and his lips unable to speak.

"Well, fuck you anyway." Torval laughed. "I've no plunder on board, so cut my throat and be about your business. I grow weary of your company."

"All in good time." Corin saw Yazrana. She glanced his way then nodded to Del and Rigan, and they leaped upon Torval and seized his arms. The man was hugely strong, but the Wolf veterans were as tough as wire and they soon had Torval's arms pinned back behind his chair. Yazrana crouched low in front of him and carefully sliced along the length of his trousers.

"What are you doing?" Torval looked afraid for the first time. Rana ignored him as she cut away the pirate's trousers and small clothes beneath. She reached forward and grabbed his sex in her hands, squeezing hard until Torval yelped in agony for her to let go.

"So you like hurting girls—do you?" Yazrana let go of his balls but lowered the knife to hover inches above them. Torval was sweating and his face almost purple.

"I don't know what you are talking about—you have the wrong person!"

"You are Torval of Crenna?"

Torval nodded and glanced at the men surrounding her, his eyes now filled with terror.

"Then you are the man we been looking for."

"Why? I've no enemies down here. Please—this is a mistake."

"What did you do to my sister, you piece of shit?" Corin spat in Torval's face again and then kicked him hard in the balls. Torval coughed and spewed on the deck while Delemar and Rigan struggled to hold him. Behind them, Shagger and Thruster stood grinning with arms folded, enjoying the spectacle.

"I . . . don't know what you're talking about." Torval coughed blood and snot on the deck beneath him. Corin readied a fist, but Yazrana urged him back.

"I said I'll handle this, Corin an Fol," she said. "I've some practice dealing with such as this one. Now . . ." She rose to her feet and wiped the knife on her sleeve. Then, as quick as a cat Yazrana pounced forward and sliced off Torval's left earlobe.

He screamed as Yazrana tossed the scrag of bloody flesh into the water behind them.

"Piece by piece, Pirate. I'll take your balls next." Rana smiled at her captive, who thrashed and wriggled in his chair. "Apt payment for a former raper." She lowered the knife, the blood dripping from its blade.

Torval stared at the steel in horror. "I know nothing," he sobbed. "Please just kill me and be done with it."

Yazrana glanced at Corin, who stepped forward and gripped Torval's beard in his fist.

"Six years ago your fleet sailed the coast of Fol." Corin yanked at the beard. "Yes?" Torval nodded emphatically. "Three ships broke away, led by one Brokka, who served under you. Is that right?"

"Yes, Brokka was my second mate." Torval's eyes shifted between Corin and Yazrana, wide with terror, like a rat in a burning barrel.

"Good," said Corin. "Well, this Brokka murdered my father while his scum crew butchered the rest of my kin. All save my eldest sister, Ceilyn, whom the bastards carried off as they fled. Oh, and I killed Brokka. I cut off his fat fucking head." Corin spat in Torval's eye and tugged hard at his beard again.

"Brokka was a wild one," Torval said. "I couldn't control him—you did me a favor killing him. Please!" He said this last word as Yazrana traced a slim slice along the side of his thigh. The blood glistened and dripped on the timber.

"What about Ceilyn?" Rana's tone was silk-soft and lethal.

"Yes, what about my sister, you bastard!" Corin spat in Torval's face third time.

"There was a girl." Torval nodded violently as though he was trying to shake his head off his shoulders. "A young lass—say, sixteen. She was taken on board."

"And then . . . ?" Yazrana caressed Torval's balls with her right hand while the left one lowered the knife.

"She wasn't touched—I swear it!"

"She wasn't touched, he says," Rana glanced at Corin and held the knife ready. "But I think he's lying. What say you, Corin an Fol?"

"I don't believe him either." Corin rounded on Torval again. "Now, say farewell to your sweetmeats, Pirate." Corin nodded at Yazrana to oblige. "Go on—cut off his bollocks, Rana."

"Wait! Please—I'm telling you the truth! I remember her face, pretty and dark. Her name was Ceilyn—yes, I recall that now. We didn't harm her because we wanted a good price."

Yazrana look at Corin, who nodded. "From whom?" Rana said. "Who did you sell her to?"

"A merchant from these parts. Yes, yes—a Permian; he bought her in the slave market outside Syrannos. We got a good price," Torval couldn't help adding, despite seeing the murder in Corin an Fol's eyes.

"His name?" Rana demanded.

"I can't remember!" The knife crept closer. "Oliam! That's it! Oliam of Syrannos. A fat, sweaty merchant. He bought Ceilyn and took her to his villa. We left for home after that—it's all I can tell you. Please, no!" Yazrana took a firm grip on her knife.

"Leave it, Rana," Corin said. Yazrana glanced at him and then nodded. She sheathed her knife and stood back, allowing Corin closer. "Let him stand," Corin told Del and Rigan as he slid Clouter free of its scabbard. They obliged, and Torval rose to his feet shaking.

"This is called Clouter," Corin said as he swung hard and fast. Torval's head bounced once and then rolled across the deck before vanishing in the dark water below.

Corin stood for a time, then fell to his knees as the tears came rolling down his cheeks.

"Will it never end?" he sobbed. "Will it never fucking end?"

***

Yazrana motioned the others to leave them as she kneeled beside her lover and gripped his shoulders with her strong hands.

"We will find this merchant, my love. Don't give up—we'll learn the truth in good time. But first we need to get back to Cappel. We've spent time enough here. Now that Imbala's gone, there'll be fresh orders coming our way."

Corin nodded as the frustration and fury colored his face. "You are right," he said. "And I can wait; if this Oliam's still alive, I shall find him too."

They joined the others and returned to the shore where their horses were tied to bushes hidden beneath the cliff edge.

"One last thing," Yazrana said as they mounted their horses. She slung her bow free of its leather holder in her saddle. Rana selected an arrow, tore a strip from her shirt, then reached inside her trouser pocket and retrieved flint and striker. Flame started, she lit the cloth, and, after waiting to see the blaze spread, nocked arrow to bowstring and pulled back.

That shaft arced high and wide, cutting through morning air and striking the blood-soaked deck of *The Red Kraken*. An hour later, as they approached the walls of Cappel Cormac, Yazrana glanced back and smiled at the dark trail of smoke cloaking the horizon to their east. Beside her Corin rode in silence.

Chapter 13

A Pause in the Struggle

A week later Corin had walked into the coffeehouse and stopped in amazement upon seeing Darrel seated on a chair and chatting excitedly with Delemar and his friend Rigan. Corin rushed forward and, laughing, embraced his friend.

The big news was half the regiment was back in Permio. There were things happening in the outside world, and as usual Darrel had the details.

"It's all about to flare up again," Darrel told them as Corin yelled to Sulina for ale and food. "Caswallon's the cause—that's what the commander says. The king's councilor claims both Belmarius and our Lord Halfdan have been secretly plotting to usurp Halfdan's brother. Of course that's ridiculous, but this Caswallon is persuasive, and already many believe him up in Kella City."

"What's Halfdan doing?" Corin thanked Sulina, who returned with a shabby tray loaded with ale flask, four mugs, and some loaves of bread. "Thanks, love," he said. Sulina smiled at him and vanished back into the kitchens.

"Staying put in Point Keep; he's out of harm's way there. Belmarius is kicking up a fuss though. Oh, Corin, I almost forgot.

The commander has requested that you accompany me back to Port Keep. He wants to ask how things are proceeding down here."

"Why me?" Corin asked. "What about Del or Rana?" Corin felt a mix of excitement and annoyance. He liked the idea of visiting Point Keep, but that just meant he'd be further from getting any news about Oliam and his sister's fate. But if the commander had ordered his presence, then there was nothing Corin could do about that now. So he might as well enjoy the trip north. "What's so special about me?"

"I don't know—I guess they're too useful, and you're not." Darrel stuffed bread in his mouth and swallowed.

"Thanks," Corin said wryly.

"No problem." Darrel, now a sergeant, had done well for himself in Point Keep running stores and supplies and creaming off a nice little bonus. Then Corin asked him about the other recruits. Darrel informed him that Greggan fared well enough, and Tomato and Sleagon stayed alternately cheerful and dour as before. But the soldier's life had changed Marric—so Darrel said. Gone was the arrogant bully, replaced by a quiet, thoughtful giant of a man whom Darrel said he'd had actually come to like. Corin found that hard to believe.

"Clorte's dead. Jorl too." Darrel sipped his ale. "That lass is pretty." He'd caught Sulina's eye and winked at her. She'd smiled and walked briskly past. "Clorte died in the forests east of the fortress."

"Barbarians from Leeth?"

"Nah, boor hunt. Poor fucker fell from his horse and broke his neck."

"What about Jorl?"

"Caught the flux a few weeks back. Died just before I left. Shame. I liked Jorl."

***

"I'll not be gone long; the commander just wants updates—so Darrel says. Once I've informed him on the bugger all that's been happening, I'll head back down." Corin lay next to Yazrana in the bed, her naked sweaty body pressed against his own. They'd just made love, and Corin lay on his back staring dreamily up at the ceiling.

"Take your time," Rana said. "You could use a break from this fucking heat—you're a northerner after all."

"I don't want to leave you."

"Don't get soft on me, Corin an Fol." Yazrana rolled free of his grasp and stood beside the drapes watching the huge white moon slide out from above a rooftop. Corin watched her nakedness and felt his manhood rising again. "You do not own me—never make that mistake."

"I'm sorry," Corin said. "I'll miss you—that's all."

"You mean you'll miss this." Rana turned and approached him again, thrusting her hips forward inches from Corin's face.

Corin grinned. "Funny you should say that." He pulled her back onto the bed, and laughing, they fumbled and sweated the rest of that night away.

Next morning, Corin rode north with Darrel and a dozen others now under their sergeant's wing.

***

"You've grown strong," Halfdan had told Corin the afternoon he'd arrived at Point Keep after three long weeks riding north. "It pleases me to see it." Later he'd explained how the Wolves had abandoned the dreary barracks outside Port Wind, preferring the isolation of Point Keep.

"This old fortress is as good a place as any," the commander told him as Corin sat in his study. "Far from Caswallon's scheming and plotting. From here we can watch and wait at a safe distance until the bright day comes when my brother the High King sees sense again and throws his councilor out."

"Is he as bad as they say—this Caswallon? I'd heard rumors he dabbles in sorcery, My Lord." Corin had reported all he'd heard while living in Cappel Cormac. There was little the commander didn't know already, and again Corin wondered why he'd been summoned back here.

"Caswallon wants me dead, and his enemies seem to disappear at frequent intervals," Halfdan said. "So I'm keeping a safe distance until I know what he's up to. As to whether Caswallon's a warlock—who knows? He's a villain for sure. Ambitious and dangerous, and slowly murdering my brother with drugs. That much I'm convinced of."

"What will you do, my lord?"

"Watch and wait. Events are taking place all over. Those savages from Leeth are up to something. Every time we fare into the forests nearby, we discover evidence of their being around. Cart tracks, boot scuffs, campfires abandoned in haste. Their king has long had eyes on our country. They're just waiting for a reason to attack.

"And sergeant Darrel informs me that Imbala's son is already uniting the tribes again. And he's good at it too—smarter than his father, so Darrel tells me. Then there is Caswallon and his plotting. But that's not all. That hornet's nest Crenna has a new ruler. A cruel, dangerous man who was once known and feared as an assassin in Kelthaine."

"The dark Prince—I've heard talk of him." Corin said nothing of his own recent involvement with Crenna.

"Rael Hakkenon, yes. No more than a street urchin from Kranek. He became a gang leader while still a boy, then after being hunted down took to the hills. Years later he showed up as a pirate chief in Sturn over on Crenna's rugged west coast, then an assassin. And now he's lord of the island. This world makes no sense, Corin an Fol."

"How long must I stay here, my lord?"

"Gods, man, are you that eager to return to the desert? Most the lads can't wait to get away. Or is it Yazrana?" Halfdan's eyes narrowed, and Corin wondered where this was going.

"I just feel that I'm needed down there."

"I have something for you," Halfdan said after a moment's awkward silence between them. He produced a gold broach shaped to resemble a wolf's head—a beautiful pin three inches in diameter. Corin was amazed by this generosity from the commander, a man he had never thought liked him.

"Delemar sent word of your deeds in Permio. You have earned this, Corin an Fol. Now return to your friends in Cappel Cormac and give my regards to Yazrana. Damn fine woman, that one."

"Will that be all, my lord?"

"Yes, ye.," Halfdan waved a hand, and Corin took the hint. He closed the door behind him and ventured back to the hall where sergeant Darrel and his men were dicing at tables.

***

Halfdan stared at the door as it closed. He ran his hands through his thinning hair and sighed. So difficult seeing the boy again, but he'd needed to know how Corin was faring. He looked older than his twenty-one years. Lean, tough, healthy and strong. A man to be proud of, and a man who—both Yazrana and Delemar had written him about Corin—had proven himself as dependable and solid as any while under attack.

Halfdan wished he could ride south with Corin and drown his worries in the Permian chaos. But he had to keep two eyes on Caswallon. Point Keep was out of the councilor's reach but near enough for Halfdan's scouts to gather what news they could. You had to keep your enemies close in this world.

And then there was Taskala. Seeing that rough scar on Corin's face reinforced Halfdan's belief that he'd been right to re-call his swordmaster. Taskala hated Corin and now appeared to hate Yazrana too. Something had happened down there that hadn't reached Halfdan's ears.

Taskala had been useful in flushing out the odd barbarian in the woods. He'd found and hanged a dozen or so. That said, he was bored most the time, and Halfdan knew the man well enough to know he couldn't keep Taskala away from Permio much longer.

***

Corin had only been back two weeks when he received a letter from the commander informing him of a special task. There was a merchant called Silon residing in Cappel Cormac. A wealthy fellow who, when Corin met him, he didn't much like.

This Silon was some kind of contact in Permio. He conducted most of his business down here and had gotten into some kind of trouble with the sultan. Halfdan's letter ordered Corin to seek the man out in Cappel Docks and escort him safely back to Port Sarfe—or, more precisely, to the huge marble villa the merchant maintained in the hills close by.

Corin had seen the merchant home and returned inside of a week. They hadn't spoken much during that voyage. To Corin, Silon seemed arrogant and aloof, and also vain—judging by the large diamond stud in his ear. But, apparently, he was a trusted ally of the commander. Corin didn't care for the man and had accomplished his task briskly and been glad to return to what he now considered home—the coffeehouse in the seediest corner of Cappel Cormac.

***

And that was where Scolly found him deep in his cups. The older Wolf had returned south with the others a few weeks back. Scolly had been out in the desert scouting and had news of new developments. "We're back on," he said, eyeing the shady clientele and sliding onto the bench next to Corin. "The tribes have found a new leader."

"His son Barakani—this is old news, Scolly."

"His army of thirty thousand strong isn't old news," Scolly said. "The sultan's panicking. Word is, he's written the high king begging for aid again."

"I bet Belmarius is happy about that."

"Caswallon has promised the loan of the Bears and us Wolves against this new threat."

"That was nice of him." Corin waved as Yazrana slid into the room and joined them.

"Caswallon has promised the Tigers too, if needed," Scolly said, smiling at Rana as she took a seat beside them. "Though I doubt General Perani's tossers will get their hands dirty." Scolly hated the Tiger regiment, as did most of the older Wolves. And for good reason, as they were clearly in Caswallon's pay, and their commander, the dour capable Perani, was now considered his lap-dog. "But as usual, we'll get the dirty work."

"What's the plan?" Corin had pulled his hood over this face to hide his fierce expression. Whatever it was, he was more than ready.

Corin liked drinking here. It kept him sharp. There was always tension and usually three or four fights every night. It was an atmosphere that ensured he stayed sober on most occasions. That said, he missed the action of the desert frontier.

"Border country." Scolly slurped his wine. "That's the weak link. Ugh, this wine is crap," he complained. "Word is, Barakani's a fox who'd run rings around that fat slug in Sedinadola. The warlord's spies will already be expecting our boys and the Bears on the south road. They'll have scouts all along the banks of the Liaho, far east as Helbrone Island and the Fallowheld. He'll plan an ambush, Corin, and we'll have to be ready for that when it happens. In the meantime, our orders are simply to watch and wait."

Chapter 14

Betrayal

"He's back." said Yazrana

She watched the long line of horsemen file south along the dusty road from Raleen. The Wolves were back. Rana and Corin and the others in Cappel Cormac had been ordered to meet the rest of the regiment south of Helbrone Island, the ancient bridge having been determined too risky to cross as Barakani's nomads were rumored to be crawling throughout that countryside.

"Who's back?" Corin grunted thanks as she handed him the spyglass. He set sights on the column, over five hundred strong, dark leather cloaks flapping in the breeze as they rode neatly two abreast. Corin cursed when he recognized the bulky rider at the front. Taskala wore a fur-trimmed cloak despite the heat. "Figures," Corin said after moment watching. "He'd not want to miss out."

The riders approached the low-lying hills where Rana, Corin, and the other scouts lay on their bellies scanning the terrain for any sign of movement from the enemy. Word had reached them that this Barakani was on the move and had sent a large force north to challenge any army crossing the Liaho from the Four Kingdoms— though most of his followers were mustering north of the royal city Sedinadola.

The rumors were correct—Barakani was better organized

than his father had been. Plus, he had the motivation of vengeance, and that promised a long and bloody war. Something Corin wanted no part of.

"Let's hope we can clear this up quickly and get back to Cappel," Corin muttered. He'd been planning to ride to Syrannos to see what he could discover about the merchant Oliam. But now he was caught in all this mess of politics, civil war, egos, and strategies. None of it made much sense to Corin.

"Some hope." Rana shook her head. "I know what you are thinking—this delays your own affairs. But this is what we are, Corin. It's our profession. So put up and shut up like everyone else."

"But it makes no sense," Corin said. "Defending South Kaelin from invasion—that makes sense. But getting stuck in the middle of a foreign war between some zealous bandit and a sultan, who I've heard is just another despot. I mean, why are we here, Yaz? Peacekeepers? That will work."

His irony fell flat when Rana didn't respond, and Corin just stared at her, then shrugged. "I know—not our place to question our orders."

Corin had seen a lot of movement during the last week, and they'd nearly been caught out twice, when nomads spotted and chased them back into the hills. Eventually they'd lost their pursuers after switching back and heading deeper into the desert. A risky tactic that had been touch and go.

But that was two days past, and they'd seen nothing of the enemy since. Doubtless Barakani—or whoever led the rebels up here—was studying the region for the best place to spring his trap. Corin suspected he knew the place the warlord would choose: Craggy Corners—a long, narrow ravine about twenty miles east of Cappel Cormac.

"That's where they will strike," Corin insisted that evening as they joined their companions and shared supper and news outside their tents. Taskala had ordered a large camp constructed on a wide, flat hill with sweeping views north to the Liaho and south across the arid brushlands. A good position, hard to attack without being seen, and from where they could scout out enemy movement and then strike the first blow in this latest conflict.

Taskala ordered ditches dug, and stakes were driven into the ground, their tips sharpened, and keen-eyed archers were posted at turns behind them. Guard duty was doubled, and grog was banned. Taskala's plan was to gather all the information he could and then strike fast and hard.

He didn't want Belmarius taking the credit as he'd done after Imbala's revolt. And that general was on his way too. The last report said Belmarius had left Wynais and was leading the entire regiment of Bears along the Great South Road—some two thousand strong. The high king's orders were to crush the nomads once and for all, doubtless following numerous messages exchanged via pigeon between Caswallon and his new best friend, the sultan.

"So why hasn't Halfdan come?" Corin was both disappointed and perplexed by the commander's absence. All but a few of his regiment had returned to Permio, and Corin knew Halfdan would want to be with his men.

"Kelsalion summoned him to Kella City," Scolly told Corin as he sat on a log and chewed a sausage he'd purloined from the mess tent. "If you ask me, it stinks of Caswallon's grubby paws. They say the high king can't take a piss without that conniver knowing which way he's aiming his cock."

"Why doesn't he stay in Point Keep? Fuck this Caswallon and his lies; the commander's risking his neck returning to Kella. An if the high king is willing to believe his brother a traitor, then fuck him too."

Scolly clicked his tongue. "That's dangerous talk, Corin an Fol; I'd keep your lips together were I you."

"I'm just saying what everyone else is thinking, including you, Scolly." Corin glared at his friend and then got up and paced around the camp.

***

"What's the matter with that boy?" Scolly asked Rana, who was watching Corin with calm, thoughtful eyes.

"It's a long story—ask Del. I'm too weary to discuss it."

"Have a sausage, sweetheart." Scolly shoved his fork in the fire and pulled out a sizzler. "You worry too much, Rana."

"It's the reason I'm still alive," she answered, cursing as she burnt her finger on the sausage. Yazrana was worried. Something told her that they were out of their depth here. Corin was right; this wasn't their fight.

***

They waited three days until the first scouts came back, led by an excited Delemar. "They're here," Del shouted as Taskala emerged from his tent, his broad face buried in soap and a steel razor in his hand.

"How many?" the swordmaster said in a growl.

"Fifty or so, all of them mounted. I suspect there are more on the way. Think you we should wait and let them gather?"

"I've waited long enough." Taskala wiped his face clean and reached for his shirt. "We ride west on the hour!" He yelled so that most in the camp could hear.

"Everyone?" Delemar rubbed grit from his eyes and looked at the swordmaster askance. "I thought Halfdan's orders were to wait for the Bears and then crush any rebels we find in a pincer movement."

"Yeah, right." Taskala pulled his shirt over his sinewy frame as Del and the other scouts watched him from their horses. "We have to pin the snake down first. Cut off Barakani's head and the tribes will scatter. To make that happen, we need knowledge of Barakani's whereabouts. And we'll only get that from questioning some of his men. Those fifty nomads will serve the purpose nicely. They might be tough, but the hot knife will soon loosen tongues. We'll catch up with them before they meet up with any friends. Kill all save a few that we put to the knife. Anyone have a problem with that?" Nobody spoke.

"I'll lead the assault myself, along with a hundred volunteers. The rest of you will break camp and follow behind with supplies and equipment."

***

"I say let him go," Corin muttered. "Let Taskala have his victory. Besides, I never volunteer. It's asking for trouble. Why should we endanger our lives in some reckless chase? Those canny fuckers will be expecting something like this."

"But we've got to, Corin, else we'll miss out." Darrel had just arrived with the main force and found his old friend seated on a log, alongside Yazrana and Scolly. "And we're always in the thick of it. We're Wolves; it's what we do."

"I keep telling him that, but he won't listen," Rana said. Corin gave her a sharp look. "It's the truth," Rana added.

"You've been away too long, Darrel," Corin said. "Things have gotten complicated. Some of us have been working while you lot were dozing up there in Point Keep. I know how these nomads operate. They're crafty. I say we will be riding into a trap."

"Well, let's keep our eyes open," Rana added. "I agree with Corin and have a bad feeling about this, but Taskala's right too. We need the information prisoners will provide. So I suggest you two stop quibbling and get ready for a long, hard ride."

They left a half hour later, Corin and his friends riding toward the rear of the column. Taskala set a grueling pace for his hundred volunteers, a steady trot that had the horses shiny with sweat after only a few miles. But Taskala's instinct proved correct, and by midmorning they had caught up with the riders.

A shout went up, and the nomads, having gotten wind of pursuit, urged their mounts to gallop toward a low range of hills. Corin recognized the place and had a sinking feeling in his stomach. "Craggy Corners—I fucking knew it. I'm not liking this!" He yelled across to Rana, who glared back at him and shook her head.

"The ravine—you were right, Corin. Glad I've got my steel vest on!"

They closed the gap on the enemy riders, whose mounts were tiring fast and would surely falter in a few minutes. At the front, Taskala unslung his horn bow from his saddle sheath and expertly nocked and loosed an arrow. Those around him cheered as the shaft struck one of the stragglers ahead, and the nomad's body pitched into the dust bedside the road.

Taskala grinned and let loose another arrow. A second tribesman fell from his horse. "We have them, lads!" Taskala kicked his mount, stowed his bow, and unsheathed the saber at his side. "Now—harvesttime!"

The Wolf volunteers caught up with their quarry just as the brown hills split neatly into two steep cliffs, as though a giant knife had sliced through them. Between those heights wound a long ravine, the rocks hanging over and freshly fallen shale spoiling the road surface and making any good speed treacherous.

Seeing the state of the road, Taskala raised his hand in warning, and his riders eased back on their steeds. Ahead, the nomads were panicking and fleeing as best they could. Taskala's riders were almost upon them as they urged their horses into the narrows known as Craggy Corners. Corin looked up at the nearest ridge, squinting as the sun dazzled his vision.

Then he saw it. Movement. Hardly more than a blur but enough to justify his worst fears. They were riding into a trap, and it was closing on them fast. "Keep your head down!" Corin shouted to Rana, as she looked up and saw figures running along the ridges on either side of the road. That was when the first arrows whistled down upon them—a storm of buzzing, whining shafts that bit horse and rider and soon had Corin, Rana, and all those around them dismounting and jumping for cover.

The arrows kept coming. Corin guessed there must have been more than a hundred archers up there, and Taskala's volunteers were trapped like bugs in a jar. He cursed the swordmaster as he dived behind a large rock and slid Clouter free from its harness.

Two hundred yards ahead, Taskala caught up with the fleeing nomads and in his rage started butchering everyone in reach, his men following suit, Delemar and Scolly included.

"Get up on that ridge and deal with those fucking archers!" The swordmaster motioned to the two veterans to scramble up the shale to their left, taking as many men with them as dared follow.

***

"Keep close behind me!" Scolly hissed as he clambered up the slope, his fingers pierced by thorns and rocks coming loose in his hands. They reached the crest and fell upon the nearest archers, killing a dozen before their comrades on the other ridge noticed the attack and starting loosing shafts.

Del fell with an arrow through his right eye. Scolly cut down four more archers, and then tripped and tumbled from the ridge, breaking a leg in his fall. A few of the archers followed and found him lying on a rock nursing his leg. Scolly killed a couple before the others worked their blades upon him, their leader cutting his heart out and tossing it off the ridge.

***

Taskala sat his horse and stared back along his column. Del and Scolly's valiant sortie had distracted the archers above him, but further back the Wolves were taking heavy losses.

"Stand firm!" Taskala yelled to those surrounding him. "We can fight our way out of this!" He sat his horse, oblivious to the chaos around him, and slowly a smile spread across his lips as he now knew what to do.

"This should see the pair of them slain," Taskala muttered under his breath. He could hear Corin an Fol screaming his name amid abuse from somewhere back in the ravine. Yazrana would be with him, and soon they'd both be dead. Taskala grinned; he couldn't have planned it better.

"We cannot help them," Taskala shouted to those nearby. "We'd best find safety for ourselves and avenge our fallen brothers later. Ride, lads, before the archers find us too!"

***

Behind the swordmaster, Greggan and Darrel stared in horror as their leader urged his beast forward along the ravine, soon vanishing from sight.

"We can't abandon Corin and the others!" Darrel wheeled his

horse around and cantered back to help his friend.

Darrel didn't get very far. An arrow pierced his shoulder and sent him sprawling from his horse. He tried to stand but was struck down by three more shafts, the third piercing his heart. He fell onto his back, his dead blue eyes gazing up at the sun.

Greggan, witnessing Darrel's death and seeing nothing but ruin, cried out in anguish, "I'm sorry!" In despair, he wheeled his mount about and followed the other riders fleeing the trap.

***

Corin could see the swordmaster turning his mount around and fleeing from the Trap. "Help us, you bastard!" Corin yelled, then ducked as an arrow scudded into the dirt inches from his hide. Rana rolled across to where Corin lay. Horrified, he noted the arrow sticking through her left thigh. Rana shrugged. "I won't be running anywhere soon. That bastard Taskala . . ."

"Betrayed us." Corin nodded and swore to himself that he would survive this terrible day just to settle that debt. "Can you hobble? Don't worry if not. I think they'll run out of arrows soon, then I'll carry you and we can—"

A second arrow thudded into Rana's chest, piercing her chain mail.

"They've got bodkins," Rana choked as blood filled her mouth. "I think . . . you better leave without me, Corin."

"Never!" He stroked her face and gently kissed her forehead. "I love you," Corin told her. Rana smiled, but Corin knew she was dying, and sudden rage surged like wildfire inside him.

He leaped to his feet, Clouter swinging in a wide arc as the first nomads emerged from their hides above and came crashing down upon them. The archers had done their work, and now spear, scimitar, and tulwar would mop up the rest.

Rana tried to rise, but a third arrow ripped into her stomach, and she let out a long slow moan. "Kill . . . Taskala for me." She choked the words out. "I do . . . love you, Corin an Fol."

Corin dispatched the first attackers and turned to reply. It was too late. Rana was dead, her almond eyes glazed over and her face oddly peaceful beneath the scorching heat of the noonday sun.

A burning, soaring madness gave Corin abnormal strength and took away any whisper of fear. Clouter felt featherlight in his bloodied hands as he turned, eyes blazing, and fell upon those surrounding him. The berserkergang, they call it in the north. That wild random fury that only a few warriors possess. Fury and loathing, and a kind of absence from reality. Corin felt no pain and knew no fear. It was though he were viewing himself through a mirror, as a man watches actors in a mummers play.

The berserkergang awarded alien strength and power to those under its sway. Some said it was a gift of the gods. And on that day it found Corin an Fol.

Screams, sobs, cries begging for mercy—Corin ignored them all as he swung Clouter back and forth with pendulum precision, hewing limbs from bodies and heads from necks. He fell once but rolled up so quickly that the three leaping at him were taken unawares and swiftly cut to pieces. He fought thus for over an hour while the rest of his comrades fell one by one, to enemy scimitar, tulwar, and spear.

At last a crafty thrust got through his guard, and then another blow knocked the helmet from his head. Corin's feet left the dirt, and he was vaguely aware of his back crashing hard onto the road surface. He squinted in the sunlight, and for the briefest glimmer of a moment thought he saw a red-haired woman smiling at him as she sat on a rock close by.

You cannot save me this time . . .

Then they were upon him, and Corin an Fol knew no more.

Chapter 15

Flies and Vultures

Haran watched as his men dispatched the last of the northerners. In a way he admired these foreign Wolf fighters. Brave and
tough, but let down by their commanders, who had no concept of
how to win this war. It was all politics, of course. But Barakani had
long studied that game, and where another man would have rushed
to avenge his kin, Haran's war chief had bided his time.

Barakani knew the sultan would secure more aid from the
north. But he also knew that aid would soon dry up. Barakani had
new friends in Raleen who were working on that. Haran had no
doubt the tide was turning in their favor. Patience was the key.

The warrior chief stepped over the pile of corpses as he approached his men, who were currently crouching and slicing the
throats of any still living.

"This one took some killing." Somal showed his toothless grin
as Haran looked down at a tall northerner sprawled on his back, his
face drenched in blood and a huge sword still gripped in his hands.
"Best make sure." Somal crouched with crooked knife and grabbed
the dead man's hair, yanking it back and exposing his throat. "He's
still breathing." Somal grinned. "But not for long."

"Wait." Haran raised his palm, and Somal gazed up at him

with curious eyes. "Let the desert finish him. We've killed enough men today."

Somal shrugged and stowed his knife. Haran watched Somal join the others and ready their mounts for swift departure. He knelt beside the young warrior with the huge sword. "Hey, Wolf. You did well today, and if you're as tough as I think you might be, then you might just survive. It's unlikely, but if you do, then go home, northerner. This is not your fight."

Haran looked up at the sky, where the vultures were circling more than a hundred strong. A strange whim it was, sparing this boy. Be far kinder to have slit his throat.

Moments later he joined his men, and together they rode west apace throughout the rest of that wonderful day. The tide was turning, and Barakani was the name it carried.

***

It was thirst that woke him. That, and the large vulture tearing at his face. Corin swatted the bird aside and groaned as pain shot up his arm. The vulture hopped backward and stared at him balefully. Corin spat at the bird, and it took sudden wing and settled feet away to feed on a corpse. No doubt it would return soon and try again. Wounded and alone, humans didn't last long out here. But Corin was determined to disappoint the vulture. He wasn't planning on dying anytime soon.

He rolled to his side, groaned again, and then in a clumsy motion that made his entire body shake with agony, he sat up and glared at the vulture now back again and hopping closer. "Piss off." The bird hopped backward again but lingered despite Corin's withering stare.

"You're out of luck, ya ugly bastard." Corin turned to see Rana's ravaged, twisted body, the three arrows sticking out at different angles, and the wide pool of blood crawling with flies and ants.

"Fucking things." Corin swiped at the insects as rage, and finally tears, shook his body. He was alive by some miracle or curse, though everyone around him was dead.

Corin checked his body. His chain mail and leathers had

saved him from being gored in several places, and somehow he'd avoided being pinned by arrows. He retrieved a shaft stuck in the dirt and yanked it loose. Rana had been right—the bodkin point was meant to piece armor. Such arrowheads were expensive and hard to acquire. How the nomads had gotten their hands on them, Corin had no idea.

He felt sick and weak, and he knew if he didn't find water fast, the vulture or one of its companions would claim its prize.

Somehow Corin staggered to his feet, leaning heavily on Clouter. After a minutes of swaying, he found enough strength to stagger across to his horse, which was lying dead close by with a cluster of arrows sticking from its hide. Corin reached down for the saddle and pulled his water canister free. It was almost full, and he downed the warm brackish contents in wild gulps, almost choking and throwing up the contents onto the ground.

He sat there for long moments shaking and sobbing, thinking of Rana lying close by and all his comrades, sightless and flesh pecked dry by the noisy cluster of creeping, hopping birds. The ravine stank of death, shit, and betrayal. One word kept Corin breathing. *Revenge.*

Giddy, Corin sank to his knees. He needed rest and shelter. He wasn't badly hurt, despite being a mass of bruises, but any small wound could get infected easily. With that in mind, he staggered along the death trail, seeing many faces he recognized. Rigan's body was badly hacked, his severed head close by, and he found Sleagon too. The latter had his arms locked around a dead nomad. On closer inspection Corin saw that Sleagon had snapped the man's neck while his enemy had stabbed him in the side.

Corin gathered as many water canisters as he could find, taking careful sips as he staggered amid corpses, crows, and vultures, the flies buzzing around his face. He drank slowly, making sure he kept the liquid down. As he walked, the vultures perched on the corpses, eyeing him warily. Corin didn't hate the birds. They were just doing their job. Plenty of time for hatred later. Survival was priority today.

Corin walked on, exhaustion and his battered body slowing

his mind, but ever present was the urge to recover and then avenge the woman he loved.

It had hurt him to leave Yazrana lying there, but there was nothing he could have done for her. At least she was at peace now. In oblivion, or whatever afterlife the Permians subscribed to. Rana would live in Corin's memory from now on.

Shortly before dusk, Corin reached the last corpses and stopped when he saw Darrel's sunny blue eyes gazing up at him. "Not so talkative now, my friend." Corin knelt down and gently closed Darrel's eyes. "Be at peace; you were a good lad." He stood and with eyes moist left the last of the corpses behind.

***

Night found Corin sheltered beneath a large rock, the stars studding the sky above his head and a cold breeze finding gaps in his tattered cloak. He had a small fire going, having recovered flint and stone from one of the horse's packs and brush wood from close by. He'd consumed a small amount of salted pork, which some sensible rider had stowed just in case. It wasn't much but would keep him alive.

And Corin needed to stay alive. He had a job to do. There was a man he intended to kill, and before he did that Corin needed his full strength back. He slept for a time, waking as dawn paled the east.

Weak and aching yet fueled by hatred, Corin started the long hot walk back to the city. It was more than twenty miles to Cappel Cormac, and in his battered state the walk took him three days. Now and then he had to jump aside and find hideouts in the shrubs as enemy horsemen rode past. At last, half starved and hobbling and leaning heavily on his longsword, Corin found the coffeehouse and staggered through the door. He hoped things hadn't changed and these were still the only people in Permio who weren't his enemies.

The girl with the hummingbird tattoo on her cheek saw Corin stagger into the taproom. She rushed over to support him, and Corin grinned at her, recalling her name: Tysha. One of the several cleaners employed by the coffeehouse owner.

"What the fuck happened to you?" Tysha found a damp cloth and wiped the blood from Corin's face. "Looks like the Djinn demons set upon you." She helped him to sit at a table.

"Tribesmen." Corin managed a wan smile. "Where's Sulina?"

"Visiting family in Sedinadola; I'm working double shifts to cover her leave." Tysha sounded resentful.

"Have you any ale?"

"Don't think you need it in your current state." Tysha scratched her tattooed cheek. "But it's your choice." She shrugged and went off to get a jug. "Here, but drink it slowly. You're half dead, by the look of you."

"I'll survive." Corin's said. "Just get that beer."

***

Corin gulped his ale down while Tysha watched him with dark, thoughtful eyes. "How about another?" Corin drain the mug and belched.

"No way—you need to rest." Tysha got one of the other girls to help her carry Corin upstairs, and together they pitched their long-legged burden onto a straw cot usually frequented by the drunks who couldn't find their way home. They left him be, and Corin slept well past noon the next day.

***

Rested and somewhat back to himself, Corin had allowed Tysha to scrub his naked body in the wash tank and pick dirt from his many wounds. She also performed another small service that he hadn't requested but enjoyed all the same.

"You'll be staying around here, then?" Tysha reluctantly withdrew her hand from the filthy water and wiped it dry on her sleeve. "I'm free most nights."

Corin closed his eyes, feeling exhausted again. He pictured Yazrana's dark eyes and felt a sudden shame. "I left her," Corin told Tysha, who glanced back at him in surprise.

"Who's that?"

"It doesn't matter now." Corin thanked Tysha and begged her to leave him be. The girl obliged with a quizzical quirk of her lips. Corin spent most of that day and the following one resting up and recovering. But at night he kept his ears sharp as he supped ale in the taproom. He learned that Barakani, after having teased and tested the Crimson Elite in a few damaging raids outside Sedinadola, had withdrawn his force and slipped back into the desert where, rumor was, he had a secret camp somewhere inland from the Silver Strand, the long white beach that ran from the royal city to Syrannos.

There was no news of any northerners having been involved. Corin assumed his regiment was still close by and was determined to ride out and join them as soon as he could. If Taskala was there, Corin would kill him. If not, he'd find where he'd gone and catch up with the swordmaster, however long that took.

He listened in as a couple of merchants shared coffee and comments on events transpiring in the west. "Going to be a long war," the merchant facing Corin said, a lean fellow with hooked nose and thick lips. He spoke with an unusual accent Corin couldn't place and seemed unconcerned that anyone might be listening. The inn was quiet that night, but Corin wasn't the only drinker.

"Let's hope it's a profitable one," replied the merchant with his back to Corin. That one's head was covered by a dark-red burnoose, hiding his features, though Corin caught the glint of something shiny and then saw the diamond stud in his left ear.

"The Crimson are overconfident," the hook-nosed merchant said. "Barakani knows he has to play a waiting game to win, and the sultan's not known for his patience any more than his soldiers are. Therein lies the warlord's strength. Barakani knows how stone and water will turn to sand if you allow enough years to pass by."

"Poetic, if a trifle irrelevant." The merchant with his back to Corin chuckled. "He'll need to act at some point, if only to keep the tribes together. You know how wild those nomads are, Nula."

Nula nodded. "Barakani is not his father. There is something about him. You'll see when you meet him next month."

"I'm looking forward to it." The merchant with the earring

chuckled slightly as if he'd said something funny. "These are high stakes we play for, Nula."

"The highest. What of the sorcerer in the north? Has he shown his hand yet?"

"Not yet, but it's only a matter of time. My contacts in Kella City say the high king's health is failing fast, and Caswallon has fed him with lies until he's paranoid that everyone is plotting against him, when the only real enemy he has is the serpent feeding him the lies. Kelsalion had his own brother arrested, you know."

This last was said in a raised tone, as if to deliberately draw comment from anyone listening close by. "It's alright, Corin an Fol. You're among allies here." The second merchant turned in his seat, and Corin stared into the dark cunning eyes of Silon of Port Sarfe, the arrogant aloof merchant he had escorted north that second time he'd left Permio.

Oh, it's you . . .

Corin hid his surprise and instead demanded to know what had happened to Lord Halfdan. "He escaped custody," Silon explained. "Lord Halfdan still has friends in that city, though they grow fewer every day, falling victim to fatal accidents at alarming rates." Silon's shrewd black eyes pinned Corin's stormy gaze.

"And why are you here, Longswordsman?"

"That's my own affair, and I could ask the same of you, Merchant."

"Who is this rough young fellow?" Nula asked his friend.

"The one I told you about," Silon replied and winked at Corin. "One of Lord Halfdan's stray Wolves."

"How do you know me?" Corin's hand edged toward Clouter's hilt. The merchant, Nula, looked nervous, but his companion shrugged.

"You're not easy to miss with that big sword, Corin an Fol." Silon smiled at Corin. "And if you're looking for Taskala, he's headed back up north. General Belmarius leads the Permio campaign now that the Wolves are to be disbanded."

"They're to be what?"

"Hunted down and killed by order of Lord Caswallon, as

their patron has been branded a traitor who seeks the high king's crown for himself." Silon raised a calming hand as Corin half-leapt from his chair, only stopping when his almost healed cuts seeped open again. "Just one of several lies Caswallon has been spreading throughout the realm." Silon continued. "Many follow that canard now, including one individual you know well. Rumor is, Taskala took gold from his new master, Perani, and is returning to Point Keep to put an end to the high king's brother."

Corin slumped back in his chair. "This is no surprise meeting, is it?" He pinned Silon with an icy stare. "What do you want from me, Merchant?"

Nula looked puzzled, but Silon smiled. "Oddly enough—loyalty, Corin an Fol. You see, I know quite a bit about you. Things you don't even know yourself. Suffice it to say, I've work for you down here in Permio, should you wish it."

"I don't want anything from you, and I'm buggered if I know what your game is. But don't worry about Taskala because I'm going to gut him open from bollocks to chin."

"That might well prove harder than you think." Silon finished his coffee and rested a tanned hand on his fellow merchant's hand. "Come, Nula, let's finish our business elsewhere. This tavern has served its purpose." Nula nodded and after awarding Corin a quizzical stare followed Silon to the door.

"Excellent coffee." Corin watched Silon wink at Tysha as she brushed past him. "I'd stay clear of that northerner if I were you." Silon hinted to where Corin sat scowling at him. "I reckon he's got a roving eye." Silon grinned at Corin and vanished into the street outside.

"What the fuck was all that about?" Tysha asked Corin as she gazed at the doorway where the merchants had just left.

"I have to leave as soon as I can," Corin told her. "Tomorrow at the latest. I don't know what that little shit is up to, but I dare not chance he's lying. I've a debt to pay, Tysha. A matter of honor. I had planned to take my time, but fresh events have forced my hand."

Tysha just shook her head, confused.

"Once that's done I'll return here, as I've business in Syrannos too. Expect me back in a few weeks."

"I might still be here." The girl looked disappointed.

Corin wondered how he would fund a trip back north when he was down to his last coin. That question was answered for him when the coffeehouse owner came in and dropped a large purse full of gold on the table where Corin was seated.

"What—?"

"Don't ask me." The portly proprietor, Gorfe, shrugged. "That merchant with the earring was here last night too. Said he was looking for you and that you would need this soon. Oh, and he said you can pay him back later."

"What does he want with me?" Gorfe didn't respond and Corin turned to examine the gold, his mind clogged full of unanswered with questions.

Despite his fear for Halfdan's safety, Corin didn't feel strong enough to leave yet. He stayed another week, practicing with Clouter in the stable yard until his arms felt like lead. He asked Gorfe if he'd heard of the merchant Oliam but he hadn't, so Corin decided to leave that task be for the moment. What difference would a few weeks make? Ceilyn's pretty face was a distant memory, but Yazrana's dark eyes haunted his every waking hour.

He needed strength and for his body to repair. Day after day, Corin exercised with Clouter in the yard outside the coffeehouse, and at night Tysha helped banish some of the desolation swamping his soul.

That last morning arrived, and Corin rose early. He gazed down at Tysha's naked brown body sprawled akimbo across the bed. "Thanks," he said. "You're a true friend I won't forget. But I've a score to settle that cannot wait."

Corin left the tavern as dawn paled the cluttered streets of Cappel Cormac and the first vendors and hawkers emerged sleepy-eyed from their dens.

He ventured down into the harbor and after an hour's steady bartering booked passage on a merchant ship bound for Port Sarfe. Once there, he traded coin for a fast horse and began the long ride north to Kelthaine.

Chapter 16

The Challenge

It had taken Corin three weeks of hard riding to reach the remote outpost known as Point Keep. He'd ridden through much of Kelwyn and Kelthaine as the weather turned increasingly colder, with frost and the occasional snow flurry whitening fields he passed. Corin had shivered throughout the journey; he wasn't ready for winter, having spent so long in the south.

At last he reached the Gap of Leeth, a wide-open plain wedged between the mountains, beyond it the vast wilderness called Leeth, a land Corin knew nothing about.

He turned south, hugging the foothills of the High Wall—the great mountain range that guarded the Four Kingdoms from the barbaric realms beyond. Centuries past, Point Keep and its sister fortress, the redoubtable Car Carranis, had been constructed as eastern watchtowers and over time were strengthened and enlarged to serve as city fortresses. Point Keep was the smaller of the two, positioned high in a defile hidden by a shoulder of the mountains.

After a few hours Corin found the track leading off and up into the hidden cleft. High above, the walls of Point Keep frowned down at him. Corin scowled as he recalled how he'd enjoyed his last trip here. But times changed. He only hoped Lord Halfdan was still breathing. He'd find out soon enough.

Believing surprise his best option, Corin waited until well after nightfall, then yelled for the gate guards to let him in. They saw a tall man on horseback with a longsword and flapping cloak, his face buried beneath a hood.

"Who calls?" Corin heard a muffled voice behind the gates.

"An old friend. I seek Taskala Swordmaster," Corin answered, trying not to shout. "I've a message from the high king himself."

"Wait there." There followed a series of bangs, thuds, and grumbles, and the sound of keys jingling, and finally one of the huge gates creaked ajar enough to allow Corin through. He didn't recognize the young guard, but that wasn't surprising as most of the men he knew were dead, their bones bleached white beneath that murderous Permio sun. "Who are you, and why were you creeping about in the dark out there?"

"Not your concern," Corin responded. The young guard caught the glint in this stranger's eye and saw the length of his sword and clearly decided not to press the matter. "Is Lord Halfdan present?" Corin pinned the lad with a steely stare.

"He's most likely resting. The commander and the swordmaster were out hunting early this morning."

"Were they alone?" Corin's voice was sharp.

"No, there were twenty or so. They ranged out into the forests hunting boar and keeping an eye out for any stray barbarian. They say Leeth has a new ruler, and that one day he'll invade our—"

"Where's Taskala's quarters?" Corin cut in. The guard blinked back at him. "I haven't got time to fuck about, mate. Where will I find him?"

"He won't like being disturbed." The young guard looked unhappy. "In the Great Hall," he said eventually. "Lord Taskala has taken that for his personal quarters, as the regiment is not what it was."

"Lord Taskala?" Corin barked an ironic laugh and left the puzzled guard behind.

"Shall I call someone to accompany you?" The young watchman looked increasingly worried.

"Don't bother," Corin shouted back. "I know the way."

Corin left the gatehouse behind and trudged up the long path leading to the castle main. The Great Hall lay within the keep, the highest tower overlooking the rest of the fortress. Lord Halfdan's quarters were above it, dangerously close to where Taskala now resided. Corin jogged across to the keep, found the narrow spiral stairway within, and took the stone steps two at a time.

***

Taskala sat alone in the heavy chair. The hour was late, and the fortress slept. But there would be no sleep for him tonight. He swilled the glass of port around his fingers as he studied his options. Clearly things had gotten out of hand, and he had been caught neatly in the middle. The agents he met with back in Kella City had been most insistent.

"The high king's brother must die," they'd told him. "For the good of the realm. Halfdan's a threat and will continue to be so at Point Keep. At some point he'll return with an army on his back. We cannot let that happen."

Taskala had listened to their lies and nonsense without a word. He knew his commander to be the most loyal of men who would never conspire against his brother. But that didn't matter a nonce. The Wolves were outlawed now, and Taskala had to look to himself. So he'd met with General Perani of the Tigers and explained his difficult position.

"You'd be a valid asset," Perani had told him. "And I would reward you with a commission that brought with it a fine salary, including a house in the royal mile. But first I need a show of loyalty."

Loyalty . . .

Taskala smiled at the irony. He had always been passionate about his regiment. He'd loved the Wolves and had served for more than thirty years. But at forty-six he was no longer young, and the thought of being hunted down like a rabid dog and then eventually hung, drawn, and quartered for treason was beyond contemplation. Untenable. So to survive, he had to betray his commander, a man Taskala respected like no other.

But what choice did he have? Halfdan had brought this on himself—and the rest of them, for that matter. Instead of seeing how things stood and allowing Caswallon a free hand in Kella, Halfdan had gone out of his way to aggravate the high king's counselor, now known to be the only real authority in Kelthaine and thus the Four Kingdoms too. Caswallon was ambitious, shrewd, and very dangerous—always had been. Taskala didn't like the man, but that was irrelevant. You had to back a winner in this life.

Halfdan had lost. And now to earn Perani's trust, he, Taskala, most loyal of captains, would have to slice open the throat of his commander. So be it.

Taskala gulped down the rest of the port and hurled the glass into the roaring fire. And why delay? He'd had several opportunities this afternoon when they'd been pursuing that boar, but Taskala knew he'd need a stiff drink before he could commit to such a task.

But now he was ready. Taskala stood and wiped the smear of port from his mouth. He was more than half drunk and dreading what he had to do. But needs must. He turned to face the door and then froze upon seeing Corin an Fol standing there.

"What the . . . ?" Taskala's hand dropped to his side, where his dagger hung from his belt.

***

"You piece of shit." Corin stormed into the Great Hall and kicked Taskala in the gut before he'd time to free his blade. The swordmaster fell backward, but drunk though he appeared, Taskala was still quick. He rolled aside and tripped Corin, who fell across him.

Taskala reached down with his left hand and freed his knife, but Corin grabbed an ear and rammed his face down hard against the slate flagstoned floor, crunching Taskala's nose and snapping the small bone.

Corin sprang back on his feet and then kicked the swordmaster hard in the groin as Taskala struggled to get up. Then Corin freed Clouter, stood over his prone enemy, and pricked the longsword's point under Taskala's chin. "I'll not slay you here and stain our regiment's name. Have you the balls and honor to face me alone?"

"You know that I have," Taskala choked as blood from his broken nose filled his mouth.

"Good. First light then." Corin hoisted Clouter up and the slung the longsword back in its scabbard. "You name the place, and make sure you come alone."

"Gardale Moor." Taskala rolled to feet and spat blood on the straw-covered flagstones.

"And where is that?"

"A lone hill, four miles south of the Gap. You would have passed it on your journey here. Its crown is encircled by beech trees and can be seen easily from north, south, and east."

"I shall find it." Corin watched as Taskala took hold of his nose with his right hand and snapped the bone straight. "I hope that hurt," Corin added. Taskala just stared at him. "First light, Swordmaster—don't be late. And remember—this is just between us two."

"I'll be there." Taskala smiled up at Corin. "I've been wanting to gut you open for years. Thought I'd lost my chance and you'd died in the desert, but they say bad pennies always roll back."

"Fuck you too." Corin turned and strode from the hall.

***

"In the morning then!" Taskala croaked after him, and then found the port jug and refilled his glass. His nose was on fire and his eyes bloodshot, but the pain in his face and groin was nothing compared with the rage Taskala felt. The whelp from Fol had bested him as he had never been bested before. He'd been drunk and caught unawares, but despite that, the knowledge still dented Taskala's hitherto invulnerable pride.

I shall finish you tomorrow, Folly.

Taskala managed a grim smile. He'd kill Corin and piss on his corpse—and by doing so stamp out the memory of what had just happened in this hall.

Taskala sat drinking for another hour until sleep finally claimed him and thoughts of his other chore were forgotten. No matter. One job at a time—first Corin an Fol and then the commander.

Chapter 17

Gardale Moor

It was a cold morning just before dawn. The wind battered his ears, and overhead, bleak slate-gray skies spilled fresh snowflakes that floated and drifted dreamily around his wind-ruddy face. Corin stood alone, waiting, Clouter's tip thrust deep in earth, the racing clouds rushing high above his head. A lone hawk cried out from somewhere nearby. A lonely sound. Seconds later and far off, its mate answered.

Corin stood on the flat grassy top of a round hill, its summit crowned by a large circle of beech trees. Tall and austere, they watched him as rose-colored light tinted the eastern horizon heralding dawn.

Corin shivered, still not ready for winter. He looked up at the trees as though expecting to see something. This was a strange place, uncanny and creepy, and today those trees would witness a death. Corin prayed silently that it wouldn't be his lifeblood seeping into the rough dead tussocks below his feet.

Occasionally the wind whipped the remnants of crispy leaves from stark limbs above, and these joined the snowflakes and danced wildly around his head. To his left, a lone tall stone marked the steep path that led up to this remote and eerie place. A place of ancient mystery where echoes still throbbed beneath the soil, hinting at rituals performed by people Corin would never understand.

Corin imagined the earth moving beneath him, felt that cold east wind bite his cheeks, and watched intently as two large ravens settled silently on the tall gray stone. Like him, the birds watched the morning light filtering in through the clouds. The sky was clearing overhead, and Corin knew it was time.

He waited a few minutes more. He felt calm and ready, despite his racing heartbeats and the knowledge that one of them would not return from this remote barren hill. Holmgang, they called it in the north. The warrior's challenge, where scores were settled between two adversaries—one of whom must die, lest Telcanna the Sky God grow wrathful and strike the earth all around. Something He had been known to do when men sought escape from their fate.

Movement below. The sound of heavy boots squelching on damp muddied ground. Corin stiffened, seeing Taskala stride past the tall stone. The swordmaster's face was flushed by cold and last night's alcohol. But he appeared confident and brash and approached where Corin waited, his manner full of swagger and smirks. Taskala carried a broadsword in his left hand, while his right gripped a single-headed war axe. Corin knew him to be a master of both weapons.

Taskala stopped a few feet from where Corin stood poised, his gloved hands still gripping Clouter's crosspiece. Taskala's gray eyes mocked this reckless fool who dared to challenge him.

Corin shrugged and let his breath out slowly, seeing it float like vapor from his lips. He must not fear. To fear is to fail. And to fail is to die. He shifted his grip to Clouter's hilt, lifting and levering the blade, testing balance and shifting his stance. He was ready.

***

Taskala glanced around and smiled at the trees. He had no dread of this place, nor did he feel the ancient stirrings and echoes of the past. Taskala had no such sensibilities. He was a killer born to kill.

Taskala thrust his broadsword's tip into the ground and

reached down with his left hand, then wiped dirt into his gloves. He felt good this morning, ready to complete this task and then move on to the next. This deed would fuel that graver action. Corin an Fol was a dog to be silenced. Lord Halfdan deserved more respect, and Takala determined he wouldn't suffer as this boy would.

Taskala smiled at Corin, who stood watching him with a calm blue-gray gaze.

"Are you ready to die, Folly? Shitting your small clothes yet?" Taskala chuckled. "I'm going to take my time cutting you, boy. Savor every moment."

***

Corin ignored the jibes. Instead he glanced up, seeing the hawk gliding past and hearing the ravens noisily mock its passage. "It is time," Corin said in a cold, dry voice.

"Then say your prayers, Corin an Fol." Taskala grinned and then attacked at once with sword and axe, a blur of motion, forcing Corin back toward the ridge shadowed by the trees behind him.

Corin blocked and swiped—no time for fancy moves today. Lunge with sword! Swing the axe; hack and slice! Stay alive! Jump forward, then swing again. Breathe. Cut low, swipe high! Lunge. Don't trip.

The swordmaster smiled as he forced Corin back again, and Clouter struggled to block the lightning-quick assault of his enemy's perfectly coordinated weapons.

Corin slipped on a stone, falling backward, and Taskala leaped in to finish him. But Corin rolled and kicking out in panic caught Taskala's shin, causing him to trip. Taskala stumbled, and Corin leaped to his feet, ramming a shoulder hard into the man's back and knocking him forward.

Taskala retained his balance and spun on his toes, slicing with the broadsword and swinging the axe down in a wild killing arc. Again Corin jumped back, heaving Clouter across, barely catching the axe beneath its head before the weapon impacted his face.

***

Taskala smiled; he was enjoying seeing the panic in Corin's eyes. "You are no match for me, boy." He watched as the lean scar-faced warrior readied for his next assault. Taskala grunted in satisfaction, seeing a warrior before him and not the youth he so despised. A man worth killing. Tall, lean, and violent with loathing.

Taskala smiled again. "And now you will pay the final tally." He leaped forward, the sword lunging toward Corin's heart and the axe swinging wide for the taller man's neck.

***

But Corin had anticipated that move. He ducked beneath the arcing axe and battered the sword aside with Clouter's edge. Seizing the advantage, Corin jumped in close, ramming Clouter's pommel into Taskala's left eye, pulverizing the muscle.

The swordmaster gasped and staggered back, blinking as blood streamed down his face and obscured the vision from his remaining eye. Taskala sliced wildly and savagely with the broadsword.

Corin backed away, bracing his feet, slowing his breath. Then he took one step forward and swung down hard.

Corin heard the whoosh of steel slicing air and knew this to be the killing blow. Taskala raised his axe to block, but Clouter's keen edge sliced through the ash shaft and cut deep into the swordmaster's shoulder. Taskala shuddered as the weight of that blow hacked down into his chest and continued through his guts. He staggered to his knees and glanced up at Corin with an ironic grin.

"See what a fighter I've made you, Folly." Taskala choked out the words, and Corin swung again. This time Taskala's broad head rolled free of his shoulders and bounced on the blood-soaked ground below.

"That's for Yazrana," Corin said as he reached down and seized Taskala's head. He stared long and hard into the cold gray eyes. "You are right. You have made me what I am. I'm the Wild Wolf, and now my task is done."

Corin felt a strange calm. He hadn't expected to survive this day and knew the consequences could still cause his death before nightfall. But Yazrana had been avenged as were his friends back there in the desert.

Corin stared at Taskala's head and smiled at the irony of life. Corin felt so alive and yet knew death still had bony fingers on his shoulders. He studied his options while Taskala's head swung from his hand.

He could flee and ride south, an outlaw hunted and tracked not only by Caswallon's people—who wanted every Wolf dead—but also by Lord Halfdan, with Corin branded as a mad dog and traitor and the murderer of the regiment's swordmaster. But Corin would not run; rather, he would face whatever destiny the gods had planned for him. Not for him the dread of a knife in the dark.

Corin shook himself into motion. Such thoughts achieved nothing. It was past time he left this dreary place.

Resigned to his fate, Corin wandered beneath the trees to where his horse stood tethered and pacing, unsettled by the smell of blood and the uncanny atmosphere of Gardale Moor. Corin stuffed Taskala's seeping head into his saddlebag and mounted his steed. The ravens mocked him, and as Corin turned, for just the briefest instant he glimpsed an old man with a wide-brimmed hat watching him from beneath the trees.

Corin blinked and the figure vanished, doubtless a trick of the light. Corin chewed his lip and urged his mount back down the steep track and eventually horse and rider rejoined the road, turning south for the fortress and the fate he knew he must prepare for.

Chapter 18

The Accused

It was Greggan who first saw the ragged rider approaching the gates alone. The weary figure crouched low in saddle, cloak and hood shrouding his features. But Greggan recognized the long-sword slung across the rider's back, and his face paled upon seeing a ghost creep in with the cold winter morning.

"Who approaches?" A spearman yelled down, but Greggan bade him to be silent.

"Open the gates," Greggan, now a sergeant, yelled at his guards below. He grabbed the spearman's collar. "Go and inform his lordship that a long-lost stray has returned." The man blinked at him, looked down at the rider, then nodded. Below, his fellow guards opened the gates and glared warily at the grim-faced horseman gazing back at them with hollow eyes.

Corin saw Greggan among them and showed his teeth. "Good to see you're alive," he said. Greggan just shook his head and stared.

"What has become of you, Corin an Fol?" Greggan stepped back in horror as Corin untied his saddlebag, then produced his trophy. He grinned savagely, then tossed Taskala's head onto the cobbles at Greggan's feet.

"This traitor has paid his debt," Corin told them, as furious guards pulled him from his horse and surrounded him with spears. "So do as you must."

Greggan watched in stunned disbelief as they dragged Corin an Fol inside the barbican and waited as Lord Halfdan emerged white-faced through the doorway. The commander saw Corin, then gazing beyond noticed the severed head. His face grew grimmer than ever, and his lips tightened to thin lines.

"That is an ill deed done, Corin an Fol," Halfdan's eyes were frosted over and his voice colder by far than that bleak winter morning. "Take this murdering felon to the dungeon and construct a hasty gallows. We will hang him ere this day is out." Halfdan gave Corin a ravaged stare and briskly turned and vacated the guardroom.

***

Corin let Greggan's men escort him to the dark hole at the back of the fortress. The oubliette hadn't been occupied in years. It was bitter cold and damp and almost as black as pitch, but Corin hardly noticed. He watched them leave and shivered as the wet stone sapped his will and the sound of dripping water somewhere close haunted his memory. He sat with eyes glazed and mind numb for several long minutes, then out of sheer exhaustion slumped forward and slept for a time. And the moment Corin closed his eyes, the dream stole upon him.

Sunshine and warmth lit on his face. Corin smiled and heard somewhere close by the sound of fast-flowing water over stone and songbirds chirping joyfully. Corin opened his eyes and saw her sitting by the waterfall, her long copper hair lifting slightly in the breeze, and in her upraised palm rested a bright-blue butterfly opening and folding its shimmering wings.

Corin was in a wood, and it was summer. He knew this by the scent of foxgloves, the buzzing of bees, and the thin green dress clinging to the woman's curves. She turned slowly and smiled at him, and those green-gold eyes tugged at his heartstrings.

"Now will you tell me who you are?" Corin asked the woman, but she turned away and lifted her hand. Corin watched entranced as the blue butterfly took wing and drifted off beyond the waterfall.

"I am one of three who watch over you," she told him. "The Fates, men call us: Past, Present, and That Which Shall Be."

"So I am dead then." Corin smiled. "And this is the wood where lost souls gather."

"Nay—rather, you are sleeping." The woman reached over and kissed his face, and Corin was filled with the urge to hold her tight in his arms, this beauty he had always loved. She traced a finger, parting the locks on his forehead. "Relax," she told him as he struggled. Try as he might, Corin couldn't move and stood rooted to the spot. "You have much yet to achieve, Corin son of Fol. Your real journey is yet to start."

"At least tell me your name," Corin persisted. "You who have always haunted my dreams."

"I am Vervandi." The woman smiled at him. "And I inhabit your every day. It is my task to ensure you reach your potential. We are in a game of high stakes. You will discover more in time."

"And who am I to have this special attention?" Corin demanded as the woman's beautiful smile faded like morning mist on water.

"You are the leaf in the wind, Corin an Fol. The harbinger, the vital pawn, and the fulcrum. You are the . . . Chosen." Her voice drifted and faded, and his vision blurred, and from somewhere close by, Corin heard the haunting sound of a solitary harp. Those clear chords floated across to him, reaching deep inside his skin and speaking to him in silent words.

Saddened by what he heard, Corin closed his eyes as the tears started to roll. The harp's song faded, the chords peeling off into distant memory.

"You must wake now," the woman told him, and Corin opened his eyes.

He blinked, staggered, and then fell face-first on the dungeon floor. Corin sobbed—not for what awaited him but rather for the loss of she whom he had always loved.

Chapter 19

Revelations

Lord Halfdan of Point Keep was seated in his study, which commanded fine views of mountain and defile below. He gazed from his window, as far below snow settled on roof and battlement. Winter had arrived, and his mood matched the gloom outside.

Down there he could see some of his men erecting the makeshift gibbet where Corin an Fol would hang that very afternoon. Halfdan closed his eyes and rested his chin in his hands. How could this have happened? What had gone wrong, and how had he missed it? A wave of weariness washed over him. He had failed and felt battered and lost.

Again he recalled that portentous day when the high king's golden vessel struck rocks in that wrecking storm off the coast of windswept Fol. Twenty-two years ago, to his reckoning. The high queen, his brother's wife, lost, and Halfdan's own beloved Celese too. And their children gone also, both the high king's heir and Halfdan's baby son. All of them taken by cruel Sensuata the Sea God, to serve in His watery halls.

"It doesn't matter what I think," Halfdan muttered to himself. "For years I've hoped, but all for nothing. Our laws make us who we are; therefore, the boy must die. I'm sorry, Corin. I have failed you."

Halfdan glanced up upon hearing a brisk rapping at the door.

"Enter." He watched the door swing open and scowled at seeing a shaggy-haired Sergeant Greggan standing there. Halfdan noted how pale Greggan looked. Halfdan was in no mood for interruption.

"What is it, Sergeant?"

"Forgive the intrusion, my lord. I have something important to tell you. Something I should have mentioned long before."

"Go on." Halfdan waved a brisk hand, and Greggan nodded.

"The swordmaster—"

"Taskala."

"Himself . . ." Greggan looked increasingly uncomfortable.

Halfdan waved his hand in irritation. "Continue, Sergeant, lest my patience desert me."

Greggan nodded. "My lord, the thing is . . . Taskala betrayed his own men down in Permio. That last raid we were caught in. The one in which Yazrana and Scolly died. Taskala could have helped them, but instead he'd urged those still in their saddles to flee the arrows cutting down our friends.

"Darrel was with me but refused to abandon Corin and so turned back. I saw him die, my lord, but I lacked the courage to follow suit." Greggan hung his head.

"So I fled with the others. At first I couldn't face my guilt and so denied it had happened. But then, over time and believing them all dead, I saw no reason to report such an action and pit my word against Taskala's, whom I've always feared. But when I saw Corin an Fol emerge from the mist like a ghost this very morning, it all came flooding back. Corin is no murderer, my lord, but rather a man of courage, nobility, and honor."

Halfdan watched Greggan for long slow minutes as the sergeant shifted from foot to foot, biting his bottom lip. "It matters not," Halfdan said at last. "Taskala is dead, and Corin will soon follow him. You know our code, Sergeant Greggan. *Any* man who takes the life of his fellow Wolf must hang—whatever the circumstances. It's the foundation of everything we stand for. I would that it were not so."

"I'm sorry, my lord."

"Leave me, Greggan. My heart is hot within me." The commander watched Greggan shuffle out the door and vanish in the corridor beyond.

And so it has come to this.

It was only then that he glanced across at the corner table and noticed the sealed letter delivered via pigeon last night. Curious, Halfdan reached across and saw the seal was stamped with a bold S, the mark of Silon, the wily merchant he knew down in Port Sarfe.

Halfdan cracked open the seal and read the contents within. He studied the missive three times and then jumped to his feet. "Greggan!"

But it was too late; they were already dragging Corin an Fol out into the damp chill of that early winter's day.

***

Corin glanced up at the scaffold and saw two ravens perched on either side. "Get rid of those birds!" Greggan ordered the three men standing up there. "Bloody things give me the creeps."

The ravens hopped and croaked as the nearest spearman waved his weapon at them. They took flight for a moment before settling again, this time higher up the scaffold. From there they surveyed with cold black eyes the scene unfolding.

"I'll not wear that," Corin told Greggan as his friend reached for the rag to cover his eyes. Greggan nodded and knelt to tie Corin's hands behind his back.

"We'll make it quick," Greggan assured him.

"Thank you." Corin managed an ironic smile. "Taskala was a traitor, Greggan. Make sure you tell the commander that." Corin gazed around, feeling the sharp cold air, seeing the white snow coating scaffold, planks, and flagstones below. He felt so alive; shame he was to die. Corin blinked back tears.

It doesn't matter—nothing lasts forever. We are dust and wind and memories . . .

Corin was determined to die well so Greggan could report that back to Lord Halfdan. At least then the commander would know him as no craven. Funny how such a thing should matter here, but it did.

Someone spoke and Corin blinked again.

"I said he doesn't need to—I already know." The voice came from behind them.

Corin and the men around him turned to gaze at the smiling face of their commander. "Dismantle that ugly monstrosity." Halfdan pointed up at the scaffold, where a guard was currently testing the drop. "We won't be needing it today. Instead, you can cut up that lumber for firewood. We'll want as much as possible for the feast tonight. It's going to be a big one."

Corin blinked backed tears of relief as the cold wind buffeted his ears. He wasn't going to die today, despite his certainty. Corin felt his legs quiver and shake and he struggled to contain his joy and relief.

The guards, including Greggan, grinned in astonished wonder as they leapt to obey their commander's orders. Halfdan turned and rested a gloved hand on Corin's shoulder. "I'm so sorry I mistrusted you, boy. Forgive me—I grow old and my wits wander."

"There is nothing to forgive, my lord." Corin smiled as Sergeant Greggan, laughing, cut the ropes and freed his hands.

***

"It was a letter from Silon, a wealthy merchant, who I believe you may have encountered before," Halfdan said.

Corin nodded as he tore at the pork chop. Close by, the hearth filled the Great Hall with glow and warmth, and three large hounds lolled sleepily in front of it. There were nearly a hundred and fifty men packed into the hall, feasting and drinking and toasting one another. Only those unfortunates on gate duty were missing out on this feast.

"It tells in detail of Taskala's treachery. Silon has spies in Kella City; he's not just a merchant, by the way." Corin nodded, having assumed that much. "How he planned to work for Perani— another traitor," Halfdan continued. "And after killing me would be rewarded with a high commission in the Tiger Regiment. And, more important, win the gratitude and favor of one Caswallon."

"Why would he do such a thing? No one liked Taskala, but we all believed him the most loyal of men." Greggan was puzzled, as were many seated there.

"He changed after that last trip to Permio," Halfdan told them. "I noticed how haunted Taskala looked at times, as though something twisted and wrong worked inside him. And he wouldn't look me in the eye as he'd always done before. I ignored the signs, believing them just a soldier's tortured conscience. We are all affected by the aftermath of battle, no matter how hardy we appear."

"So what now?" Corin wiped his mouth and slurped down a large amount of ale. He still couldn't really believe he was alive and was determined to get as drunk as he could during the next few hours.

"We stay put here in Point Keep," Halfdan replied. "That knave Perani has shown his hand, throwing in his lot with the high king's counselor, who I now believe to be the instigator of my brother's sorry demise. And your suspicions were right, Corin. Rumors have reached me that Caswallon has been steeping in sorcery for some time now. It would explain his rapid rise to power. We cannot go near Kella City, gentlemen. I don't know about Belmarius's lot, but the Tigers would hunt us down to a man. We are much depleted, whereas their number surpasses three thousand strong.

"No, my dear Wolves, it is our task to watch and wait and be prepared for any outcome. Then, if and when the time is right, we'll return and take the city back, and I shall kill Caswallon and free my brother from his invisible bonds."

They toasted their commander and cheered.

***

The next morning Corin sat in the commander's study, his head thumping and his vision blurred. "Are you sure this is what you want?" Halfdan looked displeased.

"I am. My lord, I cannot remain in the regiment. Too much has happened. And there are things I need to learn. Mysteries from my past that haunt me still. There is someone I must find down in Permio—a memory and a shadow, but a mystery I must solve. After that I desire to return to Finnehalle, my home. There was a girl there I once knew." Corin pictured Holly's smiling face and was filled with a desire to see her again.

Halfdan studied Corin's face long and hard. Finally he nodded, then he stood and reached into a closet and passed a woolen bundle to Corin.

"A cloak?" Corin untied the strings and unfolded a heavy gray cloak with hood to match.

"An officer's cloak. I wore it once, and it will suit you too," Lord Halfdan told him. "I trust you still have that golden broach?"

"Of course. It's in my saddlebag." Corin nodded thanks as he wrapped the warm woolen cloak across his shoulders.

"Comes in handy in the desert." Halfdan smiled wickedly.

"How did you know I wanted to return to Permio?" Corin was puzzled, as all those who knew about his sister's existence were now dead.

"Funny you should say that." Halfdan waved his hands. "I promised Silon swift response to any messages he sends me. It's part of our agreement to foil Caswallon's plotting." Halfdan was grinning now. "I'd not trust to pigeon alone, though I will send a few. No, Corin. I need someone reliable and capable to carry my response to Silon in Cappel Cormac, where he's currently working with the Permian Resistance."

"The Permian what?"

"Didn't you know? The sultan's Crimson Guard massacred a squadron of Belmarius's Bears after some quarrel down there. It prompted Silon to meet with Barakani in secret and together plot the downfall of the sultan. It seems they've much in common.

"There's more to it than that, of course, and I'm certain Caswallon's hand was involved in that massacre, perhaps hoping to do away with General Belmarius as well as me and let his Tigers rule supreme. But suffice it to say, our war with the nomads is over for the meantime. The sultan cannot be trusted, and it would serve us well to see his demise."

Corin blinked. "I—"

"That cloak suits you, by the way." Halfdan smiled up at him. "You are a lone wolf now, Corin. Or should I say a Gray Wolf?" He waved a dismissive hand and bade Corin to depart. "Farewell, Corin an Fol. I hope you find what you are seeking down there in the hot lands. Perhaps Silon can help you. May the gods bless your road, and may we meet again before the end."

Lord Halfdan thrust out his hand, and Corin shook it vigorously. An hour later he was on the road riding a fast horse with the wind in his face and Clouter strapped across his sturdy new gray cloak. Corin's life in the Wolves was over, but there was one task that still awaited him.

Chapter 20

Syrannos

Tysha's smile was a picture, and Corin wrapped his arms around her when the girl threw herself at him. Close by, Sulina—back from her sojourn—looked baffled and flustered.

"You did come back—and me thinking I'd lost you!" Tysha kissed him, and Corin felt a sudden warmth for this girl who had helped him at that darkest time.

"I almost didn't—though through no wish of my own. But I couldn't bear the thought of not seeing your lovely face again, Tysha." Sulina rolled her eyes upon hearing that, but Tysha beamed and kissed Corin hard on the lips.

"So how long are you staying?" Tysha demanded as she returned with a steaming coffeepot and tray full of spice cakes. "I've already asked Gorfe, and he says you're welcome here as long as you want."

"That's good of him, but actually I need to leave right away. I came to see you, girl, get a night's rest—or whatever else is on offer." Corin winked at her. "And then ride out early in the morning."

"But you've just gotten here—where are you off to now?"

"Syrannos, on business."

"Let him go, Tysha." Sulina was still eavesdropping. "You

know what these fighting men are like. Girl in every port—he'll break your heart, so he will."

"I will not," Corin waved Sulina away. The older girl sniffed in disapproval but left them to it. "There's something I have to do; it won't take long," Corin told Tysha, then looked up as Gorfe the owner appeared.

"That merchant you know left this for you yesterday. Said he knew you were on your way down here. Also said this might help." Gorfe handed Corin the crunched parchment. Puzzled, Corin quickly broke the seal and opened the letter.

Corin an Fol:

I hear you are a free agent. Seek me out in Port Sarfe if you need a contract. I pay handsomely and on time. You could do worse. Apropos, Gorfe tells me you need to find someone you lost long ago. Don't worry—he works for me as does everyone at the coffeehouse—it's why my friend Lord Halfdan chose it as a safe house for his Wolves when they were in Cappel. I visit as often as can.

Gorfe is my eyes and ears, and Halfdan wanted me to watch you—I confess I do not know why. But I told Gorfe and his girls to listen in on your conversations. So he heard about the business with Torval and the merchant Oliam and passed that news on to me.

I met Oliam once. He kept a smart villa in the street of Olives close by the temple. As I recall, it had golden gates fashioned into dragon's wings. Perhaps you should pay him a visit.

After that, think on my offer!

Speak soon,

Silon

Corin wasn't sure whether to laugh or curse. "So you are all spies," he said. "Even your little Tysha."

"Tysha knows nothing," Gorfe cut in. "Sulina is my master

spy and reports back to me all she hears. Saved a few lives over the years, has Sulina. But I didn't want to involve my younger daughter in such dangerous a pastime."

"They are your daughters? Sisters?" Corin blinked and pored over the letter again. "Well—thanks, but now that I've read this, I need to leave right away."

"What is this about?" Tysha demanded of her father, annoyed that she hadn't been a party to whatever they'd been up to.

"Let him tell you if he wishes to. In the meantime there are other customers waiting and chores to attend."

***

An hour later Corin stood with harness in hand and horse stamping beside him. Tysha blocked the stable entrance, her feet braced and long black hair tied back. She looked determined.

"I should go with you," Tysha told Corin.

"No way; you are needed here. Besides, it might be dangerous."

"I know Syrannos; our mother lives there. She's who Sulina visited last month. Sulina's close to Mother, whereas I love my father better."

Corin scratched his ear, trying to take this in.

"They are estranged," Tysha said. "Separated—have been for years."

"Well, of course I understand that, but it doesn't change anything. I need to do this alone, Tysha."

"I'm coming with you." The girl stood her ground. Corin stared at her for a minute and then smiled. Something about Tysha's determined angry expression reminded him of Yazrana. "Very well—but don't get in my way if there's trouble. I need a lot of room to swing this thing." He rested a palm on Clouter's hilt, where it hung from the horse's saddle. "You'll need a horse.'

"I have one ready."

"And you had better clear this with your father."

"He knows." Tysha grinned. "Well—are we leaving or not?"

***

Corin bade Tysha to wait behind with the horses as he slung Clouter's harness across his back and approached the huge pale-blue villa with the intricate fountains and statues of birds. It had been easy to find, lying so close to the huge Temple of Telcanna and fronted by those gilded dragons more than twelve feet high.

Corin crossed the street, glancing back to see Tysha lead the horses under the shade of palms that were everywhere in this city. Three days' ride had brought them here, and Corin was impressed by how clean and ordered this city was compared to Cappel Cormac. Tysha had told him it was nothing compared to the wealth of Sedinadola, the sultan's capital.

Corin noticed chains around the gates and a large padlock. He stopped, puzzled, and looking closer saw that the gardens that at first had looked so neat and lush were overgrown and choked by weeds.

Surrounding the gates was a stone wall perhaps eight feet high. Corin jumped at it and hauled his body over the top, then dropped silently to his knees in the gardens beyond. He squatted and gazed about. The hot sun baked his shoulders, and a bird chirped from a spiky bush closely.

A noise caused him to turn his head, and Corin cursed when he saw Tysha's brown legs straddling the wall. How the girl had climbed that, he had no idea.

"The horses are fine—tethered, safe, and watered. There's no one around, "Tysha told Corin as he gaped at her. "Look like no one's at home here either."

"How did you get up that bloody wall?"

"I used this." Tysha produced a long curved knife she'd kept hidden in her waist belt beneath her shirt. "Stuck it in the cracks and pulled myself up."

Corin just blinked at her.

They weaved through the gardens, heading for the front doors, also golden and carved with dragon faces. Oliam was evidently an opulent fellow, but if he still lived, it looked as if he'd moved some time ago. Corin prepared himself for another disappointment but froze when he saw movement to the right of the house. Corin grabbed Tysha's arm and pointed.

An old man was crouched on his knees clipping bushes; he was skinny and was clothed in baggy trousers and a loose flapping tunic. Oliam? Unlikely.

Seeing no harm in this fellow, Corin approached him while Tysha hung back, watching to see if there was anyone else around.

"Good day to you," Corin said. The old man leaped up in alarm. "Wait, sorry! I mean you no harm." The old man looked at Clouter, and his dark eyes were filled with panic. He turned to run, but Corin rested a hand on his shoulder. "I said, I mean you no harm. But perhaps you can help me—I'm looking for someone."

Corin let go of the old man's shoulder and waited as the man stopped trembling, realizing he wasn't about to be murdered anytime soon.

"I don't know anything, and there's no money here." His voice was hoarse and his gray hair long and scraggy. The old man saw Tysha standing several feet away, and he frowned. "Who is that?" he asked.

"Where is Oliam? I know this is his house."

"Gone." The old man was still looking at Tysha. She smiled at him, and he turned away, agitated. "Everyone's gone. There's only me left here now."

"Gone where?" Corin patience was ebbing fast; it now seemed that they had stumbled across some vagrant beggar.

"Over there." The old man pointed to a clump of thorn bushes fifty yards beyond the house in an area of shrub and sand at the far end of the garden. Corin raised his hand and shielded his eyes form the glare. Staring at the thorn trees, he saw two raised stones beneath their shadow and what looked to be some kind of dais. His eyes narrowed.

So Oliam was dead. That much seemed obvious now. Cori was disappointed; he'd been looking forward to killing the merchant. Now he felt cheated.

"What happened to him?" Corin grabbed the man's collar again, but tighter this time.

"Murdered." The old man spat out the word. "Nasty business."

"By whom?"

"His wife; she stabbed him in the heart with a stitched knife."

"Really?" Corin was struggling to take this in. "And what happened to her?"

"Fled with her lover—a rogue from the desert."

"Are you hearing this?" Corin yelled back at Tysha, who nodded.

"Well, that's not important to me. I want to enquire about one of his slaves."

"Oliam never kept slaves—he was a good man."

"That I doubt." Corin gazed around the garden and saw three crows watching him from the thorn bushes near where Oliam the merchant lay buried. "He purchased a slave girl at market six or seven years ago. A pretty lass from the north—sold by Crenise pirates. Do you know anything about that?"

"Of course." The old man looked indignant. "She was his wife."

"What?" Corin's hands tightened on the man's tunic.

"Ceilyn her name was—came from some distant land." The old man's eyes narrowed as he studied Corin's face. "Agh, I see it now. You are her kin—a brother perhaps?"

Corin said nothing but walked over to the tombstone and saw the words carved on it. *Oliam—much-loved father and respected merchant of Syrannos.* The grave beside it was unmarked.

"And who lies there?" Corin asked the old man as he joined him to gaze down at the stones.

"I will when I'm done cleaning up here."

"That's bit morose," Tysha said as she came alongside. "Why did Ceilyn kill her husband?"

"He beat her somewhat." The old man shrugged.

"You said he was a good man." Corin rounded on the old man in sudden rage, and the wretch took a step backward.

"He was, but everyone beats their wife in Syrannos. He was just doing what husbands do. Besides, she was wild and unruly and had a nasty temper. She nearly bit his ear off once."

Corin was at a loss for speech, but Tysha took over questioning the old man. "And her lover—you say he was a nomad? One of the desert folk?"

"Aye, one of several thousand that plague the endless sands south of here. The Crimson Guard sent a squad in pursuit, but the lovers slipped their net. That was nearly a year ago—they could be anywhere now."

Tysha thanked the old man and turned to look at Corin. He shrugged. "I suppose I should be happy," Corin told her. But he didn't feel happy; he felt confused, cheated, and utterly desolate. For years now he'd believed his sister dead, and his task would be to avenge her. Now it seemed that she still lived, albeit way out in the wilderness with some savage, whom perhaps she still loved.

"Of course, I'm pleased she's alive but I will never know for sure—just have this old man's word to go by." Corin sank to his knees, his back resting against Oliam's headstone. Tysha and the old man glanced at each other and said nothing.

"I liked Ceilyn," the old man said after a moment's silence. "She was kind to me. And Oliam loved her, but he just couldn't control her. Then one day in market this handsome stranger . . ."

Corin closed his eyes. What would he do now? Wander off into the desert for years looking for a ghost from his past? The chances of finding his sister were beyond slim. Corin stood and dusted down his trousers.

"Come on," he said to Tysha. "There's nothing for me here. Let's leave this old fellow to his memories and head home." Tysha nodded and thanked the old man as Corin turned and walked away without even a backwards glance.

"I'm glad you came with me, Tysha," Corin told her as they rode along the Silver Strand, the sun setting behind them. "You're a good lass."

"So tell me about this Holly and the other woman with the red hair?"

"How could you possibly know about them?"

Tysha snorted and patted her horse's neck. "You talk in your sleep, Corin an Fol. And sometimes I imagine hearing a woman's voice answer.

"That would be the drink." Corin cuffed her ear, and she laughed. "Holly was a girl I knew as a lad back home. The other woman—I'll tell you about her one day."

"I shall look forward to that," Tysha said and urged her horse to gather speed as they headed toward the distant walls of Cappel Cormac, its stones brushed rose-pink by sunset's refection.

Epilogue

Silon drained his coffee and made his excuses, wiping his face as the merciless Permian midday sun scorched the tents and tables of the marketplace. Silon needed to leave this place. Too dangerous to linger here. He'd spoken to Yashan, the nomad Barakani had arranged for him to meet with, and all was as planned.

Deal done, and with things to arrange back in Raleen, Silon was intent on sailing north that very afternoon. But he was twenty miles south of Cappel Cormac, and this village was heavily patrolled by Crimson Elite, who were intent on throwing any foreigners into the dungeons for questioning—or else executing them on the spot. The capricious sultan, it seemed, was once again tired of so many northerners frequenting his country.

Silon watched as a troop of crimson-cloaked soldiers strode past the market square. They looked resplendent in their polished armor and matching helms. They were sharp, efficient, and tough, but Silon thought them no match for Barakani's rebels. You had to back the right horse in this life.

Silon watched them vanish down a grubby side street. He waited a few moments, then, satisfied all was clear, jumped to his feet, folded his parchment, and strolled casually across to where his mare stood dreaming under the shade of a dusty canopy.

Just as Silon reached for the horse's bridle, another troop of Crimson Elite—some six strong—rounded a corner and stopped in their tracks, seeing the merchant untying his horse. The leader shouted at him to stop, and Silon turned, his heart sinking as the men strode briskly toward him, their weapons held ready.

"Take off that burnoose!" the leader shouted. Silon had no choice but to oblige.

"Ha! See that diamond in his ear." The sharp-eyed captain grinned at his men. "This is the fellow we're after. Now seize him, boys, and let's be off."

***

The captain was still grinning at Silon when the sword point emerged through his belly. He stared down at it in disbelief before dropping to his knees, sobbing and crumpling in a pile.

The men surrounding him yelled and leveled their spears, lunging about for the perpetrator. But their shafts were butted aside as a huge sword cut through wood, ring mail, and into soft flesh beneath. Two more fell, then Corin strode forth swinging Clouter hard and slicing the head off number four.

"I think it's time we got going." Corin gestured for Silon to mount his mare as he leapt for his own beast tied alongside.

The two remaining guards circled Corin, jabbing warily with spear and scimitar and yelling as loudly as they could for assistance. Corin blocked a halfhearted spear thrust, then jumped forward, smashing into the assailant's chest and ramming Clouter's pommel hard up under his chin, which lifted the man off his feet and knocked him out for the count.

Meanwhile, the one with the scimitar crept up behind Corin, but before he could stab him, Silon's tossed dagger caught him between the shoulder blades, and he pitched face-first into the dirt. Corin slung Clouter back in its harness and vaulted onto his steed.

Together, merchant and mercenary urged their mounts to crash through the marketplace and flee the dusty village. Minutes later, the twenty or so Crimson Elite gave furious chase north along the shimmering sun-hazy road to Cappel Cormac. Corin knew this region well, and they lost their pursuit easily enough.

At the docks, Silon bribed a sailor with several gold pieces—enough to ensure safe hasty passage so they'd not have to wait for tide or stiffer breeze as he'd planned. After biting the coins, the sailor had grinned and smuggled merchant and mercenary on board his fisher. The captain bid his crew to make ready at once, and they departed within the hour.

"You'd best come with me until the dust settles," Silon said, and nodding, Corin joined him on deck.

That night as Corin watched the coast of Permio fade to darkness, Silon joined him and thrust a large flagon of wine into his fist. "I am in your debt, Longswordsman." Silon smiled. "I would repay you."

Corin swallowed a swill and grinned. He didn't much like wine, but it was far better than water, and he was thirsty this evening. "You already have," he replied. "And, in a strange way, you saved my life too." Corin recounted the events leading to his returning to Permio to seek the merchant out.

"Well, how the Fates make fools of us all." Silon laughed and sipped his wine. "A lovely night. Let us toast it together." He raised his wooden cup, courtesy of the skipper—who, in Corin's opinion, had been overpaid—and clonked it against Corin's. "So? What will you do now, Longswordsman? You had best stay clear of my coffee-house for a while lest you endanger Gorfe and his daughters. That sword of yours will be the talk of Cappel Cormac soon. Forget the city. Mercenaries can always find good coin in the border regions."

"Fighting the sultan?" Corin shook his head. "No, thanks—I'm done with Permio for a while. Too many memories. And besides, it's so bloody hot in the desert. Nope, Master Merchant, I intend to go home. It's been more than ten years since I left."

"What about Tysha? You just going to leave her? I know that girl loves you, Corin." Silon sipped his wine and smiled.

"Yes, well, of course you know everything—and thanks for the tip about Oliam. He's dead, you know."

"So I heard—stabbed by a certain lady."

"Life is strange." Corin shrugged. "No—yes. I'm fond of Tysha, and I'll be back here sometime, but, as you said yourself, I'd best stay clear for a while. Besides, I'll only hurt the girl—I'm too restless and sure to let her down. Kinder for me to leave Tysha be, perhaps drop in now and then. I'm a warrior, Silon. A fighting man—that means I'll always be trouble. And now that I know my sister's alive somewhere but I'll never see her, I feel as if my time in the desert has served its purpose. I'll sell my sword elsewhere."

"So what will you do? Go fight in Leeth? Work for Caswallon? He's always looking for mercenaries these days." Silon chuckled and swirled the wine in his glass. "I cannot see that working for you. You're are too loyal, Corin an Fol. A warrior and a veteran campaigner, yes, but no sell-sword. You may have left the Wolves, but you'll never abandon Halfdan's trust. Work for me, and you are still on the same side. There is evil brewing up north, and soon we will all have to take sides." Silon drained his wine glass and sighed. "Go home—and I wish you luck with that. But first, join me in Atarios for a celebration."

Corin shrugged. Atarios was Raleen's first city, rumored beautiful, and sat along his way home too, should he choose horse and not ship. "Be honored to. What's the occasion?"

"Nalissa, my only daughter—gem of my soul. It's just the two of us now; I lost my wife to illness four years past. Nalissa is my darling, though a tad willful—mine own fault for indulging her. She will be eighteen next week, and I am introducing her to the nobles at Atarios. Hopefully, there will be a good match. You, Corin an Fol, can tag along and drink some ale and keep an eye out for troublemakers. I'll fill your purse with more than enough coin for your ongoing trip. Then, when you tire of rain-washed Fol, you can call on me in sunny Port Sarfe and mayhap we can fix a deal.

"These are dangerous times, Corin an Fol. And I need a strong arm with a large sword. Think about it."

Corin replied that he would give it thought. "But I'll not be back anytime soon," he assured the merchant.

"Well. The offer's there."

They shifted their discussion to the glorious evening, the dark water stirring below, and the bright stars studding the firmament high overhead.

***

Meanwhile, from the prow she watched him, her gaze taking in his stance, vigor, and the way he spoke with that gruff northern voice. What a fine man he had become—her pupil, and so well suited for their divine purpose.

A whoosh of breeze and the distant sound of laughter announced her little sister's arrival. The spiteful imp, Urdei, settled like a snowflake beside her.

"Vervandi, are you in love?" The blond child giggled. "That's forbidden for such as we—isn't it, Scolde?" A shadow stirred beside Urdei, taking form and slowly revealing a crippled old hag cowled in a black cloak and leaning on a twisted cane. The third sister had come to see what all the fuss was about.

"Hah," croaked Scolde. "Always she was soft, our sibling. Like our mother the goddess, Vervandi loves these mortals too much. They are weak things and make unreliable tools. Yonder fool will let you down just as the rest did—you will see."

Vervandi ignored her sisters, and so Past and Future let her be, returning to their stations far away. But Present remained, for she had given much to this affair. She watched and smiled as her beloved drained his wine and descended belowdecks for a well-earned sleep.

Vervandi blew him a kiss and sadly turned away. She stood on the prow and stretched out her arms. The pattern shifted, and she became an owl, gliding silently and swiftly, vanishing between the clear dark waters and brooding sky above.

I shall see you in time . . .

***

Three weeks later, Corin an Fol stood in the luxurious grounds of Silon's city mansion. He was tired and thirsty after the long ride and had been happy to help himself to wine and peruse the lovely grounds. The merchant's main establishment was his expansive white villa called Vioyamis, which lay close to Port Sarfe. But Silon also kept a spacious mansion in the Raleenian capital, run with courteous efficiency by his loyal staff.

During their ride north, Silon had informed Corin that his business in the south looked promising. Time would tell, he'd said, and doubtless there would be hard choices to make. As he gazed around the gardens, Corin could see the merchant standing close by, smiling and enjoying this beautiful evening in the city and watching his daughter dance.

Corin watched her too, as did almost everyone there. Nalissa was a sight to behold. There she swayed so beautiful and laughing, Silon's stunning daughter dancing the night away as musicians played her favorite songs, a bottle of finest Raleenian claret clutched in her hand, its contents spilling onto the grass. She caught Corin's glance and grinned at him. Corin saw Silon frowning, so he turned his head away.

Night deepened, and Silon took to his bed as did most his guests. Corin, reluctant to retire form this beautiful place, stood surveying the city, a half-empty crystal wine glass in his hand. He turned upon hearing soft steps beside him. Nalissa stood there. Her black eyes were huge, and she looked tipsy.

"Father tells me you are a good fighter." Her lips parted slightly, and she slid an arm alongside his. "You're very tall, and your hands look rough," Nalissa said, and then on a whim she reached up and planted a soft kiss on his cheek. "I like tall men."

Corin smiled into her eyes, not failing to notice that lovely tanned face, the wild black hair lifting in the night breeze, and the large gold hoops in her ears reflecting the moonlight.

"I think you might be trouble," Corin told her.

"Well, that makes two of us." Nalissa's smile widened as her gaze lowered.

Corin chuckled. His hands slid along Nalissa's curves, and he led her to the edge of the lawn where rhododendrons shaded the path leading to a patch of ferns and the secrecy they required. "Should your father find out—"

"He'll never know." Nalissa squeezed his hands. "Besides,

if you are going to be working for him, then it's only sensible we should be friends."

"Who says I'm going to be working for him?" Corin's eyes widened as she fumbled with his drawstring and unlaced his trousers.

"I do," Nalissa said as she knelt on the grass in front of him.

"I think this is a very bad idea," Corin said, but after a few moments he no longer cared.

***

Next morning Silon summoned Corin into his study, a sunlit room with far ranging views over the red clay rooftops of Atarios city. Corin wondered what it was like to be so wealthy.

"Take a seat," Silon hinted the chair across from his desk. Corin obliged and gazed around the room.

"Nice place you've got here," he said. Outside the window, Corin could see the city walls in the distance, and beyond those were golden fields of corn swaying in the breeze. "I like this city."

"I have three houses," Silon replied. "It helps as I move around a lot." He leaned forward and stared hard into Corin's face. "So. You are homeward bound?"

"Yes, I'm leaving before lunch."

"A long ride."

"It is..." Corin's eyes widened as Silon produced a heavy sack of gold and pushed it across the table toward him. "What's this?" Corin asked.

"Persuasion," Silon smiled. "I need a strong-arm around and you fit the purpose. So I'd sooner you didn't leave just yet."

"Why me? There are plenty of mercenaries available?" Corin tried to guess how much coin lay inside the sack. More than he'd earned in a month in the Wolves, that much was certain.

"Because I know I can trust you, Corin an Fol. I have Lord Halfdan's word on that. Loyalty and trust are worth far more to me than gold. Stay for a month—that's all I'm asking. If you enjoy the work, there are spacious quarters you can occupy in my villa Vioyamis. If not—at least you'll return home richer."

Corin picked up the sack and half a dozen gold coins spilled free and rolled across the table. He opened the neck wider and saw plenty more shining within. "Agreed." Corin smiled and held out his hand. Silon grasped it firmly.

"So what's my first task?"

"Protecting my daughter; If I find out that anyone's touched her, I'll slit their throat."

End of Part Two

Read *The Shattered Crown* next. Here's a sample preview...

Chapter 1

The Smithy

Corin an Fol, recently redundant longswordsman, determined cynic, and downtrodden wretch, was not having one of his better moments. His head hurt, his feet were soaked (leaky boots did nothing for morale), and it hadn't stopped bloody-well raining for three days—and worse—three nights.

He was wet through, his hands frozen and his nose running, and now Thunderhoof, his very expensive foreign warhorse, had chosen to start limping. It was all an act, of course. Thunder did this kind of thing when he'd had enough tromping about the countryside.

Corin wiped the snot from his nose and blinked through the rain. Fog and moor, moor and fog—he remembered why he'd left this place.

"It isn't my fault you were born in the south," Corin told his horse. Thunderhoof had been a generous gift from his former employer, Silon of Raleen, back in the days when they were getting on. It seldom rained down there in Raleen, it being half desert, and Thunder, worthy beast though he was, had scant appreciation for this damp northern climate.

"Besides," continued Corin, "we've only a few miles to go. You can stew in a nice warm, dry stable, and I can get soused." Thunder didn't respond, nor did he pick up his sluggish pace.

A mile marker loomed out of the murk: Finnehalle Seven Miles. The words were barely visible.

"See, look you!" Corin, excited, patted the horse's soggy back. "We're almost there, boy." But if Thunder had been impressed by the milestone, he didn't show it, which wasn't that surprising considering he couldn't read.

A lane entrance yawned off to their right, just passed a stubby clump of hedgerow. Above that a battered sign dripped and creaked on a rusty pole: Polin's Smithy One Mile.

An arrow pointed down the track. Corin reined in as he took in the sign. Down in the wooded dip he could see smoke rising crooked from the smith's cottage and forge. Polin was a stout soul. He'd been a good friend to Corin, back then.

I suppose we could always...

Moments passed. Rider sat thinking whilst horse looked mournful and did something peculiar with his right foreleg.

"Oh, sod it then. Have it your way." Corin dismounted onto the lane with a squishy thud and then hauled hard at Thunder's reins, urging the snorting beast follow him down the side track and on toward the smithy. The horse gave him that superior look—an expression not dissimilar to the one Silon used to visit upon him when he'd just said something obtuse (which happened now and then).

"Horse, I hope for your sake Polin's ale barrel is full," complained Corin. He'd had his heart set on spending a night or two in the Last Ship, the inn he'd frequented a lot—back then. Still, Polin used to keep a decent keg and it would be good to catch up. It had been fourteen years after all, and Finnehalle would still be there in the morning.

Half way down the lane, the rain stopped and a wan sun pierced the grey. Corin smiled as sunlight danced and sparkled in the puddles ahead. This was more like it. But the grin fled from his face when a woman's shriek of rage sent rooks croaking skyward.

What's this?

Corin reached the outer fence to the smithy's lands, tied Thunder's reins to a stump, and then, hand reaching back across his shoulder, slid Clouter, his heavy longsword, free of its scabbard.

"Stay here!" Corin hissed at the horse. Thunder blinked at him but obliged with indifference. Corin left him and approached the gate. He turned the latch and carefully stole inside the stockade, his wet clothes and cold feet forgotten.

Trouble. It was something Corin an Fol understood, its having been his constant companion for over fourteen years.

The woman screamed again—more anger than terror betrayed by her tone. Corin cursed and broke into a run, Clouter gripped between calloused palms and his grey-blue eyes steely hard. It had been two long weeks since he'd last had a scrap. Corin was more than ready.

***

Ulf laughed when the woman threatened him with her rusty knife. His twin, Starki, had already done for her husband, whilst the boy, Cale, had slipped inside the cottage to collect any spoils. That pimply bag of bones had his uses—sometimes.

They hadn't killed the smith yet, just brained him half senseless. The big fellow crouched spewing and moaning in the dirt just outside the stables. Ulf had forgotten him already, having eyes only for the blacksmith's wife.

She was comely, in a spitting, shrieking, red-haired, freckled kind of way. But it wouldn't have mattered if she were ugly. Ulf had never been the fussy kind.

He turned slightly at a noise to his left—Cale returning, his grubby fingers full of silver coin and his bright blue bug-eyes gawping at the scene. Ulf ignored him. Instead he goaded the girl with mock kisses and obscene hints.

Starki, lacking the finer qualities possessed by his twin, grabbed greedily for the girl. She stepped backwards, hissed, and flashed the tiny blade at his blood-shot eyes.

Starki laughed and winked at Ulf. "While you're trying to prick me with that I'm going to prick you with this." He cupped his groin with a hand and made a lewd thrusting gesture with his hips.

"Get that out and I'll slice it off!" The woman spat in his eye.

"Feisty mare, eh, Starki," observed Ulf. "Mayhap we should draw lots." Behind him the gawky Cale watched in fascinated silence.

"I'm having her first!" Starki grabbed again, but the woman knew what she was doing with her knife. She sliced hard, took a finger.

"Bitch!" Starki's meaty left fist hammered into her face, knocking her prone. He stood over her then, panting, swearing, and flicking the blood from his dripping right hand so that it splattered her linen gown.

She rolled over and tried to get up, but Ulf's studded boot thudded down onto her back, sending her sprawling again. Starki, his eyes lit with murderous rage, freed his dagger and crouched low over the woman.

He froze when the sharp kiss of steel pricked lightly at the nape of his neck.

"Play time's over, ugly," a voice said.

Starki rolled free of the stranger's blade, but only just. He looked up wild-eyed. Where had this bastard come from? A tall nasty-looking bugger clad in dun-leather tunic over a rusty mail shirt. Lean-faced—a white scar crooked up from right brow to hairline—with shaggy brown hair and scary eyes of smoky blue grey. In his hands he clutched a bloody great sword, perhaps five-and-a-half feet long.

But Starki was no craven. In a grunting blur he'd freed his axe and swung out hard and across, aiming to split this lanky impostor in two. To his right his twin watched slack-jawed as Starki's broad swipe cut through air alone.

Clouter did better.

Ulf swore as his brother slunk to his knees, Starki's fingers trying in vain to staunch the great rift opened in his belly. He wept as his guts spilled free, shuddered for a miserable moment, and then lay prone.

Ulf had his sword out, a wickedly curved blade, half sax, half broadsword. He levelled it, roared, and waded in, but the steely-eyed stranger's longsword held him at bay.

Meanwhile, the boy, forgotten by everyone, sidled slowly toward the rear of the stable, believing it prudent to vacate the premises. Trouble was the woman saw Cale out of the corner of her eye. Worse, she was blocking his escape route.

"Stay put, yer little shite," she said. Cale wasn't about to argue with a madwoman armed with rusty knife, however small. She stomped over, grabbed his wrist, and yanked hard. Cale yelped and the stolen coins spilled and sparkled to vanish in the dirt. "I've a rope just perfect for your scrawny neck," she told him. Cale gulped.

Ulf slipped a dagger into his left hand. He circled Corin, the two blades gleaming in the sunshine. Corin smiled at him. Ulf studied the stranger's nasty-looking blade. Barely, he kept a lid on his fury, hearing his twin's dying shudders behind him. Then the stranger's smoky eyes flicked across to where that idiot Cale was succumbing wimperingly to the smith's wife. He seemed half amused at the boy's antics. Ulf seized his moment, tossed his dagger hard and fast. Corin grinned, having expected that. His heavy blade sent the knife spinning away with a blaze of sparks.

But Ulf didn't waste any time. He shouldered into Corin with both hands on his curved blade seeking to hack hard into his enemy's side. Instead Corin's counterstroke clanged into the twin's blade, knocking him off balance.

Still grinning, Corin leapt at Ulf. Reversing Clouter, he rammed the wolf's-head pommel hard into Ulf's chin, breaking the big man's jaw and launching him backward. Ulf groaned once and then lay still.

Corin knelt and wiped Clouter clean on Ulf's woolly coat. He gave its steely length a critical eye before slinging the longsword back in its scabbard, hanging lateral across his back. Corin turned to the woman who had the spitting youth in a headlock.

"You get some rope, girl," he said, "and I'll hoist this fat bastard from that tree out there." He motioned toward Ulf's prone fur-clad lump and then pointed to the large ash shading the far end of the stockade.

"What about this streak of piss?" The woman yanked Cale's left earlobe and he squawked enthusiastically.

"We'll hang him too," replied Corin, grinning evilly. "By the ears," he added. "Over hot coals. Slowly." Corin winked at Cale, who for his part looked wan and sad.

"Aw...you wouldn't," the boy said as the woman left him to source the rope. Corin ignored him. Instead he went to the well across the yard, hoisted a bucket, and spilled the contents over his head.

"I'm hungry," he said to the boy then. Cale didn't reply. He was looking past Corin at someone's looming approach.

"I'm Tommo," said a gruff voice. The smith was big and fresh faced, though blood

matted his sandy hair and rouged his stubbled cheeks. "We are in your debt, stranger," he said.

"Where is Polin?" Corin asked. He didn't like being called stranger. The smithy was only seven miles from where he'd been born. Still, he didn't know these people so why should they know him.

"Father died last winter," the girl answered, returning. She threw a heavy coil of rope on the ground and then stood with feet braced and arms crossed to study Corin.

"I know you." She smiled impishly, which made her look younger, perhaps twenty-five. "You're Corin an Fol," she said, and he nodded. "I used to quite fancy you back then, but you buggered off to foreign parts. I'm Kyssa. Remember me?"

Corin recalled a freckled twelve-year-old girl with wild red hair and a mischievous grin. He nodded, "Aye, I do so, yes." Corin was awkwardly aware of Tommo's lowering brow and somber expression. "I'm sorry to hear of your father's death. He was a good man, Kyssa."

She shrugged. "Everyone dies."

Half hour later, big Tommo helped Corin hoist the kicking, fully conscious Ulf skyward while Kyssa clapped and Cale soiled his pants, this day not going as he'd planned it.

"Well," said Corin, awarding the boy a steely stare. "What have you got to say for yourself, shithead?"

"I've done nothing! I don't deserve...that." Cale's bulging eyes glanced up to where Ulf quivered and kicked.

"We will see." Corin turned and winked at Tommo, but the smith didn't look the forgiving type.

"He's a thief," said Tommo. "Thieves hang, it's the law."

"Bugger the law," said Corin. "How old are you, boy?" Corin asked Cale.

"Almost fourteen winters," Cale replied, and sensing he might have a chance, stuck his chin out. "What's it to you?" Cale was in awe of this stranger and his massive sword but determined not to show it. This bastard had easily bested the two toughest men he had ever known. They might not have been house trained but they had been his only companions.

Cale had wanted to do for them both when they were taunting the woman, but that was different. Cale didn't like that sort of thing, having his own sense of honor. Not that the wench didn't deserve it, the way she'd treated him.

Master Cale had his pride and wasn't about to forgive this weirdo stranger's executions of Ulf and Starki. For three profitable years Cale had accompanied the brutal twins, learning much as they robbed and murdered their way across the wilderness of Kelthaine and Fol.

"Thirteen and three quarters to be exact," he answered eventually.

"Well, be grateful you're not yet fourteen. If you were, I'd slit you open like an overripe melon!" Corin held the boy's defiant gaze for a moment longer, then turned away to spit on Starki's mangled, fly-clustered corpse.

Slowly his anger faded, replaced by fatigue and sorrow. Corin remembered what had occurred on his own fourteenth birthday. The memory of that day would never fade; it was branded into his skull like the sword scar on his forehead. That had been the day of the raid on Finnehalle by Crenise pirates, culminating with the death of his father and brothers, and later the loss of his mother and sister too.

"Where are you from?" Corin glared at the boy.

"It don't matter where he's from," Tommo cut in, but Corin motioned him to silence. Beside her husband, Kyssa fingered her knife fondly and smiled at Cale. He pretended not to notice.

"Kelthara," Cale muttered then, staring sulkily at the field outside. His quick mind was calculating a way out of this unpleasant situation. He heard footsteps, and turning back he paled—it was apparent Tommo's patience had finally dissolved. The ominous hulk of the blacksmith loomed over him, massive hands bunching in fury.

"Leave him be." Corin's voice halted the big man's fist. Tommo turned, glowering at the longswordsman.

"Why?"

Corin shrugged. "There's been enough retribution today," he said. Kyssa shook her head. She looked disappointed.

Ignored for the minute, Cale seized his chance. With practiced ease he scooped from the dirt the coins he'd stolen. "I'll be taking my leave now, masters," the boy announced as he spun on his heels and fled the yard. "I don't suppose we'll meet again." As Tommo and Corin gave chase, Cale turned and hurled a dagger he'd kept stowed up his left sleeve. Tommo dived and Corin ducked as the blade whooshed over their heads. Corin was angry again. His fast legs soon carried him ahead of the laboring smith, his longsword swinging behind him as he vaulted the wall with athletic ease.

To no avail. Cale was a city lad, well used to being pursued by vengeful adults down the labyrinthine lanes of old Kelthara town. He'd soon vanished into the thorny knot of woodland enclosing the western end of Polin's Smithy.

Corin yelled out to him. "If I come across you again it will go bad for you boy! Remember the name Corin an Fol!"

His only answer was the wind in the trees.

Shaking his head in disgust, Corin returned to the stockade. Before he reached the gate, the strange sound of laughter made him stop and glance up at a nearby oak. There, scarce ten feet away, beautifully balanced on the stout limb of a level branch, sat a girl. Her face was pale perfection dominated by two huge tawny eyes. These watched him with mocking humor. There was something decidedly odd about this child. Corin felt uneasy under her gaze.

"You did well today," she giggled, her bare legs swinging high above his head. It seemed odd how the chilly breeze didn't bother her, despite her only garment's being a pale blue dress hemmed well above her knees and elbows. Long golden braids cascaded down her back, and she wore shoes of softest red leather. The girl grinned down at Corin with impish delight.

"We are watching you with interest," the strange girl said. Then her lips twisted into a cat's feral grin. Suddenly she looked cruel, spiteful. "Be careful in the woods. *He* is stalking you."

"Who are you, child?" Corin managed before Tommo's heavy footsteps distracted him. He squinted through the afternoon sun to see the blacksmith approach.

"What are you looking at?" Tommo enquired. He awarded the tree a quizzical glance. Corin pointed above, then swore under his breath. The branch was bare.

"I... nothing," Corin struggled, doubting his senses. "The boy's gone," he said, stating the obvious just to change the subject. Corin wondered whether those field mushrooms he'd found yesterday were having an unwholesome effect on him. It wasn't a good sign seeing strange girls in trees.

Tommo shrugged. "I wouldn't have hung him," he said eventually, "just wanted to scare the little shite." Corin nodded. "Why not stay and sup some ale with us," Tommo offered then. "Kyssa's got a three day stew on the stove—turnips, coney, broth and all."

"I thank you, but no," responded Corin. He'd changed his mind after the fight. He desired solitude: time to think on his own. "I wish to watch the sun set on the ocean this very evening, take my leave in the taverns of Finnehalle. It's seven miles away if I read that last marker correctly, though my memory makes the distance shorter." Corin had a sudden notion. "There is a service you can do for me, Tommo, if you will," Corin added.

"Name it."

"My horse, Thunderhoof, is lame, or pretending to be. He's covered many leagues over the last week and isn't happy, doesn't like the wet. Could you stable him and see to his needs? He's a good old boy but gets a bit stiff sometimes."

"Gladly," responded Tommo, insisting once more Corin stay for some respite at least. "Finnehalle *is* only seven miles away, yes, and I've other steeds to lend you. Those rogues left shaggy mounts tied outside the north gate. They'll not be using them again, nor do I expect that young cutpurse will return to reclaim his pony."

Corin could not be persuaded. He made his excuses to the blacksmith and his wife, who joined them, insisting he wanted to walk the last few miles. It would clear his head, Corin told them. Tommo was nonplussed, but Kyssa gazed at him askance.

"You are a strange one, Corin." She yielded a shrug. Corin, feeling awkward, didn't respond. Instead he went to get the horse.

They waited in silence, both worn out by this troublesome day. Eventually Corin returned with Thunderhoof clomping noisily behind him. Then, just a few minutes later the longswordsman bade farewell to the blacksmith, his wife, and Thunder. Heart heavy, Corin took his leave from Polin's Smithy. He vowed to return after a few days' hard drinking. Thunderhoof didn't notice Corin's departure. He was already at his oats. Corin left lane and smithy behind. Time to go home. He wondered if Holly was still in town. He'd liked Holly—back then.

Chapter 2

The Dreaming

She is falling, gliding, sliding down through cold night air. Down and down. She has no fear, knows this to be another dream. Or rather the same dream in yet another guise. Down she falls encased by total blackness.

Things in that void call out to her. Dark things that hint at her ruin and try vainly to reach her. Again she is not afraid. Elanion watches over her—the Goddess of this green world, Ansu, protecting her child as She always has.

The dreamer relaxes as she glides, her pale arms outstretched and her face numbed by icy air. She sees a light, a tiny speck far below. It grows, a small distant globe rising up to meet her.

Ariane smiles. She feels the warmth of the Goddess cocooning her naked body. She is safe—nothing can hurt her now. The light expands, it reaches up, piercing the gloom, and embraces her with blinding clarity. Ariane gasps as her head fills with visions. Wild and giddy, her young mind struggles to make sense of what the Goddess is telling her.

The light takes shape. Its source is in front of her. Ariane no longer falls, instead she stands in an empty hall. Sconces flicker and faint shadows flee from the source of the light, its clarity penetrating every corner. The light, though dazzling, doesn't stop her seeing. Ariane walks effortlessly toward its center, her royal vision enabling her to see through into the very heart.

And there it is, The Crown of Kings. Source of the light. The Tekara. Crystal and radiant, its mystical benevolence banishes darkness from the realm.

Until now.

A shadow has entered the hall. It splits, becomes two shadows. Two men. Intruders. Ariane knows this, having witnessed this outcome twice before. The smaller figure reaches out, grabs the crown, then drops it as the light burns his fingers.

The Tekara falls, impacts with the marble floor.

The dream shifts.

Ariane stands alone in a glade in a deep dark wood. Ahead are tall stones, their shadows long, sloping and narrow. Above her head a diadem of stars studs the night sky. Dark trees creak and stir as she steps forward and enters the glade.

The stones watch her approach. A granite ring, dark and silent. She enters that circle within a circle, turns to her left, following the spiral into the labyrinth's heart. Ariane feels her heart beating with excitement, anticipation, and dread. Voices whisper to her from the beyond the stones.

Knowledge is power, they tell her. Power is corruption. Corruption is the world eater. Ariane ignores them, reaches the core, the very center. Ahead waits a well. Ariane steps silently forward, reaches out with both hands, eager for knowledge and power. But the well is stolen from her eyes by sudden mist. The mist deepens, clings to her face like damp, searching fingers. Ariane cries out at that touch, but her voice is muffled in the murk. Somewhere in the distance she hears the lonely strain of harpsong.

The dream shifts back.

The Tekara explodes as it greets the tiled floor of the hall, shatters into a hundred blazing sparks. Pain fills Ariane's head as she feels those crystal daggers lancing deep into her skin. She falls, bleeding and broken. All around her the shadows dance and whirl like smoky wraiths. She is cold now, icy cold.

Ariane hears laughter and knows the realm is betrayed. Sorcery and corruption. Dream Ariane closes her eyes, lets the darkness consume her again...

***

"My Queen, it is time! The council is gathering in your throne room." Ariane opened her eyes, the rough voice having jolted her back into consciousness. Outside the lofty towers and spires of Wynais, called by some the Silver City, sparkled with morning sunshine.

A cough. She turned her head, saw Roman Parrantios, her champion and trusted friend, leaning over her. Ariane blinked and grimaced as sharp pain lanced behind her eyes. She ignored it.

"I need to speak to Dazaleon. Go find him."

"But the council?"

"Bugger the council, Roman. Go get me the High Priest!" Ariane watched bleary-eyed as Roman left her, his expression grim. He was a good man, but he was a soldier, tough, resilient and practical. Not one to share the Dreaming with.

Ariane checked the hour. It was still early despite Roman's urgency. And it was *her* council, and they could bloody well wait until she was ready for them. Ariane had had Kelwyn's responsibilities thrust upon her just six months past, after her father's untimely death. She was still getting used to the governing process, and patience wasn't her strong point.

She was only twenty two, slight of build and tomboy in shape and nature, with shoulder-length black hair and dark, piercing eyes. But Ariane was clever—she was sharp of tongue and didn't suffer fools. She took after her father in that. Ariane took after her father in most things.

But not the Dreaming. Those dreams had always been her mother's province. But her mother had died whilst birthing a stillborn eighteen years past. She'd loved the Queen, but the memory of her childhood was fading fast these days and along with it Queen Cailine's gentle face.

Besides, Ariane was always her father's girl. King Nogel had doted on his daughter, always letting her accompany him on royal visits to Kelthaine, Morwella and Raleen—and even once the island, Crenna, a dangerous place infamous for piracy, dark sacrifices and insurrection.

When Ariane had asked to learn sword craft her father had indulged her. It was Roman who taught her back then: rapier, spear, knife, and bow; elbow, fist, palm, heel, and toe.

Ariane loved learning how to handle weapons. She was deft and moved like a dancer. The Queen was a fine horsewoman, too. Not for her the cozy courtesan life of other high-born ladies, like her cousin, Lady Shallan of Morwella.

But ruling her people was not so easy. She'd not been ready for such responsibility, but her father's falling from his horse and breaking his neck during a hunt had thrust it on her. Ariane was abrupt at council, easily distracted and short tempered as a rule. That said, she was kind hearted and generous. But those were not necessarily the most useful characteristics in a ruler.

She loved her country, though. Kelwyn—the second kingdom. Second in size to only Kelthaine, her northern neighbor, where the High King held court.

Or had done until last week.

A discreet cough at the door jolted her thoughts back to the immediate.

"Your Highness—"

"A moment, Dazaleon, if you please." Ariane fussed her maids get her trousers and tunic as she slid into her small clothes. She liked to dress practical at councils. They went on forever, and Ariane found court uncomfortable enough without being laden down by jewelry and fine lace. It was a point of discussion among her maid servants, though none dared speak their thoughts in her presence.

Ariane grabbed the doeskin trousers from a maid and hoisted them up her legs. She donned the green-suede tunic and girded it with a broad leather belt. Finally she stepped into short black boots of worn expensive leather.

That will suffice.

"You may enter." Another maid opened the door, allowing the tall figure outside to approach her.

Dazaleon, High Priest of Wynais, Kelwyn's royal city and Ariane's birthplace, was an impressive figure. Robed in Goddess green, he stood almost seven feet tall and broad at shoulder, his long hair snow white and thick, and his lined features nut brown around penetrating blue eyes.

Dazaleon looked to be a man of sixty, but he'd already seen his seventy fifth summer. The Goddess gave him power, they said. Strength in body and in mind. He was the young Queen's mentor, spiritual advisor, and closest confidante. But more importantly, Dazaleon was the only one who knew about the Dreaming.

Dazaleon loomed over her, his heavy brows knotted with concern. He was garbed for council, his high-priest robes immaculate emerald and the long rod of office clutched in his left fist. He shifted, fingered the rod, and waited for his Queen to speak.

"I dreamt of the crown again, Dazaleon." Ariane seated herself by the bed and bid her High Priest do the same. Stiffly he joined her, folding his long body into a chair. At her curt wave the maids scurried from the room.

"I guessed it were so, Highness. The third time, is it not?"

"The third time this week, yes."

"The same dream—the Tekara shattering."

"The same, yet subtly different."

"Tell me."

And she did.

***

An hour later Ariane sat at her throne at council whilst her court buzzed and fidgeted across the throne room. Gossip spread flame-fast throughout that airy hall, fed by hinting whispers. Rumors were afoot, the whisperers said, dire portents warning of war and darkest sorcery. Something bad had happened in the north. The Queen knew about it, Dazaleon too—and Roman. Perhaps a few others also.

The Queen raised her left hand and the court fell silent. All eyes were on Ariane and the High Priest standing tall behind her. They shuffled and waited: her nobles, notaries, priests, surgeons, steel-clad officers, silk-wrapped merchants, and other men and women of account. They numbered over fifty, each one known for their discretion and loyalty, thus trusted by the Queen. Most gathered were garbed in expensive cloth. The colors were bright, saving the priests, who wore green and the soldiers dun brown. As one they waited, their expressions tense and their manner unsure.

Eventually the Queen spoke. Despite her awkwardness, Ariane braved a confident voice, easily reaching the double doorways where the two helmeted guards stood silent with halberds crossed. Like the nobles gathered inside, these guards loved their Queen, though they were concerned she'd taken too much upon herself. King Nogel had ruled with compassion and strength. Everyone loved him, and the realm feared little whilst he was alive. Ariane had his metal in her veins, but she was so young, had not expected to have this responsibility for many years. How would she cope?

"You have heard rumors, this I know," Ariane said. "Events are unravelling fast up in Kelthaine. There is no way to say this easily, my people. High King Kelsalion is dead." There followed shocked gasps and startled looks. Everyone wanted to speak, but none dared utter a sound.

"Yes, it's true, our overlord is dead. Murdered, apparently, by Permian assassins. It happened late last week. We received word via pigeon only three days hence."

"Permian assassins my arse!" Roman Parrantios stood facing his Queen. The champion's bearded jaw was set resolute. "This is that bastard Caswallon's handiwork."

"I concur with our respected champion's opinion," Ariane told the court. Then turning to Roman, she added, "I don't, however, appreciate the interruption." Roman muttered an apology.

"There is worse news," she continued. They waited. Even the guards looked apprehensive at the doors. "The Tekara—Kell's crystal crown, which has protected his descendants and our four realms for millennia—is shattered. Broken beyond repair. I know this because for three nights the Royal Dreaming has visited upon me."

"Treachery!" This from a young officer standing to Roman's left. Fierce looking, tall, and hawkish, with long black braids spilling down the length of his back.

"It's fucking Caswallon," Roman again under his breath—he just couldn't help himself.

"Sirs!" Ariane's withering gaze silenced them both. "Hold your tongues else I'll have them removed!" Roman raised his brows while the courtiers shifted nervously. *She could do that.* "You will have your piece. In the meanwhile, I will not be interrupted." She gazed to her left, where the High Priest loomed imperious.

"As I said, the Dreaming came upon me—the Goddess Herself speaking nuances inside my head. Not once—three times. Star Bright Elanion would protect her children from the approaching storm."

Ariane shifted on the throne. "High Priest Dazaleon understands these things far better than I do. As some of you may know his interpretations of the Queen's—my dear mother's—dream-fuelled visions gave her some solace before she died. Dazaleon is the wisest among us. His counsel is without flaw, and he alone can interpret the Dreaming. So I suggest you listen. (This last was aimed at Roman and the young officer beside him.)

Ariane motioned her mentor step forward. "Come, my lord, impart the wisdom of your knowledge."

Dazaleon leaned heavy on his rod: a long, inch-thick length of ash capped by a globe of solid emerald almost four inches in diameter. The Staff of Elanion—it was this rod enabled Dazaleon speak directly with the Goddess, either in his temple or down by the lake. His heavy gaze swept the courtroom, commanding attention.

"All royal dreams are important," he told them. "Dreams direct from the Goddess are rare indeed. In my entire life I have received only two. Our Highness has had three in three days.

"These dreams bring visions we call the Dreaming. During these visions the Goddess speaks to the dreamer. Not as I speak to you today but in subtler ways. Queen Ariane, though grasping a good deal herself, has given me the task of translating those dreams so all present may comprehend what the Goddess wishes." He turned to the Queen, seated pale on her throne.

"Your Highness, tell us what you saw."

Ariane, feeling uncomfortable, kept it brief. "I fell through darkness. Then there was warmth and a light. The warmth I knew to be the Goddess cocooning me from harm. I knew I journeyed through the void—nothing else could be that dark. The light I recognized as coming from the Tekara, our holy Crown of Kings. I walked toward it. There were creeping shadows, but the light kept them at bay." She turned to Dazaleon, who nodded and stepped forward again.

"Those shadows are our enemies, Your Highness, within and without. Skulkers and deceivers. Always they have tried to undermine the Tekara's power."

Ariane nodded. "Two of those shadows became people—I couldn't see their faces, though one was taller than the other. The smaller one took the crown from its resting place..."

There was hushed silence in the courtroom, even Roman looked pale.

"That was Prince Tarin doing the bidding of Caswallon," Dazaleon told them. "Long has Kelsalion's mentor worked on that boy. Caswallon first got his claws on Tarin after the Queen's death. Torn by grief, the High King was fast losing grip over the realm, and Caswallon saw his chance. Young and impressionable, the boy Prince was easily swayed by the high counsellor's cunning."

"Little prick," muttered Roman under his breath again. "Needs something sharp shoving up his—"Ariane shot him the warning glance of a weary mother, part love, part exasperation.

"Prince Tarin dropped the crown. I..." Ariane exchanged looks with her High Priest. "The dream changed then: I stood in a wood—a sacred grove. Ahead were tall stones—a circle within a circle. I entered...saw a well...felt the Goddess calling me from inside it, so I reached out. But the well faded from view."

"Our Queen speaks of Valen Durrannin—the Oracle of Elanion. It lies deep within the Forest of Dreams in a wild corner of northern Kelthaine." Dazaleon's long fingers drummed the huge emerald capping his staff. He looked uneasy. "Are there any present familiar with this forest?"

"Well?" Queen Ariane glanced around at the faces watching her. "Someone help us. What about you merchants? You're always on the roads." She hinted to a small group of wealthy looking individuals clustered to the right of the main party.

I've been close, Your Highness." Ariane recognized the speaker as Porric of Port Wind, a city on the coast.

"And saw what?"

Porric muttered a reply.

"We cannot hear you sir!" Ariane snapped.

"I said, it's a dangerous place, Your Highness. Unsettling—even when you see the line of trees only in the distance as we did. Beautiful but sinister. Creepy—that's how I felt about it and my men were edgy too. We stopped at a nearby village. The inn's keeper hinted the forest was once the province of the Faen. The Oracle is rumored to lie deep in its midst. That's all I know."

"You have our thanks, Porric. So there it is—the Forest of Dreams." Ariane twisted in her throne's velvet-padded seat. "Back to my dreams. My visions changed again, I saw the Tekara shatter. At that point I woke because someone interrupted me." Roman had gone a bit red, the Queen's cold glare having fallen on him again. Kelwyn's champion shifted his feet and scratched an ear. She was feisty, this Queen—just like her father had been. Despite that, she needed looking after and he determined to do so.

"Three warning dreams—each one more or less the same," Ariane said. "Our realm is in peril, is it not, Dazaleon."

"It is, Your Highness. Direst peril. Your champion's suspicions are correct, I fear. Caswallon is to blame. I believe he has total power in Kelthaine. A usurper—clever and conniving. With the Tekara shattered, evil will take hold in the Four Kingdoms again. And Caswallon carries darkness with him. I have long mistrusted Kelsalion's favorite councilor. Caswallon is a twisted man. Worse by far, he is a sorcerer.

"The meaning of the Dreaming is clear enough," Dazaleon's

voice rose as he addressed all those present. "Queen Ariane must needs ride north, attend the Goddess's Oracle, and gain council on what to do next." "Forgive me, my lord—but that's total crap." Roman strode forward.

"Roman, the court will hear your thoughts," said Ariane, attempting to exert at least a semblance of control over her champion. "Please keep your tone respectful."

Roman wasn't having any of this witchy nonsense, however. "If Caswallon is our enemy, then what we need are swords and strong arms, not dream quests and portents." And the last thing Kelwyn's citizens needed was their beloved young Queen faring out on some wild caper deep within what was now enemy country. That part he kept to himself.

Dazaleon summoned patience. Roman Parrantios was beloved by all. He was steadfast and formidable, Kelwyn's greatest warrior. But sometimes he was hard work, even for a priest.

"The Goddess has spoken, Roman—her words are clear. Besides, Caswallon *is* a sorcerer, and you cannot defeat sorcery with swords. We need knowledge on how to defeat him. We also need to discover what happened to Prince Tarin."

"Hopefully Caswallon slit his throat," muttered Roman.

Dazaleon ignored that last comment. "Our contacts in Kella City sent word that the Prince fled after his treasonous act. No doubt Caswallon will hunt him down."

"So...?" Roman wasn't backing down. "Why should we care?"

"Because he shares my blood, Roman!" Ariane snapped. "The Prince may be a damned fool, but he is not wicked. I would help him if I can."

"And we need to know what happened to the shards," added Dazaleon.

"But why seek out yonder wood, spooks or not?" This came from a fair-haired noble with a lazy smile. He was easy on the eye and had a soft arrogance often shared by those blessed by good fortune and leisure. He'd just emerged from tasting wine at the far tables, where he'd been listening half-heartedly to all that was said. The newcomer was dressed in cool lapis lazuli and looked politely bored. He stood beside Roman, who glanced briefly in the new-comer's direction and grunted a welcome.

"I wondered when you would show up." The braided officer glared across at the other man. "Surprised you're not at the taverns already, Tamersane."

The blonde noble shrugged. "We cannot all be as assiduous in our duties as you, brother. But pray, what of my question, dearest cuz? Sorry I mean, Your Highness."

Ariane took a deep breath. Roman, Tolranna, and now Tamersane, his younger brother. Trouble piled on trouble. She ought to have them flogged. Trouble was she liked them too much.

Yail Tolranna and his brother, Tamersane, were both highly accomplished swordsmen. Whilst Tolranna was moody, tough, and blunt, Tamersane owned to a fondness of poetry and song. And attractive women. His idle charm and easy tongue were feared by husbands at court far more than his sword. The other thing about Tamersane—he was beyond disrespectful. Despite that, his sword play was second only to Roman's and his loyalty to his royal cousin, assured. "Isn't the answer to it obvious?" responded Dazaleon when Ariane refused to answer Tamersane.

Tamersane raised a lazy brow whilst Dazaleon explained further. "If our Queen dreams of the Oracle, it means she is needed there. Elanion's power is strongest in that forest. There we can reach her directly—nowhere else in the Four Kingdoms. And whatever knowledge she imparts will be crucial in the forthcoming war."

"War?" Ariane asked of her High Priest as the rest of the court drew a collective breath. "Is our outlook so bleak, Dazaleon?"

"I believe so, Highness. Caswallon may be clever, but his objective is transparent. That one wants to rule over all Four Kingdoms. He'll break any rebellion in Kelthaine, smash little Morwella, and then turn on us, and finally Raleen. Aided by his sorcery and with the lands no longer protected by the Tekara, what chance do we have?"

"Then I'll lead a host forward comprising two hundred cavalry," urged Yail Tolranna. "We'll escort Your Highness up there."

"Don't be ridiculous, brother." Tamersane's gaze was on the

nearest arched window spilling sunlight in from the courtyard outside. Fine autumn day. Shame he was missing it. "The smaller the
number, the safer she'll be."

"Your brother's right in this, Yail." Dazaleon stared hard at
the two brothers fidgeting either side of Roman. One dark, one
fair. Both shifted uncomfortably under his gaze, but Tamersane
couldn't help looking just a little smug.

"A host would only draw Caswallon's attention," Dazaleon
said. "We need stealth not armored horse, not yet anyway. Disguised
as Elanion's priests, a small party, including Your Highness, could
perchance reach northern Kelthaine without detection. It's risky,
however."

"But necessary." Ariane had made her mind up. Stewing in
court would achieve nothing. "I'll brook no argument," she said.
And then, raising her voice so that none could mistake her words,
the Queen announced: "Elanion has spoken to me, and my duty is
clear. I will ride north to this forest." Ariane's dark gaze then fell
on her High Priest. "Do you agree, my lord?" Dazaleon nodded. "I
believe it to be our best option, Highness, however dire. But there
is some heartening news. We have allies."

"I don't see them. Are they invisible?" Roman ferociously op-
posed this proposition. His beard bristled and his face grew redder.

"Let me explain," said Ariane. "Under Dazaleon's wise council, we reached out to sympathizers. For months we've been watching Caswallon sharpen his claws up north. Others have, too."

"We formed a secret league," explained Dazaleon. "We com-
municate only by coded messages sent via birds. Among our con-
federates are General Belmarius of the Bears regiment; Halfdan of
Point Keep, former general of the Wolves regiment and brother of
Kelthaine's late King; and down in Port Sarfe, a certain merchant
called Silon. This last contact has proved invaluable. Silon has
promised us a guide to lead our Queen to the Oracle. The man is
rumored to be coarse and ill-bred but apparently trustworthy and
useful with a blade."

Ariane studied her court. If only her father were here. King
Nogel would have known what to do. She remembered as a child

how he had single-handedly killed two armed would-be murderers with his bare fists whilst she, her mother, and the King walked the leafy streets of Wynais. Not for King Nogel a cavalcade or palanquin. Kelwyn's rulers loved their people and mixed with them whenever they could. The assassins were traced back to Kelthaine. Ariane suspected they'd been in Caswallon's pay. Even back then, Caswallon was on the rise, and he had no love for her father, Nogel having seen clean through the knave, unlike the High King, who doted on Caswallon's every word.

Father, what would you have done?

Ariane saw how Roman's face was still red with emotion. Her champion was clearly not happy, and she didn't blame him. Yail Tolranna looked hungry—eager to be part of the quest. Tamersane looked thoughtful whilst others watching looked worried and confused.

"Enough for now." Ariane stood and her court bowed obeisance. "We need a little time to cogitate and plan. I will hold a second council this evening when my mind is clearer. Only my closest advisers need attend. You few I would have return in three hours, the rest of you enjoy the evening." Ariane bid her court depart with a dismissive wave.

At her word those in the courtroom departed briskly amid chatter—all save Dazaleon and Roman, whilst Tolranna hovered with the guards at the doorway, Tamersane having already departed for the taverns at speed. Ariane turned toward her High Priest.

"Can this Silon really be trusted, do you think?"

"I don't know, Highness, but we don't have a choice but to trust him. Certainly he's no friend to Caswallon, who will most likely impose trade-strangling tariffs. Silon's artful and has many contacts. He's been around a long time, and like us, he fears the usurper's ambitions. We need cunning allies like him, not just armies with steel."

"Armies would be better," growled Roman.

Ariane stared at them both and then turned away. After a moment she spoke, her gaze still on the courtyard outside.

"Summon them back, Roman."

"You said three hours, Highness."

"I know what I said."

"But—"

"My mind is set, Roman. We ride north today. Three shall accompany me, yourself included. We leave before dusk, so I suggest you tell the others and get ready."

"First I need to know who they are." Roman was looking worried.

When the Queen told him, Roman's concerns worsened. He kept his tongue, however, just stomped moody out of the throne room. Dazaleon, watching the champion depart, raised a quizzical brow.

"Strange choice, Your Highness."

"Strange times, Dazaleon." Ariane smiled briefly up at him and then reclaimed her seat on the throne. *Father, what would you have done?*

***

It was actually quite dark by the time they left Wynais, a quiet party of riders garbed in priestly green. Few heeded their passing.

They rode north, deep into the night, finally taking shelter in a small wood beside the rocky stream marking the boundary between the Queen's land and Kelthaine. Roman insisted they take stag despite small risk of danger this close to home. Ariane complied, and the champion took first watch. Soon the other two men were snoring hard beneath their blankets.

But Ariane couldn't sleep. She was restless and edgy, her mind racing about her decision and this trip. She opened her eyes. It was hopeless—she was wide awake.

On a whim, she rolled free of her blanket and sat hunched and bleary over the fire. Roman turned, raised a brow.

"Get some sleep, old friend, I'm wide awake."

"But my Queen, the watch is a soldier's task."

"A soldier is what you trained me to be, Roman," the young Queen smiled at her champion, and he shrugged. "We are a team now, each of us must contribute. I am no exception. Besides, I really cannot sleep so you might as well turn in. I've no doubt we'll need your strength and council the next few days."

Roman smiled. "You have your father's mettle, my Queen."

"I hope so."

"Do not doubt it. I see him in you all the time. But thank you. Yes, I am weary, so I shall happily retire. Don't forget to wake that lout Tamersane. You know what he's like, and I don't want you on watch all night."

"I'll wake him." Ariane waved Roman lie down. "Go get some shut eye."

Time passed, the fire guttered. Ariane sat hunched and dreamy. Close by, Roman's snores eclipsed the other two's. Ariane was not sure how late it was. Perhaps she should wake Tamersane, but what was the point? She knew she wouldn't sleep tonight.

She felt rather than heard a noise in the bush behind her. Close by, the horses shuffled and clustered as though disturbed. By whom? Ariane turned, glimpsed *his* shadow standing there beneath the waxing moon.

King Nogel, her father.

He stood thin as smoke and pale as mist, his sad dead eyes watching her from beneath the trees.

Father!

The King turned his back on her and faded into the night.

"Father!" Ariane found her feet and noisily approached the place where he had been. She saw him again watching her from the edge of the forest.

"What would you have me do?" Ariane called after him.

"Hold to courage, little one," King Nogel's voice was dry leaves on a windswept path. "You ride into danger, a peril far greater than I ever faced."

"Caswallon?"

"He is part of it but only part. From where I stand now, I can see the bigger picture. But it is bleak, my love, so bleak."

"What can I do?"

"Follow your heart. You have your mother's intuition and my...strength. But you're smarter than I. Trust only those your heart allows. Seek out the Goddess, but be prepared. This is only the start. And be careful who you love."

"Love?"

The pale shape of her father turned away. She could see clear through him. *Love?* He was fading fast, barely a wisp of drifting fret as light paled the fields beyond the wood. Night was nearly over.

Ariane called out one last time. "Why did you leave me, father? You were so strong. I-"

"I was murdered, child."

"Caswallon." Ariane bit her lip, tasting the blood in her mouth.

"He and his accomplices, among them one we trusted."

Ariane's pale face whitened. "A Kelwynian? A traitor? Who?"

But King Nogel no longer stood there. Instead the morning's breeze put paid to the fire's last breath, and behind her she heard her men mutter and groan as they woke beneath their blankets.

Tamersane approached her with a sheepish grin.

"I must have slept through, cuz. Have you been up all night? You look awful, like you've seen a ghost or something."

Ariane glared at Tamersane. "You, my dear cousin, can take the first two watches tonight." She turned to where the others were stirring. "Galed, get breakfast underway. While you've been sleeping I've been thinking. Ten minutes gentlemen. Then we're on our way." Throughout that morning, Ariane stayed quiet. The Queen was clearly troubled. But the men all knew her well, so they let her be. Besides, they were in enemy country, and the fewer words said the better.

***

That night, whilst Queen Ariane of Kelwyn and her aids rode north, Caswallon's spy sent urgent word up to Kella City. He had the perfect guise to travel freely in Wynais, being robed in green as one of Elanion's sacred priests. He smiled. Both his masters would be pleased, and he stood to gain much.

When he returned to his quarters, a letter awaited him.

Caswallon's spy recognized the hand and paled slightly. A summoning—his other master.

Ten minutes later, shaky and worried, he tapped the door on the officer's chamber.

"Enter."

He complied and stood silent as the dark-eyed officer watched him from behind his desk—a nobleman, handsome and intelligent, and very dangerous.

"You sent word?" The noble asked him.

"I did, my lord—three birds."

The officer sighed. "It's regrettable. There are few who love our Queen like I do, but we must think of the realm. Ariane is reckless and naïve. Caswallon is invincible. He will rule all Four Kingdoms sooner or later, war or no war. So it's in our interest to court his affections. What we do is for the best, hard though it surely is. The letter I sent you bears my seal. Caswallon will reward you well."

"I'm to go to Kella?"

"Yes. One cannot rely on pigeons alone."

"But, my lord—"

"Report back on your return." The officer looked up sharply. "Well? Away with you, man! No time to waste!"

The man in the priest's garb nodded and left the highborn officer to his thoughts. As he gained the stairs, he had the nasty feeling he had been played. The sorcerer in Kella was not known for his equanimity.

Meanwhile the young noble returned to his papers. It was a difficult business. He loved his Queen and had respected her father. But he knew how the world worked. Sink or swim—the only choice. Ariane's devout passion would destroy Kelwyn, whereas were he to rule (as he could so easily with Caswallon's blessings) the country would surely prosper.

Caswallon would probably kill the spy, but that didn't matter—he would send other birds tomorrow.

Chapter 3

The Last Ship

Corin loosened Clouter's harness and sloped the long blade across his left shoulder, allowing him to walk faster and avoid trapping the hilt on branches and twigs. His second blade, a sax—broad and nasty, one-edged and slightly curved toward the tip—hung at his left hip, adjacent to a heavy knife.

This one he called Biter—good for up-close work. Gut slicing and tripe spilling. The knife he hadn't named: he hurled it at people who pissed him off. Corin knew he'd lose it one day, hence no name. He had smaller knives secreted in various compartments. You can never have too many sharp things in this world.

All Corin's blades weighed him down today. A long stiff walk and him a rider too. Still, it felt good to stretch the legs.

And he was coming home. Actually Corin had mixed feelings about that. Fourteen years and he hadn't left with the best grace.

Ahead a high ridge showed dark through a gap in the woods. Eagerly Corin crested it and gazed down past the trees at the distant smoky dwellings of his childhood home. Finnehalle.

There it lay as it always had, framed by tall bluffs; its harbor washed by the fathomless waters of the Western Ocean. Corin drew a deep breath and soaked in the sight. Finnehalle, his village, scarce more than a chaotic scattering of stone dwellings. Rain-washed houses and wooden fishing huts clustered around the old granite harbor.

Finnehalle, a place of crowded taverns and wind-swept markets, where local tradesmen plied their wares and days followed nights without event. Beyond the confines of the Four Kingdoms, few of its folk paid heed to what happened elsewhere.

Corin's eyes followed the course of a familiar stream spilling out beneath the trees and disappearing in the tangle of smoke-veiled roofs below. Beyond these the stone arm of the harbor jutted forth. Past that, the ocean's green-grey expanse sparkled and danced ever westward until it embraced the autumn sky.

Corin felt a sudden pang of loneliness seeing the storm lanterns swaying in the breeze at the harbor's end. *Come back* ...they called to him. *Come home!*

Corin shrugged away his melancholy thoughts. This was proving a peculiar day—he was a fighter not a bloody philosopher. He liked things simple and straightforward. Didn't go with moping much.

Besides, he needed to press on. The taverns would be filling by now. They'd all want to hear his story—not that Corin was much of a talker. But if they provided the ale he would happily comply.

Corin increased his pace as his thirst demanded, soon losing sight of the town in the autumnal canopy of trees. No bird song nor squirrel chatter? Odd that.

Corin stopped by an old oak. He didn't know how he knew, but someone was watching him. He turned, looked back up toward the ridge.

Silhouetted between the trees was the stooped figure of an old man, bearded features buried beneath a wide-brimmed hat. His cloak hung limp despite the keen breeze. Weird. He was a way off, but Corin could see the old fellow clearly.

The greybeard leant heavily on a long spear, its tip blazing suddenly when a shaft of sunlight pierced the clouds.

Corin slowly inched the fingers of his left hand toward Biter's bone hilt. No room to swing Clouter here. His mind was working fast, trying to recall where he'd seen this stranger before. Friend or enemy? He dare not take the chance. That hat was familiar and so was the spear.

A soft sound to his left. Corin turned sharply, sliding the sax free of its scabbard. He let out a slow breath, watched the rabbit scurry beneath a clutch of briar. Reluctantly Corin returned his gaze to the high ridge.

The old man had vanished. Gone. Disappeared in murky autumn air. There was no sound save the wind and restless sighing of trees. Corin slammed Biter back in its leather, cursed profusely, and then resumed his pace, swifter than before. He needed a drink and fast.

Something fluttered to his left. Corin saw a raven settle silent on a branch. An evil-looking bird, it glared at him in accusation.

"Sod off," Corin told it and swiftly resumed his pace. The raven croaked at him and took wing again. Corin cleared the woods. Open fields led down to the town. These he took at a trot. He reached a gate. Finnehalle—he was home.

Pushing open the gate, Corin entered the town. Slate-dressed houses loomed over him as he hastened by in long eager strides. Gulls weaved high above, their white shapes ghostlike in the fading light. Corin hadn't known what to expect really, but the town seemed quieter than it should be, despite the lateness of the hour.

Where was everybody? Corin nodded whilst passing a burley figure shouldering a sack of grain. The man glanced in his direction before disappearing behind a house. Corin frowned at the open hostility of the gaze.

Miserable bugger.

Corin shrugged off his misgivings and hastened down the main track, cursing as a dog snarled, making him jump. He needed that drink badly and sincerely hoped the taverns were still the same, the patrons happier than that grump had been.

Corin shivered, unrolled his woolen cloak, until now stowed on his back alongside Clouter. He threw the cloak over his shoulders, stopping in a doorway to clasp it with his golden wolfs-head broach. Nearly there—hearth and brew.

It was almost dark when Corin reached the harbor. At least the wind had eased. He took to strolling along the quay, not quite ready to enter the busy taverns (he hoped they were busy) despite his urgent need for ale.

Corin passed fishing huts and stinking piles of nets and ropes. There didn't seem to be anyone about. They must all be in the taverns. Maybe something bad had happened.

Despite not wanting to, Corin pictured that old man in the woods leaning on his spear. He recalled the strange girl's warning and frowned. Behind him the sun sank crimson over western water, and the sea murmured its timeless incantation, luring him to gaze into its fathomless depths.

Corin tugged his cloak close to keep out the chill. He leaned idle on the harbor wall, letting his eyes follow the moonlit waves toward the darkening horizon.

He spied movement at the far end of the harbor's arm. Someone stood there watching the water as he did. Corin wondered who it was.

He stared closer. The stranger seemed unaware of Corin's scrutiny in his silent vigil of the waves. There was something familiar about the way the man was standing. *Silon?* Corin grinned, imagining the wealthy merchant leaving his beloved vineyards and moving north to rain-washed Finnehalle. No chance.

Enough nonsense. Corin drank in the briny air one last time. He felt ready to confront his past. With a final curious glance at the distant stranger, Corin turned and briskly strode toward the nearest inn, his favorite.

A faded sign swung creaking above the well-used door, announcing the establishment: *The Last Ship*. Corin grunted as he pushed the door inwards and entered inside. This had better be the same.

***

Inside the inn a sudden welcome rush of heat greeted Corin, together with the rich smell of roasting flesh. A roaring fire cast dancing shadows across the busy room, sending bellows of smoke backwards to hang in foggy clusters beneath darkened oak beams. Shabbily dressed men glanced up warily from their mugs of ale, muttering as the rangy newcomer shouldered his way moodily to the taproom. A bald, sweating man greeted him in friendly fashion.

Corin grinned, recognizing Burmon, whose family had always managed matters behind these stout walls. The innkeeper was a merry soul and had been a friend to the young Corin. Back then he'd spent most of his time in Burmon's fine hostelry.

The Landlord looked at him askance, clearly not recognizing this hard-faced, scarred longswordsman, currently looming over the ale counter and grinning evilly at him.

"Can I be of assistance, sir?" Burmon asked, glancing nervously to the corner by the fire, where three shaggy men were seated around a table, playing dice. "Have you come far?" Burmon was evidently worried about the huge sword slung low across Corin's shoulders (Corin had loosened Clouter's harness to move through the inn.) Corin felt uneasy. Something was clearly amiss in Finnehalle if a jovial fellow like Burmon looked so strained.

"Far enough to need a large ale," Corin responded, softening his smile. "Don't you recognize me, old friend? I know it's been a while, but well I hoped that—"

"Corin!" blurted the innkeeper and then covered his mouth as the three strangers turned to glower in their direction. "Elanion bless us," he whispered, "but it is good to see you again, lad. It must be ten years!"

"Fourteen."

"Fourteen, you don't say. Where does the time go?"

Corin waited with eager anticipation as Burmon poured him a large mug of ale. "Where have you been lad? By the Goddess you've changed. I must tell Holly. She'll be delighted!"

Corin smiled. He hadn't forgotten the innkeeper's comely daughter. Ale wasn't the only reason he'd chosen *The Last Ship*. Corin had shared many a happy hour with Holly in gentler times. Warmed by ale and hearth, Corin's mood brightened anticipating an enjoyable evening ahead. Draining his tankard, he requested another before the busy landlord slipped away to serve other customers. Corin's eyes smarted as he glanced about the smoke-filled room.

The atmosphere of the inn was reserved, considering the number of folk seated at tables and propping the walls. Corin frowned. A few faces were familiar, farmers mostly and fishermen he remembered from his boyhood. None appeared overly cheerful.

Corin studied them from his half-drained ale mug. They kept their voices low as if worried to speak out loud. Corin's eyes drifted toward the tough-looking men by the fire. Mercenaries by the look of them, or else brigands like those shitheads at the smithy.

Strangers to Finnehalle, of that much he was certain. Corin suspected these outlanders were the sole cause of the taught atmosphere. He resented their presence at his favorite inn. Corin had come home to get away from bastards like this. The nearest man caught his eye, glanced at the longsword and dropped his gaze. He turned to whisper to his friends. Corin smiled and sipped his ale, anticipating confrontation.

The innkeeper returned, accompanied by a young woman who laughed eagerly when she saw who it was visited their taproom.

"I don't believe you've come back!" Holly grinned, pushing blonde tresses behind her left ear with a well-scrubbed hand. She stretched up on tip-toes, placing a wet kiss on Corin's grinning lips.

Corin recalled how fond he'd been of Holly back then; almost she had quelled his wildness. She still looked good. A bit worn round the edges, maybe, and a nonce thicker in waist. She still had that smile, though, and big cornflower eyes. Corin grinned visualizing good times in the days ahead. But then a swift glance at Burmon sobered him.

"What is it, my friend?" Corin asked, seeing the worry on the landlord's face. "What troubles you?"

"Those strangers," muttered the innkeeper. "They're Morwellan cutthroats and seasoned fighters, too. They worry me, Corin. I don't know why they came here. Some trouble back east, I expect. There is always trouble back east."

"What about them?" Corin casually turned to stare at the three. They were watching him carefully, their faces far from friendly. Corin remembered a man called Hagan, a Morwellan killer, a man from Corin's bloodstained past. His mood darkened, and a shadow fell across him, recalling bleak days he intended to bury forever. Hagan Delmorier: lethal killer with sword and knife. Cunning fox, wily card cheat, Corin's former comrade at arms.

If ever I see you again, Hagan, one of us will die.

These three Morwellans had a similar look to them. They reminded Corin of all the things he despised in himself. Unlike those clowns who had molested poor Kyssa, these three were professionals.

Burmon handed Corin a plate of steaming fish and refilled his glass. "They frighten my customers," he continued. "There was trouble the other night with some farmers from across the valley. You remember the Breen brothers?" Corin nodded. "Well those three set about them and almost beat them to pulp in this very room. Since then, folk have been afraid to speak out. Now things are worse, for one has taken a fancy to Holly."

"If he comes near me, he'll get a kitchen knife in his ribs." The woman's blue eyes flashed angrily. Corin raised a brow at the lass, admiring her spirit. Her father was looking more worried by the minute. Burmon noted Corin's hostile stare and placed a sweaty hand on the longswordsman's shoulder.

"Have a care with your expression, my friend. Those rogues are watching, and they're always spoiling for a fight."

Corin shrugged nonchalantly, then waded into his fish with hearty relish. The girl and her father left him to his meal as they saw to their guests. Corin wolfed his supper down and drained his tankard a third time. He felt much better. Burmon's strong brew soon banished the chill. From his bench in the corner, Corin could see the Morwellans still watching him with dark expressions. He locked eyes with the nearest and scowled. They didn't belong here. Well then, that settled it. Time for a bit of gentle persuasion.

Yes, ugly, I'm looking at you.

Corin unfastened his cloak, allowing it to drop to the rush-strewn floor. He unslung his harness and rested Clouter against an adjacent bench. Then he stood up flush-faced, savagely kicking his own bench out from under his feet. The room was suddenly silent. Eyes gaped and nerves tautened like bowstrings. Corin confronted the three, glancing warily at the broad blades hanging at their waists.

"Have you got a problem with my face?" Corin growled at the nearest and biggest. The inn was deathly quiet. From over at the bar, the landlord and his daughter looked on, worry creasing their brows. "I said do you have a problem, shite for brains?" Corin rested a lean hand on Biter's hilt. There was no room to swing Clouter in here.

The big one turned toward his companions and laughed. "I think he wants to die," he said. This Morwellan was even uglier than Ulf had been, a scarred, round-faced brute with shaggy beard and missing front teeth. His friends chuckled at his words, lowering their hands and reaching slyly for their blades.

"So, you are a longswordsman," spat the leader. "Can you use that bloody great thing over there, or is it just for show." He leered across to where Clouter leaned redundant. "Maybe I'll try it out on your skinny arse before I keep it as a trophy."

"Sirs, please I beg no trouble!" Burmon's plea drew more laughter from the three Morwellans.

"Be silent, porky, and pour us more ale." The leader wiped his mouth on his dirty sleeve and spat green phlegm on the straw-covered floor. "Our lanky friend here demands our full attention." He turned to the others. "I can always use another sword, however unwieldy, and those leathers would look good on me, though that mail shirt looks a bit knackered. What say you, Balian?"

"Aye," muttered the one-eyed, grizzled fellow to his left. "That sword belt would fit my waist," he grinned. "Are those studs real silver?" The third man said nothing, eying their confronter with eager loathing.

Corin stifled a yawn. "Typical bloody Morwellans," he said, "always yabbing instead of stabbing." Panther quick Corin leaped onto their table, kicked the quiet one hard in the face with his left boot, splitting the Morwellan's nose with a sickening crack.

Bearded moon-face grabbed his leg, but Corin brought his

right steel-girded boot down hard on the man's hand, snapping his fingers and making him howl in pain.

The Morwellan with the eye patch had his sword out. He lunged at Corin's thighs. Corin grinned, deftly leaping back off the table. He seized a vacant stool and hurled it into One-eye's face, sending him crashing into the crowd watching open jawed from behind.

"Come on!" Corin snarled, grabbing the bearded leader's sword arm, preventing him from freeing his blade. Corin, after winking at Big-Ugly, rammed his head hard into the leader's chin. Crack! The Morwellan's eyes glazed over and he sank groaning to the floor.

The quiet one with the broken nose stabbed out at Corin with an evil-looking sax. Corin blocked the thrust with his forearm, knocking the flat of the blade aside. He leaped forward, jammed his fingers into his antagonist's neck, and squeezed. Number three crumpled unconscious to the ground. Corin grinned. The Morwellans were a mess of groans and broken bones. The day was getting better.

Corin gulped deep breaths, then laughed. A great movement of feet announced the town folk had unanimously decided to be rid of the troublemakers once and for all.

"Found your courage at last," Corin jeered as they clustered like hornets around the Morwellans, kicking and cursing, stomping and spitting. They dragged the battered three out into the street, and then kicked and punched them some more amid hoots of gleeful laughter. Finally tiring of their sport, the vengeful posse returned to the taproom to replenish mugs and congratulate themselves on their victory. The Morwellans slunk away like mangy curs to lick their wounds.

And plot revenge.

Corin wiped the sweat from his brow. He winked at the shiny-eyed Holly and held his mug out for her to replenish. She obliged with a grin and a moist kiss in his left ear, Corin having just turned his head. Corin stooped, fastidiously removed the fresh bloodstain from his faded leather jerkin. It was nice being center of attention for a change. Or would have been if he'd had the chance to reflect on it. But someone had nudged him from behind, interrupting his reverie.

"Greeting, Corin an Fol," said someone with a foreign accent. "I see that you retain your subtle ways."

I know that voice. Corin turned, found himself staring gormlessly into the canny black eyes of Silon, his former employer.

"So it *was* you on the quay. What do you want?"

"Your assistance."

"Bugger off."

"Does the word *gold* interest you?" Silon rolled a coin between his fingers.

"It might." Corin eyed the coin as if it were a snake.

"Well then, I suggest you listen," the merchant said. And Corin did.

The End of the Sample

Enjoy the novels by author J.W. Webb

Subscribe to my weekly newsletter at

legendsofansu.com

Please review the novels—always nice to know
what my readers think.

Thank you and enjoy!
~ J.W. Webb

Made in United States
Orlando, FL
02 December 2021

11052733R00138